A PLACE OF **BLOOD** AND BONE

Also by Mark Peterson
Flesh & Blood

A PLACE OF **BLOOD** AND BONE

MARK PETERSON

First published in Great Britain in 2013 by Orion Books,
an imprint of The Orion Publishing Group Ltd
Orion House, 5 Upper Saint Martin's Lane
London WC2H 9EA

An Hachette UK Company

1 3 5 7 9 10 8 6 4 2

A CIP catalogue record for this book is
available from the British Library.

ISBN (Hardback) 978 1 4091 3255 4
ISBN (Trade Paperback) 978 1 4091 3256 1
ISBN (Ebook) 978 1 4091 3257 8

Typeset by Input Data Services Ltd,
Bridgwater, Somerset

Printed and bound by CPI Group (UK) Ltd, Croydon, CR0 4YY

The Orion Publishing Group's policy is to use papers that are natural,
renewable and recyclable products and made from wood grown in sustainable
forests. The logging and manufacturing processes are expected to
conform to the environmental regulations of the country of origin.

www.orionbooks.co.uk

This book is for Siobhan

Acknowledgements

My sincere thanks go to Louise Pye of Sussex Police for helping me understand the complex nature of the role of Family Liaison Officer. For helping me understand a little about schizophrenia, my thanks go to psychiatrist Dr K. and to two authors, Kurt Snyder and Ken Steele, who have both written movingly about the illness in, respectively, *Me, Myself and Them* and *The Day The Voices Stopped.* I also found *The Psychopath Test* by Jon Ronson to be very useful, as well as the original and inestimable fictional account of sociopathy contained in Robert Louis Stevenson's classic *The Strange Case of Dr Jekyll and Mr Hyde.* Finally, to find out more about the mysterious after life of a Victorian asylum you could do worse than visit www.simoncornwell.com/urbex/projects/ch/intro/index.html. I would also like to thank my agent, Anna Webber, for her company on the long and winding road and, at Orion, sincere thanks to stern taskmaster Bill Massey and to Angela McMahon and Laura Gerrard. Most of all, thanks to Siobhan, Kate and William for keeping me sane.

PART ONE

1

• • •

Oxford, August 1992

Martin Blackthorn had his whole life in front of him. He was twenty years old and about to start his final year at Oxford University, where he was the most promising among an already remarkable group of undergraduate biochemists. It was the last century and the new discipline of molecular biochemistry was experiencing its very first long hot summer and to Martin Blackthorn it felt exquisite to be at its cutting edge. Late into the August evenings, he could be found in his solitary research lab at Magdalen College, staring down the lens of a powerful microscope, captivated by the minute behaviours of the enzymes and amino acids as they fizzed around the human cell. That summer, one by one, the human genome was yielding up its dark secrets to talented young scientists like Martin Blackthorn.

He had decided against going home for the holidays. He despised the cramped terraced house where his parents lived: his father, a small, balding man eking out a precarious living from the decrepitude of British Rail; his mother in her floral housecoat, frittering away long evenings in front of the suffocating blue glow of the television set. Martin was their only child and there was nothing for him at home any more, so that August he got used to returning alone from the laboratory to his study bedroom with its mullioned window overlooking the deserted, moonlit quad. In the morning he would wake from fretful dreams, rise and take the bus out of the city towards Oxford Science Park, where, on the recommendation of one of his lecturers, Martin had secured himself a vacation job.

At the Science Park, he spent the day pushing a trolley around the grounds, calling in at the various offices and gleaming modern research institutes to deliver his letters and parcels. He arrived early each morning and he had three rounds to complete before he could return to the city in the afternoon and the intense stimulation of his real work in the lab.

On this particular morning the grey sack on the trolley was full to the brim. Martin shepherded it through a shady path leading between two lines of trees, his thoughts turning excitedly towards the future and all that he would accomplish once he had secured funding for his PhD. But his reverie was interrupted by the squeaking of one of the wheels of the trolley by Martin's feet. Before he set off this morning from the park office, Martin had unscrewed the offending wheel and oiled it, then screwed it back up even tighter. Now he stopped on the path and knelt down beside the trolley, tipping it up on its side and using his hand to tighten up the wheel again. It was no good. As soon as he stood up and started walking, the squeak returned. Martin felt a sudden surge of impatience and anger. Glancing down, he could see that his hand was trembling.

There were dark things inside him, things that Martin

wanted to keep secret. He knew that if they ever crawled onto his face, or, worse, if they ever moved his hand to action, he would instantly become hideous to the world at large. He didn't care a fig for the good opinion of his parents but there were others whose esteem he craved, not least of them his professors. Martin already thought of himself as a man of science and as such he knew the horrid things of his fancy were far beneath his dignity. They were the beasts he had to keep chained up.

But this morning it had all gone wrong.

During its journey through the hinterland of Oxford, the bus Martin caught to work was popular with schoolgirls from the local comprehensive. Their brazenness appalled him – they chewed gum, they fiddled endlessly with hair and make-up, they swore with shocking abandon – but still Martin couldn't help stealing furtive glances in their direction, committing what he saw to his imagination, engraving there the tender swell of an adolescent breast or the deep, tempting shadow beneath the stretched fabric of a short black skirt.

This morning, one of the girls on the bus noticed Martin staring. Swivelling her hips away from the aisle, she turned towards her mates. A moment later, when he worked up the courage to glance at the girls again, Martin saw them pointing at him and heard them giggling. Then the terrible epithet 'perv!' was thrown in his direction.

Soon the whole gang of girls were jeering at Martin. They made rude gestures too, delighting in this new low of their crudity. The adult passengers were staring at Martin now as well, the men grinning behind their hands as they twigged what was going on, the women tutting and shaking their heads. Still the girls went on hurling their abuse down the bus to where

Martin sat. His face the seared red of a boiled lobster, he got to his feet and staggered down the juddering aisle towards the exit, every step he took accompanied by more of their sluttish grunts. Lost in a torment of shame, Martin rang the bell and waited by the driver, his eyes fixed on the road ahead.

It took an eternity for the swaying bus to arrive at the next stop. During that time, like a bear tied to a stake before a pack of dogs, Martin was thoroughly humiliated in front of all the other passengers.

At last the door crumpled open and he almost fell down the steps and onto the pavement. As the bus chugged away Martin looked up at the retreating back window, where outraged faces mouthed obscenities and hands made revolting gestures.

Now, an hour or so later, Martin stood alone in the quiet cool of the woodland walk, feeling the cortisol electrify his body with a sudden and undeniable urge for revenge. In the throbbing glade Martin's beast slipped its leash and stood before him. Snarling, it pulled itself up to its full height, its breath hot upon his cheek.

June Redfern worked part-time as the receptionist at the Iona Research Institute and, like Martin Blackthorn, was late for work that morning. Her handbag banged at her plump thigh as she dashed in through the sliding glass of the front doors in time to see George, the equally rotund security guard, put down the sleek telephone headset and get up from the reception desk with a sigh.

'Oh, thank you, George, you're an angel,' June gasped, realising that, yet again, he'd taken the first call of the day on her behalf.

'Morning, June,' George replied grumpily, walking past her

to the interior door that gave access to the institute proper. He swiped his card over the electronic eye set into the wall.

Dismissing George with a wave, June plonked herself down in the chair he had vacated – it was still warm from his considerable behind – and manoeuvred the headset carefully over her wavy hairdo. She picked up the printed telephone list from the desk in front of her and fanned her face with its stapled leaves. The hot flushes were getting worse and she wasn't best pleased when the doors at the front of the building immediately slid open again to let in the first visitor of the day.

It was only the post boy. A shy young thing hiding his good looks beneath a mop of unruly hair and a pair of thick spectacles – one of those students who worked here for a few weeks every summer. Martin was his name, if June remembered rightly. She watched him push his trolley along the marble floor, two of the wheels rumbling nicely, the other squeaking.

'Morning, love,' June huffed cheerily, pulling her blouse away from her bosom to let the air in. She smiled apologetically on behalf of her own disarray but the lad was too embarrassed to hold eye contact with her. He was bent over his sack instead, rifling through the items on the top, pulling out a bundle of stuffed Manila envelopes all done up in a rubber band.

'I've got something for Dr Byron,' Martin said, holding up the wedge of fresh mail.

June pressed the buzzer that opened the door to her left. 'Take it up, love. Dr Byron's on the second floor. Behavioural Research Centre.'

Martin saw the way her jowls wobbled when she spoke. There was a tiny smear of red lipstick on her front teeth and her perfume had turned a little sour from the way she'd been perspiring. 'Thank you,' he said. Distracted, he was lost for a few moments in the image that flashed through his brain – an image of the heel of his right shoe smashing down repeatedly into the woman's startled, bovine expression.

Martin had little time for the so-called social sciences. Most of it wasn't science at all: as far as the humanities were concerned there was no bedrock of empirical truth that could be demonstrated in lab conditions. Nonetheless, Martin took the lift to the second floor and the Behavioural Research Centre. Turning left, he entered the corridor where the offices were located.

Dr Byron's room was at the end. Martin knocked twice. When there was no reply the second time, he pushed at the door and stuck his head inside.

It was just like all the other offices Martin had been in: small and square, a big computer monitor on the desk, a pinboard above flying pennants of lengthy, typewritten memos. He went inside and walked up to the desk and put the bulge of envelopes with the researcher's name on them next to a pile of papers. As he did so he caught sight of the title of Dr Byron's current research project: *Empathic thinking and levels of aggression in a norm-referenced sample of 10-year-old boys.* It sounded typically woolly but for once Martin managed to push aside his prejudice. Opening the front cover of the research proposal, he read the paragraph on methodology before flicking forward a few pages to the percentile rankings that would assess the questionnaire-based part of the research. Byron's proposal must have found a sponsor – there was big fuss in the media at that time about violent computer games – because beneath the bound document was a pile of completed questionnaires. Martin paged through these as well, seeing that they asked respondents to say how they would react to a number of carefully worded scenarios, most of them highly speculative. One especially naive example asked the boys what they would do if they encountered a baby bird on the pavement that had fallen from a nest.

Dr Byron had already marked the scripts and one paper out of the pile of twenty or more caught Martin's eye. The result was low, extraordinarily low. It fell off the bottom of the fourth quartile. Martin looked at the top of the test paper but was disappointed to find that there was just a serial number to identify the subject: the scripts had been anonymised. Martin glanced at the computer on Dr Byron's desk, where a single-colour, bitmapped version of the Iona corporate logo bounced slowly from one side of the screen to the other. He moved the mouse and the screensaver disappeared, to be replaced by a spreadsheet. Expertly, Martin navigated the pages until he found a five-digit number that matched the one on top of the test paper in his hand. He followed the scrolling column across with his index finger until it hit a name. The boy with the abnormally low score was called John Slade. Clicking back to the list of numbers that had been on the screen when he first came in, Martin left the office.

At the opposite end of the second floor was the suite of rooms where members of the public came to be interviewed or focus-grouped or whatever it was they did here. The decor was suitably modern and friendly – art posters on the wall, comfortable sofas, low tables, magazines – but it too was empty. Beyond the lounge, Martin found the rooms where the so-called experiments took place. There was a clamour coming from the first room on the left and Martin went up to it and peered in through the porthole window.

Inside, about fifteen boys of primary school age had been organised into groups of four and seated around tables, some of them holding A5 pieces of laminated card printed with a few lines of large text. It looked like they had been set the task of discussing the scenarios on the cards. As Martin watched, one of the boys got to his feet excitedly and punched the air, so anxious was he to make his point. Next to each table, a large video camera had been set up on a tripod and at the front of the room stood a middle-aged man who Martin took to be Dr Byron, deep in conversation with his research assistant.

Martin looked in at the second of the rooms, where another group of boys were eating biscuits and milling about. An elderly and harassed-looking man stood watching the mêlée from his vantage point over by the window. Martin opened the door and walked across to him. 'Is John Slade here?' he asked.

The Iona employee glanced at Martin's name badge then pointed to a boy sitting on his own at a table away from the main group. 'That's him. Strange little lad. Didn't want a biccy.'

John Slade sat alone at the back of the room from where he watched the horseplay of the other boys.

'His mum's on the phone,' Martin said, turning back to the old man and raising his eyes up towards the ceiling. 'She's going to be a little late picking him up. Traffic, she said.'

'That's all I need,' said the man. As if to prove his point, one of the boys shoved another in the chest. 'Please don't do that!' He looked at Martin despairingly. 'Savages, this lot. If I leave them on their own, they'll murder each other.'

Martin laughed. 'It's OK. I can take John along to reception on this floor and let him use the phone there. Then I'll bring him back for you when he's finished.'

'All right,' replied the man a little doubtfully. These days, however, it was unusual to meet a youngster who was so polite.

Martin walked over to the desk. The boy had blond, salt and pepper hair and delicate features and his eyes were the colour of flint. 'John Slade?' Martin asked.

John nodded slowly. It seemed the boy's IQ was likely to be as low as his scores for empathy. That was good.

'Come with me,' said Martin.

There was a pause. 'Why?'

'Your mother wants to talk to you on the phone.'

When John Slade stood up, Martin saw that he was unusually tall and well built for his age. He had no reason to be nervous of the other boys in the room: in a fight, he could have easily overpowered any one of them. Waving at the old man who'd been looking after him, Martin led John out of the room and closed the door behind them.

'Where we going?' asked the boy suspiciously.

Martin kept walking, away from the lounge. 'Bet it was boring sitting there talking to the others,' he remarked lightly.

Slade nodded.

'Why don't we find something else for you to do? Something more interesting.'

'I'm supposed to wait for my mum,' Slade objected.

'This won't take long.'

There weren't many places in the Science Park that Martin hadn't been for the purposes of his deliveries. He found the fire escape stairwell at the back of the building and, John Slade following a pace behind, descended the steps to the ground floor then down another flight to the basement. Turning, he saw the boy glance back at the concrete stairway. Martin stopped and smiled reassuringly, putting his hand on the boy's shoulder. 'It's OK,' he said. 'You're going to like this.'

At the bottom of the stairs was a large room where the air-conditioning pumps whirred and clanked. A portion of the side wall was lined with redundant computer equipment. Emptied of their magnetic tape reels, the cabinets looked blind. 'Come on,' said Martin, leading the boy past them and into a narrow corridor. Finally, they stopped in front of a door.

The institute did employ a handful of genuine scientists. They worked on the third floor and held a number of licences for animal experiments. The room that Martin ushered John Slade into was where the livestock was kept. It was brightly lit and tidy, with floor-to-ceiling metal racks on all four sides. There was no foul odour from the cages – no smell at all, in fact, other than the slight dankness of the straw and the tang of the dried food that was kept in buckets at the back of the room. In the larger cages were a few long-eared rabbits and a pair of beagles, but most of the cages – there must have been about forty – contained just mice. Martin went to stand by one of the racks. The white fur of the mice was clean and sleek and they had healthy-looking pink lips and noses. At Martin's approach they started sniffing the air excitedly, scrabbling over each other in an effort to get closer to the bars, each one ecstatic that the little silver bowl in the bottom of their cage was about to be filled with food.

John Slade was standing beside Martin now and staring intently at the rodents. After a moment he stuck one of his chubby fingers inside the cage and left it there. One or two of the mice sniffed at it then moved away but a third started nibbling at it tentatively then, maddened by its hunger, sank its front incisors deep into the flesh.

John Slade didn't yelp or yank his finger out of the cage, he just stood there impassively, staring with a detached interest at the biting mouse as if the pain it was inflicting on him was happening to someone else. At last, the creature leapt backward into its cage and the boy slowly withdrew his finger. He inspected the puncture marks, fascinated by the bead of ruby-red blood that had appeared on the pad.

Martin looked at him excitedly. 'You have an unusually high pain threshold.'

John Slade couldn't take his eyes off the blood.

Turning away, Martin walked to the middle of the room, where there was a domed glass killing jar big enough for the beagles, with tubes leading from it to a gas canister. Ignoring this, Martin pulled out the wide drawer in the side of the wooden table on which it sat. As intended, the jingling sound of metal implements won Slade's attention. The boy left the cage and came across to where Martin was standing. The cutlery drawer contained an array of stainless steel dissecting instruments. There were vicious-looking hooks and shiny scalpels and shears big enough to sever a human thigh bone. Martin picked up one of the smaller scalpels and gave it to John.

'What do you want me to do?' he asked.

'You should do whatever you want to do.'

Martin went over to the cage and took out a mouse. He squeezed it tightly in his hand, its paws clawing his fingers, its red eyes bulging. He put it on the table, lying it flat out on its back, spreading his hands and pressing with his fingers so he was holding it still.

Martin Blackthorn had done his first ever dissection during secondary school biology. It had been a rat then. He remembered its larger body crucified onto the wooden board with long pins, its belly slit open to reveal the fine layers of grey fur and skin and subcutaneous fat, its body cavity glistening with miniature purple organs. In the classroom, his classmates giggled nervously as they made their first incisions, none of them quite appreciating, in the way Martin did, the boundary they were crossing, the mystery they were being initiated into.

In the basement storeroom, the mouse sniffed the air helplessly. The bright blade of the scalpel touched its whiskers. John looked from the mouse to Martin. 'Do it, John,' urged the latter. 'Do it.'

Still the boy's hand wavered. When he looked up at Martin, indecision animated his previously stolid features. John Slade wanted very much to please his new friend but something deep within him wouldn't quite allow him to bring the scalpel down. He might be indifferent to his own pain but it seemed there was some vestigial compunction that prevented John inflicting something even worse on the defenceless creature. Maybe the empathy scores were erroneous.

In the end, Martin had to do it for him. Grabbing the boy's fist in his own, he plunged the blade into the mouse.

With a crunch, the tip of the scalpel went through the tiny skull and embedded itself into the table underneath.

'Good boy,' said Martin, letting go of the twitching mouse and turning towards John Slade. Squatting down so that his eyes were at the same level, he ran his hand through the lad's blond hair. 'I understand you, John.'

Although he was unsure, the boy nodded.

'None of the others do, do they?'

The boy shook his head.

'They think you're weird. But I know that's not true. You're not weird at all. You're gifted, John. Nature has blessed you.'

2

• • •

Brighton, November 2012

Brighton festered through its winters like only a seaside town could. On the seafront, the promenade was deserted and the slot machines were silent and on the busy shopping thoroughfare of North Street the home-time crowds were gathered at a strip of bus stops, the men and women hurriedly doing up their coats and unclasping umbrellas.

They knew the rain was coming. They could smell the metallic bloom on the breeze and even feel it behind their eyes – that subtle change in the pressure of the air that made the tubers open somewhere deep inside their skulls. Sure enough, the wind began to bluster up the shopping street, knocking sideways into the cars that crept up and down the hill, their red and yellow lights peeping through the darkness as, overhead, bruised and blackened clouds wheeled into position. It was coming.

Trevor Liddle, the relief manager of Phones4U, turned off the lights in his narrow shop and locked the door behind him.

As he scowled up at the sky, the first raindrops fell – big, fat ones that splashed onto the pavement. Trevor swore under his breath. He was tired. He resented so many hours spent on his feet serving younger customers who knew more about the phones than he did, and older customers who knew nothing at all – and worst of all this morning he'd forgotten his coat. Gasping, he took a supermarket ciggie out of its aluminium-coloured box and lit it and as he inhaled his first long drag, another drop of rain spattered its white length.

Shielding his cigarette with the bridge of his fingers, Trevor hurried across the road at the traffic lights, slipping in front of a nudging car, making the pavement on other side. The rain pelted down now hard enough to strike Trevor's scalp through his gelled hair as he scampered to join the clump of people sheltering in the doorway of a shop, gently backing himself into the throng until he was finally clear of the cloudburst. He stared down the hill at the three double-decker buses idling at the end of the queue of cars, straining his eyes to see if any of the electronic displays above the drivers' cabins promised him a number 25.

'No!'

It was a woman's voice, somewhere off in the middle distance: a dark, foreign accent. Alarmed, Trevor craned his head to see the crowd begin to part a little between the last bus stop and one of the alleyways that led to the Laines. A moment later a young black woman plunged through the people and splashed drunkenly into the gutter about twenty yards down the road from where Trevor was standing. 'No, I won't!' she shouted, the rich vowels seeming to roll round her mouth for a moment before she spat them out defiantly. She had brown skin and mad hair that sprouted from all over her scalp in topknots and she was wearing a pair of ripped jeans tight enough to make her bottom stick out even more. She righted herself and started stomping up the hill.

A moment later, a huge man in charity-shop clothes stumbled into the gutter and shouted. The wild-looking tramp had a funny way of walking as well, his gait short and awkward as if hobbled, his body swinging from side to side as he made a desperate effort to catch her up. He was a lot older than she was and his colourless clothes were torn and dirty, his face cast in deep shadow by the brim of his pork-pie hat.

As the vignette developed, the people closest to the woman began to inch away. The citizens of Brighton were no longer disturbed by the way some people yelled incoherently in the streets, or waved their arms at passing traffic, or mumbled in strange tongues as they waited in the supermarket queue to buy their tubes of alcohol: they merely paused to calibrate the level of threat these screamers represented, then they went about their business again. And yet, as the rain fell down on North Street and the shouting match continued, at the back of everybody's mind was a base note of fear. It was born of some news report they had in common about a person with a severe mental illness who had tarried too long in some waking nightmare and who, returning to earth with a bump and whatever sharp implement came to hand, had loomed out of nowhere to strike down an innocent passer-by such as them. No wonder they turned their backs. Far safer just to leave them to it. Let the dogs eat the dogs and, when they'd crunched the last of the bones, let them eat the refuse, too.

One by one, the buses started pulling in at the three stops, the foremost forcing the man and woman back up onto the pavement, where they disappeared into the surging crowd.

In front of Trevor, the doors of the number 25 opened with a hiss and, as the bus engorged the grateful passengers, he allowed himself to be swept towards it. He dug his bus card out of his jacket pocket and flipped the wallet open to show it to the driver before shuffling his way into the stuffy, brightly lit interior of the bus. When he tried to steal a glance back at the arguing man and woman he found the windows were too steamed up for him to see.

Down a quiet alley, in front of a lonely chocolate shop that had closed up half an hour before, the tramp was just behind the woman's shoulder now. He put his arm out and grabbed her above the elbow, pulling her back, spinning her round. His grip was strong but she shook it off. 'I told you to fuck off!' she yelled into his face. She stared contemptuously at his straggly beard and the odd, faraway expression that had come over his jellied eyes. She laughed, opening her mouth wide as she did so, showing him her white teeth. 'What is he, then?' she cackled. 'Your lord and master?'

It turned into an almighty storm. A few minutes from the seafront, outside Kemptown police station, uniformed officers at the start of their evening shifts sprinted through puddles to get to their cars and on Edward Street umbrellas were upended and the drains regurgitated their contents into the road. On the fifth floor, the rain was drumming against the window of the interview room, where a man named Clements was getting increasingly fed up. He'd been stuck here for more than two hours and he still had no idea why the cops had asked him to attend. In the time he'd spent in this empty room the light had melted from the sky and a host of officers had come and gone, each one assuring him that Detective Chief Inspector

Beckett wouldn't be long, that he was on his way over now from Hollingbury nick, that all Clements needed to do was sit tight. But he had had enough of sitting tight.

The door opened and two plain-clothes officers trooped into the room and stood side by side on the other side of the table. *Tweedledum and Tweedledee,* thought Clements, although in truth only Tom Beckett leaned towards the tubby side.

'You've put on weight, Tom,' Clements said.

Tom Beckett stared down at him, an expression on his features like he'd just stepped in something.

'But you've gone up in the world,' Clements went on in his wheedling tone of voice. 'A DCI, no less.'

Both officers sat down facing Clements. Beckett introduced his colleague. 'This is Detective Sergeant Minter.'

Clements's eyes swivelled to take in the younger officer. Smooth, ambitious, hatchet-faced, Beckett's sidekick looked like he would be playing things by the book this afternoon. 'Minter?' Clements said, savouring the word. The name rang a bell but, after a moment's careful consideration, he dismissed the thought and turned his attention back to the organ grinder.

Beckett thumped a buff-coloured file down on the table. It was an old-fashioned Murder Book and it was stuffed with papers, some of them peeking out from beneath the dog-eared cardboard flap. A scrawl of felt pen on the front bore the legend *Anna May* and the date of her death: *12th July 1995.*

Clements made a sour face. 'For fuck's sake.'

'You still got the pet food business?' Beckett said.

Sitting back in his chair, raising his face to the ceiling, Clements said in a weary voice, 'Just say your piece and fuck off.'

Tom Beckett fixed him with the kind of look that suggested

he, at least, wasn't happy to do things by the book. 'I asked you a question, nonce.'

Clements checked the video camera and the tape deck, neither of which were on. 'No, I haven't got the business any more. I lost it when you sent me down for five years. Remember?'

Beckett nodded. 'Like a pig in shit, you were. I mean, there was the business. Then there was the salary you drew from the council.' He leaned forward. 'You even had your accommodation thrown in, didn't you? A flat of your own, if I recall rightly. Somewhere you could use when you needed a bit of privacy.'

Clements leered at him. 'There were certain fringe benefits to being the house father.'

Beckett nodded slowly. 'That's how you thought of the girls, was it? A perk?'

The silence in the room lengthened. Clements nibbled a fingernail. He grunted, said in a rush, 'I fucked her but I didn't kill her, all right?' He waved his hand dismissively in the direction of the Murder Book. 'This is ancient history, Tom. It happened twenty years ago. You can walk down memory lane if you want to but you can do it on your own.' He looked at his watch. 'Now, I think it's time I went home for my tea.'

'Seventeen years,' said Detective Sergeant Minter.

Clements looked at him. 'What?'

'Anna May was killed seventeen years ago,' Minter said. He was twenty-seven, with blue eyes and dark brown hair that he usually kept short, although right now it was curling up a little from the collar at the back because he'd been too busy to get to a barber's.

The reopening of the cold case had been Minter's idea, not

Beckett's. He wanted justice for Anna May and he'd pursued that aim relentlessly over recent months, devoting spare weekends and rest days to tracing the other children from the home where Anna had been living – the home at the edge of the city where Clements should have been looking after her. Minter had pulled in favours where he could, chivvying Forensics to have another go at the evidence, snatching any moment from his catastrophic workload to find something, anything, that might persuade his bosses to officially reopen the investigation. Now, at last, he had Clements sat in front of him and as he opened the Murder Book and took out a crime scene photograph from the top of the pile, laying it on the table in front of Clements, Minter's heart was pounding in his chest. 'Have you seen this before?'

Clements was in his fifties, tall and bony, with swept-back hair and a reedy moustache he'd added the last time he'd come out of prison. Once upon a time he might have been considered quite dapper but now he was just seedy, the skin of his face blotchy, his hair greying in long, oily streaks. Today, like most days, he was dressed in shapeless jeans and a grubby old sweatshirt that was frayed at the collar and cuffs. His face hadn't seen a razor for a week and the nicotine stains at the ends of his fingers were deepening, turning from yellow to shit brown. He moved the photo round so he could see it better.

The colours had bleached a little and the background was fuzzy – just a few points of diamond light to suggest where the river flowed and dark green patches where the thicket began – but the detail of the crime scene in the foreground was intact. There was light and shade on the grass where Anna May lay on her side, one of her hands reaching out in front of her, fingers closing around a thick tuft as if she was trying to hang on.

Minter glanced down at the photo as well, shocked to realise that at the time of her murder Anna had barely been a teenager. At the time, she'd seemed so much older.

'Yeah,' Clements replied in a bored, sing-song voice, 'I've seen it before. You know I have.'

Minter took a second photograph and an autopsy report out of the file. He put the photo down on the table. 'The victim was a fourteen-year-old girl,' he read aloud from the report, adopting the dispassionate, even clinical tone of the pathologist. 'She had semen in her vagina, although the deterioration indicted that the sample was already at least twenty-four hours old at the time of her death. There was no evidence to suggest that the murderer had sexually assaulted the victim.'

'There you go,' said Clements triumphantly. 'That's what I just said. I fucked her but I didn't kill her.'

All the time he'd been sitting opposite Clements in the interview room, Minter held an icicle of fear in his stomach. Now, for the first time, he made himself look Clements in the eye. 'It was a brutal attack. Anna May was struck repeatedly around the face and head with a metal bar – a thick metal bar, judging by the extent of her injuries.' He put the autopsy report down and looked at the photo. Her head resting on a pillow of long grass, Anna's round face had been reduced to a pulpy, unrecognisable mess, fragments of white bone peeping through the smashed left cheek. 'Did she threaten to go to the police about the things you were doing to her? Was that why you argued?'

Sighing, Clements folded his arms.

Minter said, 'We've had another complaint.'

Clements's eyes flicked across the table. 'Who?'

'Janine Stephenson.'

Clements shook his head. 'Don't remember her.'

'Janine was thirteen when she came to Hillcrest. She said you forced her to have sex with you.'

Clements laughed. 'She suing, is she?'

'Did you have sex with her?'

'No, I didn't.'

'I've found out a lot about you, Clements. Things the children were too scared to mention to the police at the time. I know what that feels like, you see. I know what it feels like to be scared.'

Clements stared at Minter. Suddenly, it dawned on him. 'You were there, weren't you? You were the kiddie who discovered the body. I remember now. Yeah. I knew I'd heard your name before.' He sniggered. 'Quiet little fucker, you were, back then. Haven't changed much, have you?' He shook his head. 'So that's what this is all about. I thought it was Tom here getting all antsy about his legacy, but it's got nothing to do with him, has it? This is about you.' He nodded at the photograph of Anna May's smashed face. 'Your memories keeping you awake at night, are they?' Clements liked the fear and vulnerability he could see etched on Minter's face. He was in control now, just like he'd been all those years ago. 'Y'know, you kids never ceased to amaze me, the way you talked about your parents. How they didn't want to let you go. How they hated you being in care. How, one day, they'd come back and rescue you and you'd all live happily ever after. It was pathetic. None of you could face up to the truth.'

The wind shivered the window, throwing a handful of darts against the glass. Minter might have started digging into the facts surrounding Anna May's death at Hillcrest, but he'd never enquired too deeply into the circumstances of his own childhood and the reasons he was taken into care at the age of six. Even then, Minter always had the sense that there were things he'd rather not be told. So, for someone so methodical, he went about that other investigation with a surprising lack of focus. He was like a crab making its way along the shoreline: whenever he encountered an obstacle or a dead end, he stopped completely, pausing to consider before moving off in another direction. All he had really achieved to date was to retrieve a copy of his original birth certificate that bore an address for a house on the Moulsecoomb estate – a house that had been demolished long ago – and a blank space where his father's name should be.

'You tell me, then,' Minter said to Clements. As a child, he had been told that his mother couldn't look after him, that when they had lived together she used to leave him on his own in the flat, sometimes for days. 'What is the truth?'

Clements grinned. 'You really don't know, do you?'

'Know what?'

'There was a fire,' Clements said.

'The fire was an accident. My mother forgot to turn the stove off when she went out.'

Clements grunted. He tapped his finger against his own temple. 'She was sick in the head. She set the place on fire deliberately. She left you inside to burn.'

'That's not how it happened.'

'I was the house father at that poxy home. I saw all the files. Every one. And yours, well, it kind of stuck in my mind. Your mum wanted you gone, Minter. She tried to kill you.'

When Minter stood up his chair clattered to the floor behind him. He turned on his heels and left the room.

The echo of the slam died slowly. Clements looked at Beckett. 'Do you think I upset him?'

Beckett got up himself and came round to the other side of the table, and in one swift movement yanked Clements out of his chair, slamming him against the wall.

'What kind of nick are you running here?' Clements jabbered.

'Next time,' said Beckett, 'it'll be *me* coming for you.'

Outside, Minter stood in the glassed-in stairwell. He gripped the handrail tightly, a vile taste in his mouth as if he was going to throw up, his forehead resting against the coolness of the glass. When he looked out over the seafront he could see the white horses chopping at the Palace Pier and the strings of lights swinging wildly from lamp-post to lamp-post as they stretched away along the promenade. He heard the moan of the wind and the distant roar of the sea. Minter put his hand against the glass but when he touched it with his palm he found it wasn't cool any more.

It burned.

He woke and cried out. He was six years old, standing inside a room filled with smoke, in front of a closed door outlined in bright orange. He was coughing and the intensity of the heat pulled fat beads of sweat from his scalp. On the other side of the door the fire crackled and the door itself was moving, rippling like the fur of an animal, the paint blistering, bubbling. 'Help me!' he cried, but no one heard because there was no one else but him at home. The flames were raging out there but all the little boy knew was that he had to get out of his bedroom before he choked to death on the smoke. So he closed his hand over the door handle and pulled.

'You OK?'

Minter turned round to see Tom Beckett standing in the shadows. He nodded.

Beckett stuffed his hands into his pockets and walked over to where Minter was standing. For a few moments, the two men stood side by side, watching the lights of the speeding cars as they drove through the rain along the seafront road.

'You know,' said Beckett, 'Clements is a scumbag of the first order. He might be winding you up about your mum.'

In all the years Minter had spent in care, his mother had never come to visit. 'I think it happened just like he said it did.'

Minter was a rising star in Brighton and Hove but now he seemed to shrink before Beckett's eyes, becoming smaller, greyer, almost insubstantial. Like a ghost.

'We'll let Clements go, then you and I can go for a beer.'

Minter said nothing.

Beckett broke the silence. 'Tell me about Janine Stephenson.'

Minter made a mental effort to marshal the facts. 'I interviewed Janine in prison. She's got a long history of substance abuse. Three convictions for possession of crack cocaine and another for intent to supply.'

'Yeah, and now we know why she took all those drugs, don't we? Have you got any corroboration for her story about the abuse?'

Minter shook his head.

Beckett asked, 'Forensics?'

'There's no probable DNA match to anyone on the database, and certainly not to Clements.'

'So Janine's testimony is all you've got.'

Reluctantly, Minter nodded. 'I need more time, sir.'

Beckett sighed 'It took guts to do what you did just now,

fronting up to Clements like that. But you know what things are like, Minter. I can't afford to have you chase something like this into the sands.'

'I've turned up Janine,' Minter protested. 'There's more to come. I can feel it.'

'You can keep tabs on Clements and you can keep going with the investigation in your own time if you like, but for the moment at least I'm not going to ask for a case review. There's no point. It will just get knocked back. I'm sorry, Minter.'

Minter turned away. He looked out over the promenade again.

Beckett said. 'You never asked me why I spent all afternoon at Hollingbury.'

Minter turned to look at his boss.

'I'm being seconded.'

Because of the latest budget cuts, all the detective squads in Brighton were being reorganised. Temporary posts and secondments abounded. 'You're going to CID?' Minter asked.

'Afraid so. In their infinite wisdom, the powers that be have decided the force does need a second murder squad after all. I've been asked to set it up.'

'When does all this happen?'

'I've already started on the list of officers I want. There'll be the usual argy-bargy about your transfer, of course.'

'Are you telling me that I'm going to be seconded as well?'

'You up for it?'

Any ambitious officer needed to serve time on a murder team. 'Of course I am, sir.'

'Good. Although a certain rather tasty detective sergeant is already giving me earache about the detective inspector's job.'

'You mean Kevin Phillips?'

Beckett nodded. 'Do you think you two can work together?'

'I never had a problem with Kevin.'

'I hoped you were going to say that.'

'But that's not to say he won't have a problem with me.'

'You leave Kevin to me.'

'When do we start?'

Beckett looked west, out across the city. 'As soon as we catch ourselves a nice, big, juicy murder.'

3

The echoing concourse of Brighton railway station was an immense, cavernous space. Its interior was illuminated by outsize sodium lights, their tulip-shaped bulbs glowing yellow-orange as they dangled from the roof, their fittings topped with vicious-looking spikes to keep the seagulls from settling. 'What the hell is it now?' said the early morning commuter as she watched the delays riffle down the departure boards. Across the ticket turnstiles all the barriers were closed. Behind them, the first London train of the day was standing stationary and silent, its doors agape. All along the platforms the signals had turned red.

A real voice instead of a clipped digital recording cleared its throat nervously and crackled over the tannoy. 'Sorry to have to announce, but all services have been temporarily suspended because of an incident in the station.'

Immediately, a groan went up from the commuters. 'Do you think they have any idea how much we pay for our damned season tickets?' said the woman.

Minter hurried across from the concourse to the part of the

station hidden between the WH Smith's concession and the toilets, where two uniformed officers were already erecting a small white marquee and a well-built man wearing the peaked cap and fluorescent green vest of the British Transport Police was talking to a third.

'This is Constable Ellis, sir,' said the PC when Minter arrived. 'He found it.'

Underneath his cap Constable Ellis's ginger hair had been shaved to within a whisper of the back of his neck. The Transport Police – not-quite coppers who nicked the serial fare dodgers and intimidated the drunks – were recruited for their meatiness. 'I've been on the railways a dozen years,' Ellis said, a blink of terror still in his eyes. 'But I've never, ever seen anything like that.' Behind him, a white-suited Scenes of Crime officer went into the little marquee.

The officer in dark blue said, 'We've got a description of the man who left the case.'

'Who from?' Minter asked.

'One of the train drivers saw a man carrying a suitcase wander into the station about twenty minutes ago. The guy looked like he was homeless.'

'Did the driver see him leave?'

'Afraid not, sir.'

Minter traced his eyes over the yellow bricks of the station wall, which had been grubbied by a century and a half of steam and diesel fumes. Halfway up, a single CCTV camera had been screwed into the brickwork. It was a good angle. 'Where does the footage get recorded?' Minter asked Ellis.

'Our office on Queen's Road.'

'How old is the system?'

Ellis shrugged. 'A good few years.'

Minter nodded. They'd probably have to take the hard drive out. He glanced the other way, to where the crowd in the concourse was thickening by the moment and a hapless-looking ticket inspector was being surrounded by an angry knot of passengers. 'Close the station and get all those people off the concourse, but don't let any of them leave,' Minter told the PC. 'Hold them outside. We'll interview them there. Tell the station manager to make the announcement now. Then lend the staff a hand to clear the place.'

The constable looked over at the swelling crowd. 'They're not going to be happy.'

Minter lifted the flap of the tent. 'Tough.'

Inside, the Scenes of Crime officer was on his knees, crouching over the suitcase. The case itself was cheap-looking; the sides bulged. The SOCO had a strip of tape in his hands which he was using to carefully lift prints from the fabric of the handle. Here and there, the ground around the case was shadowed with more of the sooty grey powder. 'Lots of prints,' the SOCO muttered over his shoulder. 'Good ones, too.' Still on his knees, he scrambled to the side.

The suitcase was big and blue with a pair of wheels attached to the bottom, the kind of thing that people staggered off the Gatwick Express with every day. Looking down, tilting his head this way and that, Minter spent a moment trying to make sense of its contents.

The woman was naked. The tops of the arms were wrong – pushed up like that against her shoulders in the tight confines of the suitcase, they looked too thick, too bulky. Then Minter realised the quartered dead woman had been jumbled up. Those weren't her arms at all. They were her legs. They'd been stuffed in either side of her torso so that her thighs were shoved against the bloodied joints of her shoulders. Suddenly, the full grisly horror of the dismembered body dawned on Minter and he had to look away.

His mouth was dry and his head was aching because he hadn't had a wink of sleep last night. When he'd finally gone to bed he'd just lain awake waiting for the morning to creep down his window pane, his mind turning in smaller and smaller circles until it felt like the flywheel was about to come off the gears. He was glad when the telephone rang and it was Beckett giving him something other than the truth about his mother to think about.

Minter had seen all kinds of death. His job was to offer up an account of who had done these terrible things to the woman whose body had ended up there in the suitcase. That was what the public in the station were entitled to: an explanation; things put back in the right place. So, looking back at the contents of the case, Minter's brain stretched for rationality. The blood was pooled a couple of inches up the sides. Not a lot of time, then, between her death and the body being stowed inside the suitcase. 'Anything else?' he said to the SOCO.

The SOCO nodded at the floor beside him. 'A couple of partial footprints.' Minter looked down at the drops of drying blood. On the mica-flecked concrete they were the colour of rust. 'How much more do you want?' said the SOCO.

He had a point. The CCTV, the eyewitness description, the fingerprints – assuming they could find him, the perp was as good as banged up. This would be about the body. About who she'd been and where she'd gone and why someone had marked her out for slaughter.

Minter made himself look again. The suitcase was splayed

open. She had brown skin. The hands were gone, as well as the head, which was going to make identification difficult.

He stepped outside the tent to gulp at fresh air. He stood on the concourse for a moment, his eyes tracing the blue-painted metal columns up towards the canopied glass and steel roof of the station, behind which the milky light of dawn was streaking the dark sky. In a saner world, disgruntled commuters were being herded out of the concourse by a small and ragged line of station staff.

4

• • •

In his new office at the CID headquarters in Hollingbury, DCI Beckett downloaded the preliminary post-mortem on the dead woman. One by one the grisly images opened on his computer screen. There were forty-three stab wounds in total, the accompanying report from the pathologist explained, most of them flesh wounds but a few of them much deeper, delving right down to the bone. The pathologist estimated that eleven different knives had been used, ranging from a clasp knife to a nine-inch hunting blade.

According to the pathologist's report, the reduced function of the dead woman's kidneys might indicate damage caused by alcohol, a blood infection or early onset diabetes. At this stage, before detailed toxicology, it was impossible to say which. What they did know was that the woman in the suitcase was in her late twenties or early thirties and of African descent and that the last meal she had eaten had been a couple of days before. Most of the ingredients had already been digested and absorbed and the matter the pathologist had found in the intestines was now on its way for further analysis.

Beckett emailed back to the pathologist, asking him to take a section of the femur and send it to the national forensics lab in Nottingham where an isotopic analysis could be carried out. There was no telling how long the woman had been in the UK before her death but if she was a recent visitor or, worse, an illegal, then the bone scan might be the only way they had to establish a place of birth. If nothing else, it would give Beckett a place from which to start.

Like the rest of Sussex House, Beckett's room was lit day and night by overhead strip lighting because the windows had been covered in white plastic laminate to prevent people spying in from the road outside. His office was virtually empty. Facilities had put in the phone lines and the computers but very little else, just two big desks pushed beneath the window – one for Tom Beckett, one for his putative detective inspector – and a blank association board screwed to the wall with a pair of new marker pens sitting ready in its gutter. The meeting table that seated six might still be on order but at least the investigation had a name now – Operation Ghillie. Beckett didn't know what the hell a ghillie was but it didn't really matter. The names were selected sequentially from random lists of nouns held somewhere in the bowels of the Home Office: operations might be named after a type of shoe or a type of sword and sometimes this could cause amusement, like the anti-terrorism investigation some bright spark wanted to call Scimitar, until someone pointed out that it might offend Muslims.

Beckett glanced again at the post-mortem photographs on the screen. A lot of serial killers took trophies from the bodies of their victims, most commonly the extremities. Some killers needed to touch what they killed with their hands, delighting in the skin-to-skin contact afforded by strangling; others, like this one, wanted to stab and cut with knives. It was a frenzy called picquerism and it was a pleasure that would invariably prove too compulsive to stop at just a single victim.

Beckett read through the post-mortem report again, searching for any telltale clues the killer might have left on the corpse. There were plenty of traces on the suitcase but nothing at all on the body itself – no thread of cotton, no partial fingerprint, not even, as yet, any DNA.

It worried Beckett. Worried him a lot.

The CCTV room was just along the corridor. Little more than a broom cupboard in size, it was not a popular assignment but this morning Minter was taking great pains with his edit of the footage from the railway station.

The first sequence he had copied from the hard drive had been recorded by the camera covering the entrance. The grainy black and white image track showed a handful of commuters creeping under the arches and over to the ticket barriers, their faces little more than smudges. A moment later, a big man in a long black coat followed them onto the concourse. He was wearing a hat and carrying a heavy case – so heavy, in fact, that he had to use both hands to lift it, his body twisting over to one side with the effort. A few yards into the station, the suspect stopped and put the case down. He looked around, his head moving jerkily from side to side as he took in his surroundings. 'Jesus,' Minter said under his breath, thinking about the cheek of the man in bringing the suitcase and its dreadful contents into such a public place.

On the screen, a tubby man in a grey suit with a satchel over his shoulder passed nearby. It was the train driver who had given the suspect's description. He could only have been ten feet away when he broke his stride to look across. He had certainly taken a good look – no defence lawyer was going to say otherwise. Once the driver had gone on his way, the man in the dark coat picked up the suitcase again and staggered out of shot.

The second sequence was taken from the camera behind Smith's. The man with the suitcase walked into the top right-hand corner of the frame, struggling even more with the heavily laden case, glancing warily from side to side. It was a closer shot and when the man looked up he stared straight into the camera lens. 'Gotcha!' Minter said, freezing the frame on the screen and peering at the set of enormous features beneath the brim of the pork-pie hat. Minter selected the Print function from the pull-down menu and a moment later the laser printer to the side of the monitor started to wheeze. Minter pressed play again and watched as, without any kind of warning, the suspect dropped the suitcase. It fell heavily to the floor, stood upright for a moment, sagged, then collapsed onto its side. At the same time this was happening, the suspect turned and hobbled out of shot. After a minute – Minter logged it from the time signature as 6.08 a.m. – a British Transport Police officer came to stand over the unattended luggage. Minter stopped the tape and started the DVD burn. On the bottom shelf of the rack, the machine chugged away.

In his office, Tom Beckett opened the email from the pathologist. The section from the femur would be prepared and sent off by lunchtime but the police surgeon warned the Senior Investigating Officer that the lab in Nottingham had a minimum two-week turnaround.

There was a knock at the half-open door and Minter came in. 'Hard copy from the station, sir.'

Beckett got up from his chair and grabbed the photo Minter was holding. 'This'll do us,' he said, getting his first glimpse of the man they were hunting. He paced over to the association board and used a bit of sticky to put the photo up next to one of the hideous photographs from this morning's post-mortem, the one showing a deep knife wound to the woman's shoulder. 'This guy looks pretty memorable. Get an enhanced copy sent to every officer in Brighton and Hove. Some plod might have moved him on from a doorway last night.'

'Yes, sir.'

Beckett nodded at the silver disc Minter was holding. 'That for the briefing?'

Minter nodded.

Taking the DVD in its plastic case from Minter's hand, Beckett said, 'Get on to all the other forces in the country. Send them the PM and ask them if they have any unsolved murders where the perp has used knives – lots of knives.'

'What about a profiler?'

'I've already contacted someone at the Home Office. Apparently, he's reliable, down-to-earth. He won't spin us any yarns.'

Profilers had changed a lot in recent years. 'Good,' said Minter.

'And go over to the mortuary and talk to Dr Hunter. We all know the good doctor hates to speculate but we need to find some way of identifying this body.'

Minter jogged down the stairs of Sussex House and pushed open the front door to find Detective Constable Vicky Reynolds waiting on the doorstep, her finger poised over the entry buzzer. She was a couple of years younger than he was, tall and statuesque, with long, dark hair and something very different about her appearance.

'Vicky,' Minter said.

'Don't worry,' she replied. 'I'm not stalking you.' Vicky had spent three years as a detective constable in Tom Beckett's Serious and Organised Crime Unit team, the last of them alongside Minter. 'I'm here in an official capacity. I've come to present my credentials to CID – let them know there's a new family liaison officer in the division. And by the way, Minter, thanks for telling me about your secondment.'

'I only knew it was going to happen last night.' It was Vicky's clothes, Minter realised. At Kemptown, he was used to seeing her in the standard issue outfit of a dark skirt and jacket and white blouse – the kind of smart but anonymous workwear female detectives deployed in order to ape their male counterparts. This morning Vicky had dressed very differently in a wine-coloured jacket with white stitching around the lapels and a skirt that went above her knees. The sudden reveal of her femininity snagged Minter's eye. Being a family liaison officer suited Vicky Reynolds very well indeed.

She asked, 'Is it the body they found at the station?'

Minter nodded. 'I was first on the scene.'

'As bad as they're saying?'

'Worse.'

There was an uncomfortable silence, as there always was between them when neither Minter nor Vicky could quite find the words to move things on. 'Well,' said Minter, floundering a little, 'congratulations on passing your FLO units.'

'They weren't exactly hard,' Vicky demurred. The law degree Vicky had studied for meant examinations held no terrors. She looked down at her watch. 'I'm ridiculously early. Have you got time for a coffee?'

A coffee would go brilliantly with the cigarette Minter had been promising himself ever since he had arrived at Hollingbury from the station. 'OK.'

Just around the corner from Sussex House, tucked inside the gates of the neighbouring industrial estate, was a fast-food shack. It was open all hours, serving the stallholders from the fruit and veg market that took place in the early morning and the lorry drivers making deliveries to Asda through the night. It was known to make the best bacon sarnies in the city, with doorstep-cut white bread and thick rashers. With no time for breakfast, Minter fetched two coffees from the serving hatch and walked over to where Vicky was sitting under a gazebo to keep the drizzle off. There were two other tables huddled under cover but both of them were empty. 'Are you still going to be based at Kemptown?' Minter asked, lighting his Benson and Hedges.

Vicky sipped her coffee and nodded. 'I'm assigned temporarily to any squad that needs me, but SOCU is still my home team.'

'So you think you're going to enjoy it?'

Vicky thought she detected a dismissive edge to Minter's question. It was common enough. 'It's not all tea and sympathy, you know. FLOs have broken big cases in the past.' What had started out a decade ago in Traffic – where the first family liaison officers helped the loved ones of road-accident victims through the traumas of identification and post-mortem – had grown into a much wider role. 'My specialism is Major Crime,' Vicky insisted. When it comes down to it, I'm still an investigator.'

But Minter was worried about Vicky for a different reason. If an officer wanted to be sure they still had a job at the end of every month, they had to be right at the front of the so-called front line. 'It's still the victim route instead of the offender route.'

'I know,' said Vicky. 'This might be the dumbest career move I've ever made. But I was burning out in SOCU, Minter. If I'm going to continue as a police officer, I need a whole different slant on the job.'

Minter nodded his understanding.

Vicky watched him smoke. 'If you don't mind me saying, you look like shit.'

'I didn't get a lot of sleep last night.'

'I thought the body was only discovered this morning.'

'It was.'

Vicky said, 'You interviewed a man named Clements last night didn't you?'

'Did Beckett tell you?'

Vicky knew about Minter's childhood spent in care. 'You might find this difficult to believe, Minter, but Tom Beckett is worried about you. So am I.'

Minter could feel his face reddening.

Vicky put her hand over one of Minter's. 'Missing Persons is what I do now, mate. If you want some help in finding her, all you have to do is ask.'

Minter took his hand away. 'Why the hell would I want to find her?'

'Aren't you curious? Don't you want to ask her why?'

Minter stubbed his cigarette out in the little silver foil ashtray. 'You're a cop, Vick. You know how low people sink.' He stood up, jamming his cigarettes back into his jacket pocket. 'For all I care, she can go to hell.'

*

Inside Sussex House, Detective Sergeant Kevin Phillips slipped out into the corridor to take the call.

'Well, Mr Phillips,' said the Asian voice on the other end of the telephone line. He was speaking from a call centre in Mumbai. 'If it's not a good time to speak,' he went on with exaggerated politeness, 'I will be pleased to put you down for a call back tomorrow.'

'Listen, you halfwit,' Phillips hissed. 'I'm a police officer and I've started a murder case. I haven't got time to talk to you today *or* tomorrow.'

'Would it be more convenient then,' asked the man from a thousand miles away with a target to meet, 'if I ring you this evening? Perhaps it would be easier for you if I availed myself of the landline number you have listed on your account?'

At the moment, the only bright spot in Phillips's life was that he'd managed to keep his money worries secret from his wife. 'No! I'll call you.'

'But Mr Phillips, we at the bank feel it is imperative that we help you out of the tight spot you've got into.'

Phillips's debts were racking up by the week. He'd rolled over his overdraft and he'd missed the last five mortgage payments and now he was even using credit cards for food shopping, sliding each of them in turn into the machine at the supermarket checkout then waiting with a queasy feeling in his stomach until, finally, *Approved* flickered magically onto the grey LED.

Phillips ended the telephone call. 'Fuck you, mate.' He slipped his phone back into his pocket and leaned against the wall. He wasn't stupid. He knew he couldn't go on like this.

He was in big trouble and if he was going to dig himself out he needed to get the DI's job on the new murder team. The only thing that stood between him and a significant boost to his income was a certain pushy young officer called Minter. But Phillips had been a DS a lot longer than Minter and he had experience of working a murder. By the time Mumbai called again he was sure he'd be sitting pretty behind the other new desk in Tom Beckett's office.

Minter drove along the seafront road, passing the long line of Regency terraces that faced the English Channel. There was just a hunched-over dog walker making his way along the blustery footpath, the choppy sea a pencil-grey colour behind him. Stopping at some traffic lights, Minter lit another cigarette.

The sea mist came up out of nowhere. It rolled across the waves towards the land, spreading out all the time as more of the salt spray condensed in the freezing air until, in less than a minute, it started to engulf the old West Pier. As Minter watched from his car, the rusted, skeletal iron girders – all that remained of the derelict Victorian structure – began to disappear. The mist unfurled across the road and suddenly the temperature inside Minter's car plummeted, making him shiver. The houses on the other side of the road became invisible to him. The black front doors, the buttermilk walls, the terracotta chimney pots – they all began to blur and dissolve.

Then, as quickly as it appeared, the mist began to clear. The seafront emerged once more and the gulls shrieked in relief. Through the last wisps, Minter saw the traffic lights change from red to green. He drove further along the road that divided the sea from the land, turning his mind to the interview he was about to conduct with the pathologist and the pressing need to establish the identity of the body in the suitcase. Like Beckett, Minter knew they didn't have much time.

5

• • •

'Who we here for, then?' asked the sergeant in the blue Kevlar stab vest.

Minter gave him a copy of the suspect's photo. Looking down at it, the sergeant grimaced.

'Vincent Underhill,' Minter said. 'Male homeless schizophrenic with a previous conviction for wounding.'

The sergeant shook his head. 'I fucking hate the schizos. No telling what they're going to do.' He eyed Minter. 'You want me to do the caution?'

'I'll do it. And if at all possible, let's do this softly softly. My boss wants him in a good state for the interview.'

The sergeant looked at Minter. 'That rather depends on Mr Underhill.'

The light was draining quickly from the sky and the rain was teeming down as Minter led the snatch squad of six officers out of the car park and along the parade of darkened shops, at the end of which St Michael's church rose high above the iron railings, the steeple illuminated by a pair of floodlights set into the ground. As he splashed through the puddles on the pavement and into the churchyard, Minter's pulse began to quicken.

Inside the glassed-in modern porch was a display board with a handwritten message welcoming the homeless to St Michael's and an arrow pointing down the stone steps towards the crypt. A young man with a stubby, undyed Mohican was waiting at the top of the stairs. He had an ID card on a lanyard round his neck and Minter moved quickly towards him. 'Mr Hall?'

'Yes,' said the manager of the night shelter.

'We spoke on the phone. Is Underhill still here?'

Hall glanced round at all the weaponry – tasers, batons, see-through shields – stashed about the bodies of the officers behind Minter. He nodded apprehensively. 'He's still here. He's right at the back, sitting on his own. He always sits on his own.'

Minter nodded to the crypt. 'Show me.'

The steps down were steep and had been dipped smooth by the tread of many centuries, and with every step that Minter took the air grew a little colder. At the bottom, Minter saw that the crypt ran right beneath the church, a maze of stone columns supporting the weight. Spotlights lit a lot of the interior but there were still areas of deep shadow over by the walls. In front of Minter were four rows of camp beds, about twenty in all, each one made up with army surplus blankets and thin pillows. It was raining hard outside so quite a few early birds had already claimed their pitches. One of the men was lying down and flicking through a copy of the *Argus*; another had taken off his woolly socks and was peeling strips of skin from the blisters on his feet. As Minter walked between the lines of beds, all of the homeless men turned to look at him. He glimpsed unshaven faces and hostile, rheumy eyes, he smelt the dampness of their clothes, the tang of their unwashed flesh. Then, through the forest of columns, he caught sight of the man he had come here to arrest.

Vincent Underhill was sitting right at the back of the room, at the table closest to the long trestle where a tea urn gently steamed. Nearby, at the other canteen tables, a handful of other men were sitting in little groups, drinking and chatting, their low voices murmuring through the stone crypt. As Minter approached, their conversations died out one by one until he could hear nothing but the shuffle of his footfalls against the stone floor. He had ventured into nightclubs after stabbings and crack dens during raids but at least there was an excitement there, a thrill of the chase. Here in the crypt there was just a brooding sense of unease.

Dressed in the same black greatcoat and pork-pie hat, Underhill was hunched so far over his mug of tea that Minter couldn't see his face. He was a huge man – much bigger and taller, in fact, than the high-angle cameras at the railway station had been able to convey. Six foot six inches, Minter estimated his height at. The black woollen greatcoat draped his frame like a cloak, its tails hanging down either side of the chair, two pools of water on the stones where the rain had dripped from the sodden material. Minter glanced down at Underhill's mud-spattered walking boots and thought about the footprints in the blood. He was breathing through his mouth now because the man had a stink all of his own.

'Vincent Underhill?'

No reply. Underhill didn't even look up.

On his back, Minter could feel the baleful stares of the other men in the night shelter. 'Sir,' he said, his voice a little louder this time, the sound echoing in the crypt.

Underhill heard him this time. His fingers clasped the mug a bit tighter, his broken fingernails encrusted with grime. They were big hands, Minter noticed, thinking about the knife wound in the shoulder of the butchered girl and about the power that would have been needed to plunge a blade in that deep.

Minter pulled up a chair and sat down opposite the suspect. From beneath the grey pork-pie hat, Underhill's black hair fell in long matted corkscrews. The lower part of his face – which was still all that Minter could see of him – was drowned in an extravagant beard that was likewise matted and flecked with grey. Underneath the greatcoat Minter could see the layers of clothes he was wearing in an effort to keep out the cold and wet: a threadbare suit jacket, a V-necked jumper, a collared shirt, a couple of vests, each article turned a dirty kind of grey. Underhill seemed monochrome, as if he'd stepped straight out of the CCTV footage. He said something under his breath – not words exactly but strange, half-strangulated mutterings.

Minter tensed, expecting trouble. Underhill looked to his right into the corner of the crypt, where a Calor gas heater had been turned on. Minter followed the direction of his gaze.

All three of the heater's panels glowed bright orange through the gloom and in the deathly silence, Minter could hear the gas jets make a soft purring noise. When he looked back, Minter saw that Underhill hadn't taken his eyes off the fire. He studied the side of Underhill's face, comparing its features to the image from the CCTV, certain now that the man in front of him was the same man who had left the suitcase at Brighton station.

Underhill looked ancient, almost ageless. Years of sleeping rough, of exposure to all kinds of weather, had turned Underhill's skin into leather. His features were swollen, almost waterlogged. There were huge bags under both his eyes and the end of his nose was spider-webbed with purple veins. He looked like one of those mummified prehistoric men who rise through boggy ground to be rediscovered thousands of years after their original death. Still he stared at the purring fire, saying nothing.

Minter stood up. He raised a hand to beckon the other officers forward, then he started to deliver the caution, placing Underhill under arrest on suspicion of murder of a woman as yet unknown.

'Come on, sir,' said Minter when he was finished. 'It's time to go.'

The silence deepened again and Minter and the other officers readied themselves for action. Underhill placed his mighty hands on the table top and slowly levered himself up until he towered over Minter, his yellowy, bloodshot eyes taking in the group of body-armoured officers gathered behind. The gas fire purred and Underhill turned his head to the right until he was staring into the ripple of orange flame once more. Then, after a few moments' consideration, he turned back to the police officers and his shoulders dipped.

Minter relaxed, too. 'This way, sir,' he said, indicating the stairs at the other end of the crypt.

Calmly, almost meekly, Vincent Underhill allowed himself to be led away.

'That guy's head is like a radio mast,' said the police doctor. 'He's receiving signals from everywhere.'

Beckett had come across the GP before. Previously, he had proved to be an amenable fellow but right now, standing outside the interview room where Vincent Underhill was being held, Beckett could see he was on the edge of pronouncing his prime suspect unfit for interview. 'How about time limits?' he suggested, trying desperately to rescue the situation. 'Twenty minutes of questioning followed by ten-minute rests.'

Agonising over his decision, the middle-aged doctor rubbed his hands together. 'I'm not sure what use that would be.'

'This is a murder charge,' Beckett said. 'We've got forensics linking Underhill to the crime. So you tell me, what time limits would you consider safe?'

The doctor looked at him. 'I'd put it the other way round. Ten minutes questioning followed by half-hour gaps.'

The custody clock was ticking loud and clear in Beckett's ear. He did the maths. That would leave him a maximum of ninety minutes. It wasn't enough, not with someone as confused and meandering as Underhill would inevitably be, and they'd already wasted a couple of hours booking him in and then the doctor speaking to him. Beckett had decided to do the interview in the small suite on the top floor of Sussex House instead of the custody centre next door, where the clanging doors might tip Underhill over the edge. This interview was going to be done nice and friendly, with no eyeballing and no leading questions. The last thing Beckett wanted was some beaky pretrial judge ruling Underhill's statement inadmissible because of the circumstances of the interview.

'OK,' he said. 'Done.'

Beckett shook the doctor's hand and asked a PC to show him out. He was about to go back into the interview room, where Underhill was waiting with the duty solicitor, when he caught sight of a prim-looking woman hurrying towards him along the corridor.

'At last,' Beckett said under his breath. The appropriate adult was social worker Evelyn McIllroy. They exchanged an unfriendly greeting. 'You done one of these before?' Beckett asked.

McIllroy was chippy. 'One or two.'

'We've asked you to attend to help us ensure that the suspect understands the nature of our questions, and to help us understand the meaning of his answers. Mr Underhill will have a lawyer present at all times to represent his interests.'

'Thank you, DCI Beckett,' Ms McIllory said, 'but I'm already very familiar with section seventy-six of the Police and Criminal Evidence Act.'

Nodding, Beckett opened the door to the interview room. 'Let's get started then.'

In the middle of the large square room four chairs had been arranged in a circle but Underhill was standing up over by the window, his back turned to them. Beckett and the social worker took their seats either side of the solicitor. After a few moments, Beckett said, 'Can you come and sit down now please, Vincent.'

Underhill stayed exactly where he was. Beckett glanced at the woman PC standing by the door. She shrugged, as if Underhill had been standing there for ages.

'Vincent,' Beckett said more loudly. Underhill turned around to see where the noise was coming from. Glancing across, Beckett could tell that McIllroy was a little overawed by his extravagant appearance. That was no bad thing. It was a monstrous act that Underhill had been accused of.

Slowly, Underhill came and sat down in the empty chair. One by one, he stared at all his interlocutors.

'Thank you, Vincent,' said Beckett, mentally ticking off another wasted minute. He did the introductions as quickly as he could, naming everyone and explaining their function and describing how the time limits would work. Beckett began. 'You are Mr Vincent Underhill?'

After a moment's consideration, Underhill nodded.

'And at present you do not have a permanent address?'

Underhill looked at him as if he didn't understand.

'The detective is asking you where you live, Vincent?' put in the social worker.

Sounds tumbled out of the suspect's mouth like marbles. 'Word salad', the police doctor had called it. It was a condition that afflicted a lot of schizophrenics. Beckett pressed on regardless. 'Can you tell me where you were at six o'clock this morning?'

Underhill reached into the pocket of his greatcoat and took out a tobacco tin, prising off its lid with a long and filthy fingernail and fishing out his makings. The PC by the door started to object but Beckett held his hand up to stop her. In the few short minutes he'd spent with the doctor, he'd gleaned some useful information. The brain chemistry of schizophrenics was unique. Nicotine worked differently on them than it did on other people. Cigarettes were a kind of self-medication: rather than being stimulants, they calmed schizophrenics down and sometimes even took the edge off their hallucinations. Caffeine had much the same effect. Beckett asked, 'Can I get you some more coffee, Vincent?'

'Y-' Underhill stuttered. When the effort became too much for him, he nodded instead.

'PC Daniels,' Beckett said, 'can you get Mr Underhill a cup of very strong coffee, please.'

The constable opened the door and had a word with someone outside.

Underhill licked the cigarette paper and folded it over the tobacco, his hands shaking. Beckett took a box of matches out of his pocket and struck one, holding the flame out for Underhill. The vagrant leaned forward and allowed Beckett to light his pipe-cleaner-thin roll-up, the twist of Rizla flaring until he blew it out with his first exhale. A flake of charred cigarette paper floated down through the air between them.

Beckett, who had been careful to avoid eye contact, said, 'Perhaps I can remind you where you were, Vincent.' He took the enhanced version of the suspect photo from the station out of the evidence folder and held it for Underhill to see. 'Is this you, sir?'

The vagrant glanced down at the photo.

Beckett watched the reedy cigarette burning down. 'We have an eyewitness statement as well.' He took that out of the folder and read aloud the description given by the train driver. 'It sounds like you, Vincent.'

Underhill smoked greedily.

The coffee arrived. Underhill sipped at it and smacked his lips and went back to his cigarette.

Beckett took another photograph out of the folder. 'This picture is from a different CCTV camera at Brighton railway station. It shows a man carrying a suitcase.' He showed Underhill the photograph. 'Can you tell me what was inside the suitcase?'

The solicitor looked askance at Beckett. Underhill offered up a volley of his curious mumblings.

'Sorry, Vincent,' said Beckett. 'I didn't catch that. Could you repeat what you just said, please?'

The solicitor glanced down at his wristwatch.

Beckett tried again. 'Can you tell us where you were at six this morning?'

Another thirty seconds passed. The social worker sighed. Beckett shot her a look. 'Vincent,' he said, 'this is a murder investigation. It would very much count in your favour if you could give us an account of your movements.'

'I make that nearly ten minutes,' said the solicitor, closing his file.

Looking at the ceiling, Beckett offered up a silent prayer. 'OK,' he breathed, getting up from his chair. 'Half an hour break.'

It was then that Vincent Underhill muttered something a little clearer.

'It's all right, Vincent,' said Evelyn McIllroy reassuringly, 'you can have a rest now.'

Underhill's eyes flickered across to the social worker.

Beckett said, 'What was that, Mr Underhill?'

Underhill made another determined effort to speak. At first, his jaw was clenched so tight that the sounds got stuck behind his teeth but then his cracked lips parted a little and the words spilled out in a rush. 'Suitcase to the station.'

'You took the suitcase to Brighton train station?' Beckett echoed.

'DCI Beckett,' snapped the solicitor, 'you can carry on with this line of questioning in thirty minutes, but now it's time to stop.'

Ignoring him, Beckett tried to seize his chance. 'Why did you have to take it to the railway station?'

But words had failed Vincent Underhill again. And when he stared up into Beckett's eyes his rigid features had recomposed themselves into an expression of abject, helpless terror.

Downstairs, on the second floor, plain-clothes officers hurried in and out of Operation Ghillie's Major Incident Room, where a long piece of paper Sellotaped to the wall represented Vincent Underhill's recent movements. Other than arriving at the night shelter at five thirty-six that afternoon, it was blank.

Tom Beckett stormed into the room. 'Please tell me we've found some forensics?' he asked Minter.

'Still nothing on the body.'

Beckett's brow furrowed. 'So much for the killer always leaving something behind.' He remembered the enlarged kidney. 'What about toxicology?'

'Should be with us tonight. I was going to give the hostels another spin. A lot of the homeless won't be turning up until now.'

Beckett looked at his watch. He could start the interview again in sixteen minutes.

'Got the bastard!' said Kevin Phillips, walking into the MIR and pushing past Minter. He handed Beckett the stapled sheets of a two-page statement. 'Just had a walk-in,' he explained triumphantly. 'A man named Liddle. He's the manager of Phones 4U on North Street. Last night he saw a man answering Underhill's description having a row with a black woman by a bus stop near where he works in North Street.'

'What time?' Beckett asked.

'Right after he shut up shop. About five thirty.'

It fitted with the time of death. Beckett read the description of the woman. Right age bracket, right height, right ethnic background. *Bingo.* 'Where's Liddle now?'

'Downstairs doing an e-fit.'

It was the breakthrough they needed. 'Sharpen up this description,' he told Phillips. 'Get hold of an actress who looks like the e-fit and set up a reconstruction. Five thirty is rush hour – there would have been hundreds of people on North Street.'

'Yes, sir,' said Phillips. As he paced out of the room he caught Minter's eye and grinned.

Back in the interview room, Beckett put the new evidence to Underhill straight away. But Underhill just picked up his tobacco tin and took the lid off and started rolling yet another cigarette.

Beckett reached out with a match to light him up. 'Vincent,' he said, blowing out the match, 'can you at least confirm whether or not you were on North Street last night?'

Underhill's eyes darted around the room, from the winking red light of the video camera to the wristwatch on the solicitor's knee to the statement Tom Beckett was holding in his hands.

'Vincent,' Beckett persisted, 'I don't think you realise the seriousness of your position. We have a witness who says he saw you arguing with a woman we believe to be the victim. Your fingerprints are all over the suitcase in which her body was found. Have you got anything at all to say that will help us understand what happened between five o'clock last night and six o'clock this morning?'

Underhill put the cigarette to his lips again. His hands trembling, he hunkered down in his chair. Suddenly, the atmosphere in the room changed. Something teetered on the edge of a precipice. Everyone in the room noticed it, except for Evelyn McIllroy. 'Are you all right, Vincent?' she asked. 'Do you need a break?'

With an astonishing burst of energy, Underhill launched himself out of his seat. The impact of his huge body knocked the social worker backwards out of her chair, sending her sprawling onto the floor. He was on her again in a flash, his hands closing round her throat, the grip so tight that Beckett couldn't prise his fingers away. Underhill snarled ferociously, spittle falling from his mouth into the terrified woman's face. PC Daniels helped Beckett try to push him off but, showing an incredible, almost superhuman strength, Underhill shrugged them away easily and pounced on his victim once more. His hands closed around Evelyn's throat, making her artery bulge like a rope. Her face turned purple. The door to the interview room burst open and Minter rushed inside to join the fray.

Vincent Underhill ended up in the custody centre after all. It took six officers to get him there.

'Right!' said the custody sergeant, banging the cell door shut behind him and locking it. He looked at the ring of bedraggled officers surrounding him. Only PC Gregory looked like he didn't need medical attention. 'You take first watch, Gregory,' he said, hanging an orange booklet from the hook beside Underhill's cell. 'Write him up every fifteen minutes. I'm not having any nutcase topping himself on my watch. Not without the correct paperwork anyway.'

Inside the cell, Underhill sat on a seamless rubber mattress on top of a concrete plinth and listened to the heavy footsteps retreating down the corridor. When they had died down, he slid himself onto the floor, crawling into the gap between the lidless toilet bowl and the side of the bed and folding his massive frame to make himself as small as possible.

The prisoner in the next cell started banging on the door. 'Cunts! You're all fucking cunts! Do you hear me!' The shouting went on for a minute or more but finally he gave up and there was silence in the cell block.

They began as whispers. They always began as whispers. Then, at the very edge of his vision, Underhill could see the bends in the light. They scuttled across the rubberised floor towards him and leapt into the air. They brushed his matted hair, chanting his name. *Yes, you did,* they chorused, their voices shrill. *Yes, you did, Vincent. And now you're going to pay.* Underhill covered his ears with his hands and drew his knees up even more but they giggled and crowed even louder, stopping only to whisper to each other about what Vincent had done and how he was going to be punished for it. *You should have killed yourself when you had the chance. You should have jumped off that building when you had the chance.* Mumbling, Underhill shook his head. *They know what's in the suitcase, Vincent.* 'No!' Underhill moaned. 'No!' *So much blood Vincent! Who would have thought there'd be so much blood!*

A few minutes later, when PC Gregory looked into the peephole to check on the prisoner, all he could see was Underhill sitting hunched up by the toilet, his hands covering his head, his elbows resting on his drawn-up knees. Unlocking the door and swinging it open, Gregory hesitated on the threshold of the cell. 'Do you want to see a doctor?' he asked.

Underhill's eyes slid towards the door. After a moment, he shook his head.

'Suit yourself,' muttered the police officer, looking around the cell to check there'd been no damage. He took the orange booklet off the hook and wrote a note about what had just transpired.

His head in his hands again, Vincent heard the door clang shut. The key turned in the lock and then the voices began again.

On the dark promenade, Minter shivered in the wind. For the first time in what seemed like weeks it had stopped raining but now the clear sky had brought with it an icy night. He stamped his feet to keep himself warm, raised the collar of his jacket, watched a van slowing almost to a halt along the seafront road. It bumped up the kerb and trundled towards him over the grass of Brunswick Lawns, the diesel engine chugging. It stopped a few yards away and the driver squeaked the handbrake on and turned the engine off. He jumped out of the cab and hurried across to the doors at the back. A moment later the serving hatch built into the side of the van opened and a wedge of yellow light split the darkness.

Minter headed over. 'Bad night for it,' he said, looking up into the bright interior, where the driver was busying himself stirring something that smelt like Heinz tomato soup. He glanced down at Minter's warrant card then went back to stirring. He was balding on top and late middle-aged and the cravat around his neck gave him a raffish air. 'Certainly is, old boy,' he said, the accent making Minter wonder what ups and downs the man had experienced in the course of his life. Most people wouldn't dream of coming out on a night like this for the homeless soup run: compassion like that was a rare commodity. It was something to be mined from painful circumstances. 'You been a volunteer long?'

The man was working quickly now, ladling steaming orange soup into Styrofoam cups. 'Three years,' he said, wiping his hand on a tea towel and reaching down from the serving hatch to shake hands with Minter. 'The name's Bill Simpson.'

Minter introduced himself. 'You busy at the moment, Bill?'

He was lining up the cups. 'I should say so. The hostels are full every single night. More snakes than ladders, these days. Lots of people losing their jobs, their houses.' He sighed. 'Not a good time for us to be losing our funding from the council, either. No one made a fuss about it, of course. The homeless aren't cute, are they? Not like cats and donkeys are cute.' He looked at Minter. 'Couldn't do me a favour, could you?'

'What's that?'

'Jump up here and give me a hand with the table?' Frowning, he touched the small of his back. 'Slipped disc.'

Minter went round and climbed into the van and helped him carry out the little square table. Once the metal legs were unfolded and it was set up on the grass Bill went back into the van and came back with an outsize plastic container full of half rounds of ham and cheese sandwiches.

Minter checked his watch. He'd come here after drawing a blank at the hostels. It seemed Vincent Underhill kept himself to himself: none of the homeless would admit to knowing who he was, although Minter couldn't be sure they were telling the truth. There was no love lost between the police and the homeless. To the cops, the vagrant population of Brighton were an irritant. They moved them on from doorways, hassled them for begging and arrested them for endless petty crimes. As far as the police were concerned, the homeless – and the large proportion of the homeless who suffered a mental illness in particular – caused a great deal of aggravation for very little reward. The men and women who visited the soup kitchen on Brunswick Lawns were the hardcore, the recidivists who'd lost the knack of sleeping under a roof a long time ago. Shunning the outreach programmes, they slept outside whatever the weather.

Bill Simpson put the tub of sandwiches down on the table. 'Thanks,' he said.

Minter took the opportunity to show Bill the photograph. 'This gentleman is in custody at the moment. You ever seen him?'

The picture had been taken at Hollingbury just before they threw Underhill into the cells. A bruise was beginning to bulge just above his right eye. He looked deranged, his hair bedraggled and his face turned away from the camera, his intense gaze trained on something no one else could see. Tomorrow morning, people all over the city would wake up to find this image in their newspapers and on the television and it would remind them of all those other wild-eyed custody photos they'd seen of men who attacked their victims out of a clear blue sky.

'Yes, I've seen that chap,' said Bill Simpson. 'He's not what I would call a regular but he's here from time to time.'

Heartened, Minter took out his notebook. 'When was the last occasion?'

Bill thought about it. 'Must have been three weeks ago. The day of the snow.' He shook his head. 'That was a busy night.'

Disappointed, Minter asked, 'Do you mind if I stick around? Show this photo to some of your other customers?'

Bill smiled. 'Good luck with that one. And, by the way, it's service users.' Minter looked at Bill quizzically. 'It's not customers,' the older man explained. 'It's service users. Got to be politically correct about that kind of thing.'

Minter nodded. 'I'll try and get it right next time.'

Bill looked past Minter's shoulder. 'Here they come.'

The beacon of light had attracted the homeless to the van. They came walking across the road or trundling along the promenade, dark and solitary figures moving slowly in and out of the pools of light. As they neared the van it was difficult to tell the men from the women because they had all swathed themselves in overcoats and thick gloves, woolly hats and balaclavas. Standing in the shadows, Minter watched them gather to slurp the soup and munch the sandwiches. There wasn't any conversation – they just stood still or milled about, their watery eyes darting to and fro, watching intently for the first sign of trouble.

Minter stepped from one solitary figure to another, showing them Underhill's photograph, asking them the same questions in the same low, discreet voice. Seeing his suit and sniffing the reek of officialdom it brought with it, most of them refused to say as much as a word, just grunted and turned away. One of them even cursed and flung his arms up to ward Minter off, as if he was some kind of devil. Minter moved on to the next, all the time keeping his eye on a figure standing at the very edge of the little crowd. Eventually, when the black bin liner was full of empty cups and Bill had started packing away, he made his way over to the lone figure.

'Not having much luck, are you?' she said in a cracked voice. Under her bobble hat she had messy, long, grey hair and broad, raw cheekbones. She smelt of cheap cider and of clothes that had got wet too often. She used her purple tongue to lick the last, glutinous threads of soup from the side of the cup.

Minter showed her the photograph. 'I'm interested in a man named Vincent Underhill.'

She let the cup fall onto the ground. The wind caught the inside of it, rocking it back and forth. 'Never heard of him.'

Behind Minter, the engine of Bill's van started up throatily. He watched as a sudden gust picked up the white cup and sent it tumbling along the dark promenade. 'Shame,' he said. 'Right now he really needs a friend.'

'Time to go,' said the woman, wrapping her coat tighter around her.

Minter put the photo back in his pocket. 'Looks that way.'

The woman didn't move. 'Weegee.'

Minter said, 'What?'

'His name's Weegee.'

'Like Ouija board?'

The woman coughed. It was a hacking, bronchial cough. She hawked up phlegm and spat on the pavement at Minter's feet. 'How the fuck should I know? It's just what he's called.'

Minter nodded. 'But you've known him for a while?'

'He's been on the streets longer than I have. And that's saying something.'

'Has he got a pitch?'

The crone laughed. 'A *pitch*! Weegee doesn't beg!'

'How does he live then?'

Another cackling laugh. 'How do any of us live?' She glanced up and down the prom and confided, 'He told me once he's got a hovel out on the Downs.'

'Any idea where?'

She shook her head.

Minter asked 'When was the last time you saw Weegee?'

She looked up at the stars. 'Oh let me see,' she said, teasing him now. 'That's it. Last night.'

'What time last night?'

'All night. I was with him all night. Why do you want to know?'

6

• • •

Blake was a drummer. Just seventeen. Past midnight he was pedalling his push bike through the Hove back-streets, his mobile throbbing reproachfully in his knapsack. He was supposed to have been at the recording studio half an hour ago. He'd missed the last bus into the city. He was late.

Tucked behind the Brighton seafront, where a few hours before Minter had been talking to the vagrants at the soup kitchen, the square mile or so of Brunswick Old Town was a rabbit warren of infill. There were boarded-up pubs, blind alleys, decayed lodging houses and streets that ended nowhere. Blake sped up one of the few thoroughfares, past a looming five-storey townhouse with a broken, gurgling drain.

It was going to be a long night. Apart from his phone, Blake had in his knapsack his beloved sticks, a bottle of Lucozade, a bar of Yorkie raisin chocolate, some weed, Rizlas and ten Marlboro. He crossed Western Road, dodging the late-night traffic, pushed hard on up the hill, turning left into a quiet old mews. His bike bounced jarringly over the potholed tarmac, sending up splashes of rainwater. The mews was arranged round a square courtyard, with a fire escape leading upstairs. Brighton was something of a creative hub and a couple of years ago the small units for business start-ups had seemed like a good idea. The recession had put paid to all that and now the jewellery maker and the web designer were defunct and on the ground floor only the metal fabricator and the music studio survived: there was money to be made from scrap metal and money to be made from the dreams of musicians. The studio was owned by a friend of a friend at Blake's college and he had said that Blake's tech metal band, The Obscene, could use it to record their all-important demo as long as they cleared up after themselves and were out by daybreak. Blake had been here yesterday to get the vibe, when the courtyard had resounded to the constant beat of hammers and the whine of angle grinders, but now the metal fabricators were silent and Blake hurried past a heap of twisted iron and slipped inside the studios.

The rest of the band was already there, gathered behind the glass that separated the sound booth from the rehearsal space. The Pearl drum kit was in a state of splendid isolation in a booth all of its own. It was a cool set-up.

'About fucking time,' said Matt. He was The Obscene's lead guitarist and liked to think of himself as the pathfinder, the one who pushed The Obscene to be original.

'Sorry, man,' Blake apologised, shrugging off his knapsack. 'I had to look after my little brother.'

There was a chorus of ridicule. Babysitting wasn't rock and roll.

Matt picked up a piece of paper from the mixing desk. 'Let's get started.' He had written out the set list for the songs they were going to record for the Brighton record companies. 'We'll start with "Burned Skin".'

Jimmy, the singer, lit a cigarette with his Zippo and blew a long plume of smoke up towards the ceiling. '"Trick of the Light" is the stand-out track,' he drawled. He liked to keep things hard and fast, the guitar chords thrashing, the rhythms nice and chopped. That way he could bellow out his lyrics over the top in a rasping, last-ditch voice.

Matt squared up to Jimmy. '"Burned Skin" has the middle eight.'

'All that twiddly guitar shit?' said Jimmy, for whom melody was anathema.

It was always like this. Blake ignored them both, getting on with changing the right-hand drum kit to a left-hand drum kit. He only stopped when he saw Jimmy's cigarette. 'Hey,' he called, sticking his head out of the drum booth and pointing at the *No Smoking* sign on the wall. 'Guy's doing us a favour.'

Looking Blake up and down, Jimmy drawled, 'Like, you've still got your bicycle clips on.'

Even though he hadn't worn any, Blake glanced down at his jeans. Even Ed, the bassist, laughed.

'Let's just do it,' said Matt, who had enough ambition for the lot of them.

They worked hard all night, Blake and Ed swaggering a blistering rhythm, Blake's big snare sound driving every song, Ed's bass crunching away in time. Matt ripped out chord after chord and Jimmy did what only Jimmy could. They were on the groove good and proper, and didn't stop until gone three, when they gathered in the sound booth to listen to the playback and Matt finally pronounced himself satisfied. The band came together for a salvo of high-fives across the desk then

Blake mixed down the four songs to an MP3 and burned ten CD copies. Even he forgot the *No Smoking* sign as he built a celebratory spliff.

'Shit,' he said, glancing back at the drum booth as the others sloped off for the night. 'I've forgotten to put the kit back together.'

'You were awesome tonight, man,' called Ed from the front door.

'Cheers,' said Blake.

Matt tossed Blake the keys to the studio. 'Later.'

Alone, Blake went into the booth to swap sides on the high hat and bass drum. He sniffed at the air, hoping the open door would go some way to alleviate the worst of the smell of dope. A couple of minutes later, he left the studio.

It was freezing outside. Blake locked the door and did the buttons up on his jacket, his hands moving quickly in imitation of the fill from the last song. There was no doubt about it, The Obscene were on their way. All that gigging had paid off.

Undoing the padlock and swinging his bike around, Blake glanced up at the galleried landing. Immediately, he knew something was wrong. He didn't know what it was and he thought for a moment it was just the skunk still trailing through his frazzled brain but something about the vibe out here had changed completely. The feel in the mews was different, as if something bad had gone down. There was a rhythm to all things. It might be hard to make out sometimes, it might be as subtle as the ghost notes Blake loved to play, but there it was all the same. A missed beat.

Leaving his bike, Blake put his foot on the metal grille of the first step. Maybe a burglar was hiding somewhere up there in the abandoned units, he thought, a burglar intent on stealing the valuable equipment from the studio. Well, fuck that, he wasn't having any of it. Guy was doing them a favour. That Pearl kit alone was worth over five grand. In the inadequate beam from the security light downstairs, Blake slowly climbed the steps.

From the top of the landing, he could see over the mews. In the moonlight, looking out over the zigzag lines of TV aerials and chimney pots, Blake heard the low moan of the sea on the beach. His breath turning to mist in the cold air, he turned left and came to the door behind which the jewellery maker had once plied her trade. She must have left in a hurry because the door had been left open. It creaked a little as he went inside.

It was pitch-black. Blake fished his lighter out of his pocket and sparked it. The long room was divided into two. He was standing in what used to be the retail space – the yellow flame from his lighter multiplied in the glass of empty display cases. On the other side of the shelving was the maker's studio itself. It was deep in shadow. Blake held his lighter aloft and called out, 'Anyone there?' His eyes adjusting slowly to the darkness, he walked past the shelves and into the workshop. There was a big table at which the maker would have sat to assemble her bits and pieces. On the table top something had been covered up with a large canvas sheet. The air in this part of the room was laced with a strange aroma.

Suddenly, Blake slipped and lost his footing, landing on his back in a heap. 'Fuck!' He rolled back onto his knees as quickly as he could and scrabbled on the floor with his hands in an effort to locate the lighter he had just dropped. 'Jesus!' he muttered into the complete darkness, feeling something wet on his fingers. This was a bad trip. His heart was beating a drum roll in his chest. The wet stuff on his fingers was much too sticky to be just a pool of rainwater. 'Fuck!' Panicking now, he scooped up his lighter and sparked it. That's when he saw, roughly at the level of his eyes, the arm hanging down from the table. It was a human arm but there was no hand at the end.

PART TWO

7

• • •

Oxford, June 1993

A bully is a bully. There's always an explanation – someone hurt them too, some real or imagined slight working its way out of their minds like a splinter – but the plain truth is, bullies have a cruel streak. They enjoy what they do.

'Lick it!' yelled Kelvin, gripping the back of John's neck harder, pushing his face close to the dog shit on the pavement. 'Go on! Lick it!'

The yellow, slimy mess was making John Slade gag. Tears prickled at the back of his eyeballs. He wouldn't cry, though. They wouldn't make him cry.

'Come on, Kelvin,' said the bored-looking teenager watching from his bicycle, his foot idly spinning its chain round and round in reverse. 'Let's go to the shops.'

'Why bother?' Kelvin said, shoving John sideways. 'You already stink of shit.'

John sprawled across the pavement, getting to his knees as

Kelvin sauntered after the bicycle. 'I've got cigarettes,' John blurted out from the ground.

Kelvin turned around. 'What did you say?'

It wasn't just the bullies who had John Slade pegged down as different, as detestable. At school, the other boys in his class never picked him for their football teams and the girls who patrolled the playground in little groups at lunchtime never deigned to stop and speak to him. John only had one set of clothes and that was his school uniform. He wore it every single day and even his old class teacher who remembered John from the days before he became so sullen and withdrawn – even she was put off by the smell. But worst of all was Kelvin.

'I've got cigarettes,' John repeated.

'How many?'

'A pack.'

Kelvin affected connoisseurship. 'What brand?'

John stared at Kelvin vacantly.

'See you later, Kelv,' called the boy on the bicycle over his shoulder.

Kelvin put his hand out to John. 'Hand them over.'

'I haven't got them on me.'

'Where are they, then?'

'In my den.'

Kelvin's gang could use a den. He decided to take that off John as well as the cigarettes. 'Where's this den?'

John pointed across the road, towards some trees at the edge of the housing estate. 'In the woods.'

Kelvin looked over. It wouldn't take five minutes. 'Show me.'

The wood was the last bit of nature left hereabouts. The canopy of the trees prevented most of the sunshine from getting through to the ground and soon the light around Kelvin and John became thickly green. When they'd walked for a couple of minutes, Kelvin picked up a fallen branch and used it to thrash the nettles as they went. He was imagining what his mates would say when he showed them their new headquarters. Every gang needed a den.

'There,' said John.

They'd reaching a little clearing, in the middle of which was an old shed. It might look a bit rickety but it was big enough for four or five of them and there was a door with a lock on it. 'Have you got the key?'

John took it out of his pocket and waved it under Kelvin's nose. Walking over to the shed he undid the padlock and held the door open. Kelvin leaned in. It was dark inside and there was a funny smell.

Using all his might, John came up behind him and shoved Kelvin in the small of the back. The other boy landed in a heap on the floor of the shed. John slammed the door behind him and Kelvin heard the scrape of the padlock against the rusted old latch. 'You're dead, you are!' yelled Kelvin, flying at the door and banging it with his fist. 'Do you hear me? You're fucking dead!' He stood there for a moment in the pitch-blackness, listening to the sound of John's laughter. 'Bastard!' The kick Kelvin aimed at the door made it bulge but the big padlock held it shut tight.

Kelvin put his ear to the door. He couldn't hear a thing. Maybe John had run off and left him. Maybe that was his plan – just to play a stupid trick. He started to wonder how long it might take for someone to find him. He could be here for hours. He'd miss his tea. 'John?' he said in a little voice, 'if you let me out now, I won't hurt you.'

The funny smell inside the shed was getting worse. It made Kelvin want to retch.

'Kelvin?' said an adult voice.

Kelvin thought he was about to be rescued. 'I'm in here!' A moment later, he heard the key in the padlock and, with a creak, the door opened.

Blinded by the light, Kelvin didn't see the cricket bat sweeping through the air but he felt the crunch all right. With a thud, he landed on his back on the wooden floor of the shed. It was then that he saw what had been making that awful smell. A few inches from Kelvin's face, the carcass of a small animal had been nailed to the wall. It had been skinned, its flesh red, the sinews laced with white fat. There were lots of others. The side wall was full of them. Rabbits, foxes, even cats and dogs.

Terrified, Kelvin scrabbled to his feet. He put his hand up to his face, touching his own blood. He had a split nose and a cut above his left eye and as soon as he realised this they both began to sting like mad.

'Come out here,' said the man with the cricket bat in a posh voice. He wasn't from the estate where Kelvin and John both lived.

Kelvin emerged blinking into the sunlight. John Slade was standing just behind the man, slightly in his shadow. 'Are you his dad?' Kelvin asked the grown-up. He started to beg for mercy. 'It was the others. They made me do it.' He looked past the man towards John. 'We were just having a laugh, weren't we?'

'Take your clothes off,' the man interrupted.

'What?'

Emboldened, John took a step forward. 'You heard him. Take your clothes off!'

Kelvin looked back towards the man but there was no clemency there. Kelvin yanked his school shirt over his head. He took his shoes off and pushed his trousers down, laying them on the floor beside him. He stood there in just his pants. His voice trembling, he said, 'What are you going to do?'

At school, John Slade's stare was blank and lifeless but now his grey eyes had taken on a different aspect. They flickered over Kelvin, taking in every part of him.

'Walk over there,' said the man, pointing to the edge of the clearing. It was the man who was in control, Kelvin realised. All this had been his idea. At the edge of the clearing he had dug a shallow grave. 'Get in,' he said.

'Please,' Kelvin begged, still thinking this was about his bullying. 'I won't do it again.'

'Get in!' the man commanded.

Kelvin stepped into the gashed earth.

'Lie down,' said the man.

Lying down, Kelvin felt the cold, clammy earth on the bare skin of his back. Looking up, he saw the two figures silhouetted against the green canopy – the taller one of the man, the shorter one of John Slade. In shadowplay, he saw the man lift the cricket bat high over his head and lean over the grave. 'Close your eyes,' he said.

In the silence of the deep wood, Kelvin began to whimper and a moment later he lost control of his bowels. He closed his eyes and awaited the first blow.

There was a stifled laugh then Kelvin heard the shutter-click and wind-on of a camera. Daring to open his eyes, he saw that John was taking his photograph. Removing the camera from his eye, the boy looked into the grave and cried in a delighted voice, 'Now who smells of shit?'

Calmly, the man said, 'If you ever pick on him again, I'll print these photographs and give them to the people in your class. Do you understand?'

'Yes,' said Kelvin.

'Now get out of here.'

Climbing awkwardly out of the grave, sobbing tears of horror and relief, Kelvin ran over to the shed where he'd left his clothes. He used his shirt to clean himself off as best he could then he threw it onto the ground. Pulling on his trousers and grabbing his shoes and socks, he ran headlong out of the clearing, pausing just the once to look back and check that the dreadful pair were not pursuing him through the woods.

In the clearing, John Slade was belly laughing like he'd never done before. 'He really thought we were going to do it!' he exclaimed, pleased as punch at the humiliation he'd wrought upon his long-time persecutor. 'Did you see his face? He really thought you were going to kill him!'

Martin felt the smooth edge of the cricket bat. 'Who's to say I wasn't, John? Or that I won't.'

Worried, John looked at his champion. 'It's all right,' he said. 'Kelvin won't be picking on me anymore. Not now. Not after we took the photo.'

Martin put his hand on John's shoulder. 'People like Kelvin don't change,' he said almost sadly. 'He'll want to get his own back. And I'm afraid I can't be with you all the time.'

John swallowed hard. He hadn't thought of that.

Martin smiled. The boy's lack of intellect made him a very easy dupe but there was another reason why Martin wanted to string him along a little longer. The scientist in Martin wasn't satisfied with these theatrical devices anymore – the hunting of rabbits, the revenge on little Kelvin. He wasn't satisfied with the blood and tissue samples John Slade had donated over the course of the last year or so. It was time for the experiment to take another turn.

Martin tapped his palm with the cricket bat. 'What would you have done, John, if I *had* bludgeoned Kelvin to death just now? After all the things he's done to you, would you have tried to stop me?'

John looked up at the only friend he had in the world. 'We were teaching him a lesson.'

'I told you, John, people don't change their nature.'

John's brow crinkled as he thought about what Martin had just said. Other people were a mystery to John, but Martin knew everything there was to know about them.

'Go on, John,' said Martin, digging the boy in the ribs with the handle of the cricket bat. 'Take it. Feel its weight.'

8

'Six seconds and we're out of VT,' said the voice in Abi Martin's ear. After four years on the sofa, it always surprised Abi how nervous she got at the top of every breakfast show.

It was 6.29 a.m. 'Go,' Abi said impatiently to the make-up girl bending across her to fix a highlight on her brow, furious that the girl hadn't spotted the problem when she'd been sitting in the damned chair just twenty minutes ago. The voice in Abi's ear started babbling. 'Go!' she commanded again. Apologising wretchedly, the girl with the make-up brush scurried off.

On playback, the electronic theme music bounced to its crescendo. Abi watched the fingers of the floor manager disappearing into his fist. *Three ... two ... one, and in.* She beamed into camera as brightly as the backlit orange panels of the set that were intended to warm up the winter bleakness of the central London skyline behind the plate-glass windows of the studio. A mid two-shot discovered Abi and co-host Simon sitting side by side on the small sofa. It still felt cramped to Abi but the sofa was one of the many changes the show's new producer had insisted on in search of what he called 'chemistry' between the hosts.

'Good morning!' they cried in unison, as, out of the corner of her eye, Abi saw the Steadicam operator hurrying over for her first close-up. The Steadicam was another one of the producer's ideas to enliven the show and put a few more percentage points on the ratings. It had taken Abi a few rehearsals to get the knack of finding the shouldered lens but now she'd mastered it completely. She smiled into the camera and then delivered some of her autocued lines over a recording of yesterday's kangaroo bounding about the back of the studio, its antics fetching guffaws of laughter from the assembled crew. The VT finished then Abi looked down the lens of camera number one and said, 'It's a *great* show today as well. There's a *very* moving story about the hundreds of women victimised by an unscrupulous internet dating agency.'

Back to the master two-shot.

'And on a lighter note,' said Simon, 'we have an *exclusive* interview with Ben Rafter coming up at half seven.'

'That's right.' Abi took over. 'Ben's new movie, *Hand in Glove,* premieres at the Odeon Leicester Square this week and I caught up with the world's favourite romcom star at his West End hotel suite.'

'I heard some rumours about Ben and his co-star,' Simon leered.

Abi nodded. 'He certainly seemed smitten with Fliss Stewart. You can find out more at eight.'

Simon raised an eyebrow. 'Remember where you heard it first.'

Abi dealt with the news in twenty seconds, ticker-tape

headlines moving below her on the playback screen as she trailed the seven o'clock bulletin. 'And at half past eight *X Factor* winner Ethan May will be joining us on the sofa to talk about last night's triumph.'

A smattering of cheers and applause from the crew. Two-shot, Simon saying, 'Fresh-faced Ethan's single went on release today, and if downloads are anything to go by it's heading straight for the Christmas number one spot.'

'Exciting stuff,' chimed Abi before she put on a serious face in order to introduce the first location report. There'd been a shocking twofold increase in binge drinking among the youth of Torquay.

'Coffee!' called out Simon as soon as they were out. 'I must have coffee!' Instantly, one of the production assistants hurried over with a mug emblazoned with the show's logo.

Crap editing, Abi thought, *kicking off with a soft news story.* She glanced at her bleary-eyed co-host. Simon was in his late twenties and dressed in a beige-coloured cashmere top. He was smoothly good-looking, easy on the eye and, there was no getting away from it, younger than she was.

Abi Martin's face had great structure, with high cheekbones and a small, dimpled chin and striking green eyes that popped brilliantly under the lights. Her body was honed to perfection by daily visits to her private trainer in a gym off Covent Garden. For the show Abi had designer dresses sent over every morning from a selection of her favourite shops in Bond Street and her jewellery sent round from Asprey's. Tony Evans, the show's new producer, had tried to get Abi to wear less bling and once even dared to ask her to consider wearing high street brands, arguing that her look needed to reflect the target demographic, but on that score at least Abi had seen him off. Tony might understand ratings but he most certainly didn't understand women. Even at this time of the morning, in fact especially at this time of the morning, they wanted glamour. Today Abi was wearing a short dress in blue satin from Burberry that revealed her knees and had a plunge zip front. The shimmer was driving the cameramen nuts but the high hemline was knocking spots off Simon's beige.

'Out of VT in three,' the director said in Abi's ear as Simon plonked his coffee cup down on the table and dabbed at his mouth with a make-up tissue.

The first shot was Abi's and she picked it up seamlessly, shaking her head sadly at the Saturday night antics of the young men of Torquay. She turned and fed an easy ad lib to Simon which, to give him credit, he hit out of the park, bringing another guffaw from the studio floor. Abi changed gear for the segue into the next item.

Christmas presents under a tenner.

'Mercy Mvule,' said Kevin Phillips.

Beckett took the photo from him. It had been taken on Brighton Pier, the candy-striped helter-skelter rising up into a blue sky. Standing in front of it, looking every inch the tourist, was a tall, shapely woman with a wide, flat nose and braided hair teased upward from her brow. She smiled at the camera, handsome and full of life, her brown skin lightened by a sheen of yellow.

'She was born in Togo,' Phillips explained.

Beckett nodded. It fitted. The analysis of the contents of the digestive tract belonging to the woman in the suitcase had led the ethnologist to conclude that the victim's diet had been West African. 'Who reported her missing?'

'Her flatmate. Freema …' Phillips consulted the witness statement in his hand, stumbling a little over the unfamiliar spelling. 'Ag-ye-man. She's in the custody suite now.' Phillips looked pleased with himself.

'What do we know about Mercy?'

'She's been a UK resident for the last couple of years. She's legal. Rents a studio flat off the Lewes Road and waitresses in the city.'

Beckett looked at the photo. So Mercy was a citizen, he thought, paid tax and national insurance just like everyone else. But now she was dead. 'Good work, Kev.'

'Thanks, sir.' Emboldened, Phillips asked, 'Have you made up your mind about the job, sir?'

Beckett hesitated. 'It's not good news, Kev. I'm asking DS Minter to ride shotgun.'

'Minter?'

Beckett didn't like having his decisions questioned. 'Yes, Kev. Minter.'

'I've worked my arse off in the other murder team. Two cases, two convictions, both perps going down for life.'

'I know what you've done here. You're well thought of.'

'So why don't you give me the job?'

'This investigation isn't about jobs for the boys.'

Phillips's voice was shaking. 'I *need* this job.'

'And I told you. Your time will come.'

'Yeah. Just not right now.'

'I'm afraid not.'

Turning on his heels, Phillips walked out of the room, slamming the door behind him.

Beckett went over to the association board, where he stuck the photograph of Mercy Mvule next to the crime scene images of the second victim taken at the mews in Brunswick where the body had been discovered in the early hours of the morning. She was around the same age as Mercy and her clothes had been removed, but this second victim was a white woman and a good few inches shorter than the first. The killer didn't seem to have a type. Yet the profile of an opportunistic murder – someone who hunted his victims randomly – didn't fit with the habit of moving the bodies after death. He'd taken the hands again but this time he hadn't decapitated his victim. He'd used a blowtorch on her face instead, holding her features in the flame for what may have been minutes on end, until the flesh had all melted from her face. Behind Beckett, there was a knock at the door. He turned to see the female press officer he had met a couple of days ago on his whistle-stop induction tour of CID – the day before all hell broke loose. He walked discreetly away from the board and met her in the middle of the room, where she handed him a press release. She said, 'I thought you'd better see this before it goes out.'

Beckett read the release. The first paragraph advised women in Brighton not to venture out on their own after dark. It was a sensible precaution but also guaranteed to start a panic. Which was why, Beckett realised, the press release went on to announce that this afternoon Brighton and Hove police would start taking DNA samples from every male in the city aged between seventeen and forty-five. It was the first Beckett had heard of it. 'Was this the chief's idea?'

Gingerly, the PRO nodded.

'And where am I supposed to get the manpower to resource all these mobile units?'

The PRO shrugged. 'Sorry, sir. I'm just the messenger.'

Beckett sighed. 'Does the chief really think the murderer's

just going to stroll into one of the trailers and stick his tongue out for us?' But no matter how he moaned and groaned, the press release would still be going out. He handed it back. 'Fine.'

'I'm afraid there's worse,' she said, swapping the release for another sheet of paper.

Beckett looked down at the colour proof of the front page of the Brighton *Evening Argus,* where today's date was smudged onto the top right-hand corner. It wasn't the twenty-point banner headline – *Second Body Found!* – that shouted out the loudest, nor was it the jowly-looking photograph of Beckett they had chosen to place beneath it. It was the sidebar story – *Are City Cops Missing the Obvious?*

'Believe me, I tried,' said the PRO, 'but the editor is running with it. He said he only sent it over as a courtesy.'

Beckett read the quotes attributed by the newspaper to *former murder detective Andy Griffin*. 'Some fucking courtesy.'

'You know that Griffin lost his job here last year,' said the PRO. 'He was your predecessor as SIO. This is sour grapes. He's getting even.'

Beckett nodded. According to the conditions of service it was impossible to make warranted officers redundant, so those with more than twenty-seven years of service had to be put out to grass and forcibly retired. That was what had happened to Andy Griffin. At the time, Beckett had felt sorry for him.

'I spoke to the crime reporter on the *Argus,*' said the PRO. 'He owes us a favour or two. He said that if we issue a rebuttal straight away he'll try and get the editor to run it in tomorrow's paper. It might be an idea if you speak to him directly.'

Beckett gave her back the front page. 'You handle it. Griffin's got no inside track. Tell the paper he can go fuck himself.'

'Or words to that effect, sir?'

'Or words to that effect.'

On her way out of Beckett's office, the PRO passed Minter in the doorway. 'You wanted to see me, sir?'

'Come in, Minter,' Beckett said. 'When did the hostel manager say Vincent Underhill arrived at St Michael's?'

'We got his call just after six.'

'Dr Hunter's best estimate for time of death for the second victim was eight thirty p.m.'

'Which puts Underhill in the clear. He was at the hostel.'

'How's his alibi for the first murder?'

'Pretty solid.' The time line of Underhill's activities was beginning to look full. 'We've found two other homeless people who said they bumped into Underhill and his lady friend wandering around the seafront. They waited for the last patrol to finish and then they dossed down in a doorway about one. We've found an outreach worker who says she woke up the woman at four. Then at five they were both woken up by the bin men.'

'You checked with the council?'

'Yes, sir.'

It wasn't looking good. The strongest parts of Underhill's alibi coincided with the probable time of Mercy's death. There was a possibility, of course, that in the dead of night Underhill had stolen away from the shop and his slumbering companion and killed Mercy Mvule, cut up her body and stuffed it into the suitcase, then put it somewhere safe before returning to the shop doorway for another forty winks. It was a possibility, of course. But it hardly seemed likely.

'I found a plastic surgeon at the Princess Alex with experience of reconstructive surgery following severe burns,' Beckett said. 'He's doing us a bust of how the victim would have looked. We've got dental casts, too. This won't take long.'

Minter nodded.

'I want you to give Underhill another spin,' said Beckett. 'He might not be the killer but he sure as hell knows something about how Mercy Mvule ended up in that suitcase.'

'Where is he now?'

'They sectioned him and took him to Meadow View.' Minter was already on his way out of the room when Beckett called him back. 'There's one bit of good news.'

'What's that?' said Minter.

'I'm naming you as DI.'

Minter was gobsmacked. 'Thanks, sir.'

'It's on an acting-up basis. You'll have to do the board.'

Acting up or not, at twenty-seven, Minter would be the youngest detective inspector in the division. He was delighted. 'Of course.'

Beckett knew how much Minter had on his mind right now. 'Don't let me down, Minter. I need you right at the top of your game.'

'I won't, sir. I promise.'

Kevin Phillips sat alone in the Major Incident Room, taking it out on a computer keyboard. When his home mobile rang he thought it was Mumbai calling again. He was just about to switch it off when he saw from the screen that it was Fiona, his wife. Kevin answered, saying hello in the most placating voice he could muster.

Judging from the traffic noise in the background, Fiona was outside. 'I've just rung the bank, Kevin,' she said accusingly.

It was the call Kevin had been dreading. 'Hang on,' he said, getting up and hurrying over to close the door. 'What's up?'

She was breathing heavily. 'You bloody well know what's up. Don't *lie* to me any more. I needed to buy petrol, Kevin. I needed to get the kids to playgroup.'

'Calm down, Fi. Tell me what's happened.'

She was stranded on a garage forecourt and there was some kind of commotion in the background. Kevin's children – Martha, two, and Max, who wasn't yet a year – were getting impatient in the back of the car, like they always did. 'Mummy's just talking to Daddy!' Fiona yelled. She turned away from the car and hissed, 'Have you any idea how humiliated I feel, Kevin? All my cards were declined. All of them! I was standing in that queue for what seemed like for ever. I could feel the way everyone was staring at me. They felt sorry for me, Kevin! They *pitied* me! How the fuck could you let it get this bad? Why didn't you tell me?'

Phillips decided that attack was the best form of defence. 'You knew what was going on. You just pretended it wasn't happening.'

The accusation stung Fiona. 'You've always looked after the money.'

There was a silence, broken only by the sound of the children crying. Sounding tearful herself, Fiona said, 'I telephoned the mortgage company. They told me we're five months behind on the payments, Kevin. We're going to lose the house. We'll be thrown out on the street!'

9

Ignoring the gaggle of autograph hunters, Abi Martin's silver Mercedes swept through the security gates of the car park behind the television studios. It was driven quickly across the river then crawled through the endless red brick of south London. Charlie, Abi's driver, had worked for the TV station for years now and in that time he'd driven all the big stars. Unlike most of them, Abi Martin always remembered his name and always got him a little something for his Christmas box, usually a bottle of single malt. In return, he'd do anything for her. He knew her moods too, and this morning Charlie could tell that Ms Martin was preoccupied. So it wasn't until he was finally bowling down the M23 that he dared to look into his rear-view mirror and ask, 'How was the show?'

'Great,' said Abi. 'We had the *X Factor* winner on.'

Charlie nodded. 'Seems like a nice lad.'

'They always do, don't they.'

Charlie glanced in the mirror again. 'Never last though, do they?'

Abi shot him a glance. In showbiz terms, her longevity was

indeed remarkable but this morning she was hypersensitive to any reference to her age. Right after this morning's show she'd had another run-in with the producer, Tony Evans. Abi looked at the line of hills in the mid-distance and calculated it would be another half hour before they got home to her house in Rottingdean, just east of Brighton. Her phone started chirruping and she fished it out of her handbag.

'Abi!' proclaimed Jean Dawson, the legendary doyenne of London's Soho. 'So glad I caught you! Great show!'

'Thanks,' said Abi frostily.

'I tell you, Abs,' said the agent, 'I've been *frantic* on your behalf. I've just come out of a breakfast meeting with Kitchen Sink.'

Kitchen Sink was the production company that made the breakfast show. Abi's existing contract ran to more than seven figures, and she could easily double that with her other work – the column in the *Daily Mail,* the ghost-written biographies, the lucrative personal appearances – but now her contract was up for renegotiation.

'And?'

Jean Dawson's voice became steely. 'The ratings for the show are in free fall. I've never seen a more depressed-looking bunch of suits. You can forget the idea of a fifty per cent increase.'

From the back seat, Abi shot a glance over the headrest at the bald patch on top of Charlie's head. It seemed like he was doing his best not to listen. 'Tell them to ditch Simon. Tell them to get me someone with some sex appeal. And go for thirty-five.'

Jean sighed. 'In the current climate, I think we have to be more realistic.'

Abi couldn't bear to have her expectations managed in this way. She'd lived her life in the gossip columns and on the front pages. Her back story had the kinds of rollercoaster twists and turns that enabled her many fans to draw on a well of shared experiences every time they saw her in the papers or in a magazine. Abi was a survivor, she'd triumphed over adversity, and for two decades now she'd stayed at the top of an industry run by snake-hipped men like Tony Evans. If Abi courted controversy every now and then that was OK too, because it offered her fans a pleasure even more piquant than aspiration – envy. Abi's life was an open book. There was no one like her.

'Are you saying,' she told her agent, 'that you haven't got the stomach for the fight any more?'

'No, of course not. It's just—'

'Was Tony there? Did he bang on about the demographic?'

'Apparently, he sent another memo. I saw him yesterday, in fact. In the Ivy. He was having lunch with Sonia Lewis.'

Abi snorted derisively. 'That little tart.'

This time last year Sonia Lewis had been presenting children's TV but since then she'd had a well-publicised affair with an England football player and her stock had risen dramatically. Right now, Sonia Lewis spelt trouble for Abi Martin. Her rival was young and bubbly and blonde and just the kind of airhead Tony Evans would go for if he had his own way. Simpering Sonia would make even Simon look authoritative.

'Tony was squiring her around the room,' Jean went on. 'He didn't bring her over to my table but I knew it was all for my benefit. Silly bitch even waved at me. I ignored her, of course.'

'This is what we do,' Abi said. 'Book us a table at the Wolseley. It has to be a table by the rail so everyone in the room can see. Tell them it's me and they'll bump someone. Then ring Sky Living and ask their top producer to come along to talk about that breakfast show they're always threatening to get off the ground.'

'Excellent idea,' said Jean with relish. She could almost smell the whiff of showbiz grapeshot. 'What time, Abs?'

'Half past ten.'

Abi cut the call. Pleased with the arrangements, she settled back into the grey leather plush of the Mercedes. She was in the back seat of a limo and on the front foot again. She was where she belonged.

Charlie turned left at the roundabout and headed over the top of the Downs towards Rottingdean. Five minutes later, the car was idling in front of the black iron gates that protected Abi's property. She handed over the little remote from the back seat and Charlie pointed it at the gates. They began to slide open, moving slowly left to right, clanging a little when the leading edge met the brick pier.

Abi's ranch-style house sat at the top of a winding drive, commanding fine views over the English Channel. It was painted white, with seven bedrooms spread over two asymmetric wings. There was a formal rose garden at the front and a heated outdoor swimming pool in the back, where a locked door led out onto the Downs and a high wall kept out prying eyes. Charlie parked the Merc beside a Lexus and a Porsche and turned round to face her. 'See you tomorrow morning, Ms Martin.'

Every weekday morning at four he'd arrive at the house in the same car and every day he'd hand her the same thick envelope containing her briefing notes for that morning's show. On the drive up to town, Abi would read everything, even down to the bio of the first guest, whose interview took place when most of their viewers were still fast asleep. There might be some context in the notes that Abi could use, some lip-smacking detail that would unlock the entire interview, turning it from another piece of fluff into something special. This was the kind of journalistic habit Abi had acquired years ago and the kind of thing a lollipop like Sonia Lewis would never even bother with. 'Can you pick me up on Piccadilly tomorrow, Charlie?'

'Oh,' said Charlie, maintaining the pretence he'd heard nothing of Abi's conversation. 'No worries, Ms Martin. What kind of time?'

'About twelve?'

Charlie had already rehearsed the route in his head. 'That's fine, Ms Martin. I'll be waiting.'

'Wonderful.'

Charlie was already out of the driver's seat, coming round to her side and opening the door. As she stepped from the back seat in one practised and sinuous movement, Abi bestowed on her driver a smile. 'You're a treasure, Charlie,' she said, sealing his lips with a touch of her hand on his arm as surely as if she'd waved a magic wand in his direction.

Charlie almost touched an invisible cap. 'See you tomorrow, Ms Martin.'

On the other side of the solid oak front door was an enormous hall with a wide, carpeted staircase. There was art all over the walls, including Abi's trophy Tracey Emin neon piece. Popping her remote control into the bowl, Abi ran her index finger along the bottom edge of the antique walnut table to check the housekeeper had done the dusting properly then she shrugged off her flame-red Aquascutum mac and put it on the coat rack. She went into the lounge and kicked off her Strutt peep-toe platforms and sank into one of the barge-like white sofas.

'Hi, babe,' called a voice from the kitchen.

A moment later Jack Bellamy was standing under the archway between the two rooms. He was in his late twenties, with intense, baby-blue eyes, a pair of biceps that strained the sleeves of his grey T-shirt, and a year-round tan he topped up every day in the solarium upstairs. He was wearing a pair of designer jeans with panels built artfully into the denim. He came over to the sofa and gave Abi her decaf double espresso and a lingering welcome-home kiss. 'Good show?'

Abi ran her hand down his arm. 'I was brilliant, of course.'

'Of course. Can I get you something to eat now?'

Abi stood up. Suddenly, she had an appetite for something else.

The word 'minimalist' didn't do the en suite to Abi's master bedroom justice. It was ethereal. Heavenly. The walls were made of pale grey stone, each slab a foot square. The fixtures were all snowy white, the bath in the middle of the room a high-sided, geometric oblong surrounded by large pebbles at its base. Abi took a bottle of Frédéric Fekkai shampoo and a bottle of Frédéric Fekkai glossing cream out of the recessed shelf cut into the angle of two of the walls and walked naked across the heated Italian marble. She passed a hand under one of the sensors on the side of the chromium bar and, immediately, steaming hot water poured forth from the rain jets overhead. She stepped underneath, letting the water cascade down her body. As she did so, Abi laid one palm across her stomach, reassured by the firmness she discovered there.

A minute or so later, the bathroom door opened and Jack walked towards her through the billowing mist. She reached out for him. He resisted a little at first, as if he didn't want to get his clothes wet, but soon relented. She pulled him under the jets, his T-shirt darkening straight away. She yanked the top up over his head and threw it onto the marble floor, running her hand down his body, feeling the bumps of his iron six-pack. All the time, Jack was licking and biting her ear, his hot breath echoing deep somewhere inside her brain. Expertly, Abi used one hand to pop the buttons of Jack's jeans, peeling the sodden trousers down over his thighs, taking the heft of his stiff cock in her hand.

Afterwards, when they were lying in the bed that Jack had strewn with red rose petals, they talked about their plans for the rest of the day. Abi had a Skype call with her publicist and an email to compose to her London publisher about the third volume of autobiography she'd foolishly agreed to write, while Jack was going to get his chest sugared. Turning to her boyfriend, Abi said, 'That thing we talked about last night? Did you mean it?'

Jack nodded. 'Of course I did.' Reaching over to the bedside table he took a cigarette out of the packet. When Abi didn't protest, he knew she was in a good mood. He lit his ciggie. 'What about you? Did you mean it?'

Abi smiled. 'Why not?'

Jack blew smoke. 'And there was me thinking you only wanted me for my body.'

Abi laughed sexily. 'Well, it's certainly not for your mind.'

Jack laughed too. He put up with Abi's little teases. He put up with a lot.

*

Outside Meadow View Hospital in Brighton there were no parked ambulances, no patients hobbling out of Casualty on crutches. Meadow View didn't treat injuries to the body. It treated injuries to the mind.

Clever landscaping, Minter thought, parking his car. The hospital had been hidden from the semi-detached houses that ringed it on three sides by a wide apron of grass and a high perimeter fence. In this *Daily Express*-reading part of the city, having a mental hospital as a neighbour could seriously damage your equity, especially if potential buyers ever took the trouble to discover the kind of inpatients Meadow View locked up at night. Minter stayed in his car to finish his cigarette. The mental hospital looked modern and inoffensive enough – red brick with a white-painted concrete bulge in the middle where the main entrance was – and Minter had been here a couple of times before in connection with other cases. He didn't like it, though. Something about the hospital made him feel very uncomfortable.

As soon as Minter opened the door to his car, a big black dog stood erect in the back seat of a nearby old Datsun and started barking loudly. Enraged, it glared at him then clambered from the back seat to the front in an effort to get closer, its thick tail drumming against the window of the car, a trail of slaver hanging down from its mouth. As its furious barks echoed round the hospital grounds, Minter hurried past it towards the entrance. He rang the buzzer and waited, peering through the safety glass at the reception area inside. After a minute without answer, Minter tried the door and was surprised to find it open.

Inside, there was no seating, just an expanse of polished white flooring with an empty cafeteria on one side and a couple of anonymous-looking offices on the other. Minter heard some shoes squeaking on the floor and a moment later a young man dressed in jeans and a short-sleeved shirt appeared around the corner. If it hadn't been for the photo ID hanging on a lanyard round his neck, there was no way Minter could have been certain if he was a resident, a visitor or a member of staff.

'Can I help you?' he said politely.

Minter showed his warrant card and introduced himself. 'I've got an appointment to see Dr Jones.'

The orderly scrutinised Minter's photo, comparing it to his face. 'That's fine. I'll just go and get him.' He turned and disappeared again past the cafeteria.

Minter walked over to one of the strange drawings that had been framed and put on the wall. Some kind of art therapy for the patients, he supposed, scrutinising the scenes on one of the A3 pieces of cartridge paper. The pictures could have been done by a child: the stick figures represented as female by the addition of triangular skirts, the faces little more than circles with lips curving up into exaggerated smiles. Having drawn them, however, the artist must have found the images too awful to preserve. Each face had been obliterated by angry-looking scribbles in black biro. Minter leaned forward, trying to decipher the multitude of tiny letters crammed into all four corners of the paper, although it was difficult to tell whether they made words or had just been used as decoration.

'Detective Inspector Minter?' said a voice from behind him. Minter turned to see a slightly older man in a checked shirt and corduroy trousers, a photo card clipped to his belt. 'I'm Dr Jones,' he said, extending his hand for Minter to shake. The psychiatrist's fair hair was the messy side of tousled and the smudges under his eyes suggested he was owed more than a bit of sleep. 'Vincent Underhill is in my care.'

'How is he this morning?' Minter asked.

Jones looked at Minter slightly askance. 'Calmer. You know, your men were not very gentle with him.'

Minter nodded. Dr Jones was a couple of years post-qualification, he guessed, a little bit of idealism left, then, but not very much – hanging by a thread, most likely. Apart from the police force, which had welcomed him in when he left care for good at eighteen, Minter didn't much like institutions, or the people who worked in them.

'Funny,' Minter said, 'anyone would think Underhill was upset about coming here.'

The psychiatrist indicated the doors behind Minter. 'Shall we have a chat in my office?'

Jones used his swipe card to unlock the double doors, leading Minter along a corridor with strip lighting overhead. They passed a window looking out over a courtyard, where there was an algae-strewn pond and two plastic garden chairs looking disconsolate in the permanent drizzle. The hospital was eerily quiet and tense. Ahead of them, the corridor seemed to stretch out for ever.

'How long have you worked here?' Minter asked, partly to break the silence.

'Six months. Acute psychiatric hospitals are punishing places to work. I'll be moving on soon.'

A door to one of the wards opened and a young woman appeared. She looked like a ghost – gruesomely thin, her cheeks sunken, her eyes hollow. Behind her, through a crack in the door, Minter saw a blur of beds and a woman bending over a chair where someone else was sitting.

'These are the open wards,' Jones explained. They walked on a few more yards until Jones stopped outside a door on the left. 'This is me.'

It was a cramped office with barely enough room for a desk. There was a red panic button on the wall and as they both sat down Minter wondered about the occasions when Jones had reason to use it.

The psychiatrist looked at his watch. 'They'll still be doing the drug rounds. Not a good time to go on the wards. We should give it a few minutes.'

Minter raised an eyebrow.

'Not every patient is cooperative,' Jones explained. 'Some of them refuse to take their medication. I'm afraid it then becomes necessary to administer the dose by force.'

Minter nodded. 'Tell me about Vincent Underhill.'

'He was an inpatient here five years ago,' Dr Jones said. 'Although I can't find any medical records prior to that.'

Minter wasn't surprised. The police hadn't much luck either. The one thing that seemed certain about the homeless man was that he hadn't been born in Brighton. 'What was the reason he came to here?' Minter asked.

'Vincent was arrested following a disturbance in Brighton. He presented with the classic symptoms of schizophrenia.'

Minter started taking notes. 'Which were what?'

Dr Jones consulted the file. 'Vincent told the psychiatrist here that he first started hearing voices when he was sixteen. They came out of a television set his father had just purchased. Within a few weeks he was hearing the voices at school as well. That's when he realised the teacher was saying things to him that none of the other pupils could hear.'

'What kind of things?'

'The usual aural hallucinations. Persecutory in nature. They told Vincent he was disgusting and vile and that he should commit suicide.'

'Was there any history of violence?'

Dr Jones flicked through the pages. 'Some altercations with the other patients but nothing that would have been considered particularly worrying for someone like Vincent.'

'Why did he leave?'

'He'd been taking his medication for two months and as a result the severity of his hallucinations had decreased significantly. Vincent's section was ended on the recommendation of the medical board.'

'They just let him go?'

'You can't keep people locked up for ever, DS Minter.'

Minter indicated the file. 'What else does it say?'

'That's it,' Jones said, closing the file and putting it on top of the little pile. 'That's as much as we know. Vincent probably stopped taking his medication very soon after he left Meadow View. Unmedicated, he'd soon be living back on the streets, where he would have abandoned all but elementary self-care. Without any insight into his illness, his delusional system would have become more entrenched and what most people would see would be a gibbering wreck of a man. He'd be the lowest of the low, an outcast, even among the homeless.' Dr Jones put the papers back and closed the file. 'Believe me, I've treated a lot of older patients like Vincent Underhill. I call them the Rip Van Winkles.'

All very interesting, Minter thought, but not what he was here to find out. 'How dangerous might he have been by then?'

Jones looked at Minter warily. 'You know, statistically

speaking, schizophrenics like Vincent are far more likely to become the *victims* of violent crime.'

'Statistically speaking,' Minter replied, 'there's been two murders committed in Brighton in as many days.'

Dr Jones sighed 'There are isolated instances of paranoid schizophrenics killing people,' Jones admitted. 'It's called, rather poetically, the moment of denouement. That's when the delusion under which the schizophrenic is labouring suddenly comes into focus and the victim leaps out at them. But just imagine, DS Minter. Imagine that you believe that I am the devil and I'm about to rob you of your immortal soul. Or, better still, imagine that I am about to flick a switch that will bring the entire world to an end, killing everyone on the planet. What would you do?'

'I'd stop you.'

'That's right. But now imagine that you were arrested for stopping me. What would you tell the police?'

Minter could see where this was going. 'I'd tell them why I needed to stop you.'

'Of course you would. You'd tell the police the truth without hesitating for one moment, because in your situation any sane person would do the same thing. And that's how it is for delusional schizophrenics, DS Minter. You have to understand that as far as they are concerned their delusions are real and they are merely acting in a sensible and logical manner. They've got nothing to hide, nothing to hide at all.'

'If that's true, then Vincent Underhill would have just left the body where it was?'

'Almost certainly. And he would have been only too ready to admit to the killing when you interviewed him. If he had killed this woman, Vincent would probably have been furious that you didn't approve of his actions. He would have regarded you as stupid, or as part of some conspiracy.'

Minter thought about the way Underhill had stared into the gas fire in the church crypt and wondered what messages he'd been hearing. 'Have you talked to Underhill since he came in?' he asked Jones.

'As I told your boss last night, Vincent explained to me how he found the suitcase in town. His voices instructed him to pick it up and take it to the railway station, where he was intending to put it on a train. But he became confused.'

'Do you believe him?'

'I have no reason to disbelieve him.'

'We have an eyewitness who saw Mr Underhill arguing with a woman on North Street.'

Dr Jones looked surprised. 'The same woman whose body was in the suitcase?'

'We think so.'

'You think so,' Jones repeated, peppering Minter's word with doubt. The psychiatrist looked at his watch again. 'The rounds should have finished by now. Why don't you ask him yourself?'

Outside the office, as they walked along the corridor, Minter asked what had happened to the other so-called Rip Van Winkles.

'The side effects of the antipsychotics we have in our armoury now are not nearly so bad, and they are much more effective. Patients like Vincent Underhill might never lose their voices altogether but they can come to understand them for what they are. Accept them as part of their illness.' He looked at Minter. 'Vincent has already consented to taking Risperdal. It doesn't look like he's addicted to either alcohol or drugs, which is another huge factor in his favour.' By now, they had come to a second set of locked double doors. 'These are the closed wards,' Dr Jones explained, using his swipe card to gain access.

On the other side, the corridor and the decor were exactly the same but the doors that led to the wards no longer had any windows and access to them was controlled by a videophone entry system.

Minter asked, 'What kind of illnesses do these patients have?'

'A variety,' said Jones as he pressed a button to one side of the door. 'Mostly bipolar and schizophrenic – that's our bread and butter – although some are a lot more troubling. There's psychopathy of various kinds, or sociopathy, as we must learn to call it now.' The electronic lock was thrown, the door was opened and Dr Jones was greeted by name by a middle-aged woman. It was warm inside the ward and there was a cigarette fug hanging in the air. 'This is Detective Inspector Minter of Brighton and Hove police, Wendy,' said the doctor. 'He wants to talk to Vincent.' Around the edges of the ward, each patient seemed to have their own room, although the six doors had been left open so their interiors could be inspected at all times from a central station. Only one patient remained in the association area, a balding man in his fifties who was sitting in an easy chair in front of a television set with the sound turned down, his head in both his hands. 'This is a male assessment ward,' Jones told Minter in a low voice.

Minter followed the psychiatrist into room number five where Vincent Underhill was sitting in a high-backed hospital chair beneath the window. 'Hello, Vincent,' said Jones as he and Minter entered.

Underhill looked up at the two men in turn. His bruised right eye had almost closed completely and he had a cut on his left cheek which had been treated with a butterfly stitch. An ugly rash ran down his throat towards his chest. His long, lank hair remained unwashed and he was dressed in his now familiar greatcoat. Its smell pervaded the room.

Last night, before they put him in the cells, they'd made Vincent Underhill give up all of his possessions in case he used something to try and harm himself. Minter had visited the custody centre to go through the odd assortment of items, wondering what significance the rolls of string, the twists of silver foil paper and the fragments of seashells, each one bleached by tide and sun, might hold for the man. Lodged inside the crown of Underhill's hat Minter had found thick pieces of cardboard and wads of more silver foil. He suspected that Underhill had wedged them there to stop the messages getting inside his brain. Now, as Minter looked at the vagrant, he wondered what other odds and ends they might find if they ever discovered Underhill's hovel on the Downs.

Dr Jones sat on the edge of Underhill's bed. 'I'm Dr Chris, Vincent. Remember? We spoke earlier this morning.' Looking over at the psychiatrist, Underhill nodded slowly. When he held his hand in front of him it shook uncontrollably. 'I understand. We can maybe look at reducing the level of your medication tomorrow. The Risperdal is probably causing that rash on your face as well, Vincent. But that's normal. It's nothing to be worried about.' Again, Underhill nodded slowly. 'Good.'

'Vincent,' said Minter, moving a plastic chair and sitting a few feet away, 'do you remember me?' After a moment, Underhill's dark, watery eyes widened in apparent recognition.

'I've been talking to a friend of yours. A woman named Rosie. She told me that your street name is Weegee. Is that right?'

Another flicker passed over Underhill's features.

'So you know Rosie, do you?''

A nod this time.

'When was the last time you saw her?'

Underhill's closed lips hummed for a long moment before, with a painful slowness, they began to form the words. 'N-ni – night. B – b – before l-last.'

'The night before last,' Minter confirmed. He could even detect the faint echo of an accent. It seemed that Vincent Underhill was not a Brighton native. 'What time?'

Another stream of grunts. ''leven.'

'Eleven o'clock?' said Minter.

Underhill nodded.

Minter asked, 'How did you know what time it was?'

Underhill ground his teeth in frustration. Giving up, he rested his head against the back of the chair.

'Keep trying, Vincent,' Dr Jones encouraged him.

'P-per-pu-'

'Pubs?' said Minter, catching on.

Underhill's alibi was stacking up right in front of Minter. 'You mean the pubs were kicking out?' he said.

Another nod from Underhill, this one almost of triumph.

'How long did you stay with Rosie?'

'Sl-slept. In, a, doorway.'

Minter changed tack. 'Vincent, where did you find the suitcase?'

Underhill looked wrung out by the effort. Dr Jones got up from the bed. 'I think that's enough for one morning. If he's going to continue with his recovery, Vincent needs some peace and quiet.' Minter went to protest but the doctor ignored him. 'Thank you very much, Vincent – I'm sure DS Minter appreciates your help. And I'll make a note about the Risperdal.' He nodded kindly at the schizophrenic then he looked at Minter, his expression indicating they should leave.

Minter looked up at Underhill. 'I'll be back tomorrow.' Reluctantly, he got up from his chair and followed Dr Jones out of the room.

'Will his speech improve with the medication?' Minter asked as they walked back out of the ward and along the corridor.

'It usually does. Tell me, is Vincent still a suspect in this case?'

'There have been some developments.'

'Yes. I saw the newspaper.'

'Vincent Underhill remains a person of interest. What difference does that make to you?'

'Vincent is here under a forty-eight-hour supervision order,' said Jones. 'The tribunal meets tomorrow to decide whether to escalate that into a section.'

Beckett had got the jargon wrong. 'Would that be a problem?' Minter asked Dr Jones.

'I wouldn't think so, but you never know.' Jones sighed. 'It's not the same as it was for the clinicians at Broke Hall all those years ago. Those guys had it easy. The tribunal here tomorrow is multidisciplinary and it will be chaired by Vincent's social worker.'

A couple of minutes later, having arranged a time to come back to speak with Underhill again, Minter was walking to his car. The Datsun had gone, taking with it the big black dog.

*

At the house in Rottingdean, Eden Martin was home from school. She put her keys back in her purse and slung her bag onto the chair in the corner of the hallway and gave her full attention to her BlackBerry, her nails clacking gently against the tiny keys as she arranged to meet with Katie and Lloyd at the cinema tomorrow.

Katie liked Lloyd. Eden knew that. Her thumbs agitated the machine. Katie insisted that Lloyd liked Eden more. She had texted that she wasn't sure if she could make it. Frowning, head down, Eden walked into the kitchen-diner, fretting that going to the cinema alone with Lloyd would be way too embarrassing.

The room ran from the front to the back of the house. It was enormous – a hyper-modern, state-of-the-art kitchen with red-black storage cupboards, a dizzying array of spotlights in the ceiling and a marble floor that extended thirty or forty feet into the dining area, where a modern dining table seated eight in comfort and a line of fold-back doors overlooked the garden and the swimming pool. In the other wing of the house there was a more formal dining room decked out with antique table and chairs but it was in the kitchen-diner that the family gathered every day. Eden drifted through the space, her fingers flying across the keypad of her phone. Now Lloyd was saying he might have to go out with his mum instead. She swore beneath her breath.

She opened cupboards, looking for snacks, finding Ritz crackers. Fetching down the box she grabbed a handful from the cellophane liner, leaving the carton out on the counter and snatching up her mobile as she went to the oversized fridge to look for half-fat Philadelphia. A text belled her inbox and she opened it. Katie wanted to see the film, after all. Good and bad at the same time.

'Hello, darling,' said Abi, padding into the room. 'How was school?'

'Forgotten,' Eden mumbled, concentrating hard on the composition of her text to Lloyd.

'Sometimes I wonder if it's worth all that money,' Abi sighed, glancing at Eden's smart green blazer.

Inwardly, though, Abi was very proud that her daughter went to the most expensive private day school in the city. Abi's own parents had no such aspirations for her. Abi had to make do with the grotty local comp, spending three miserable years there before escaping to the stage school where her real life finally began. From the doorway, Abi glimpsed past Eden to the vast picture windows at the front of the house, admiring the uninterrupted view of the English Channel. She'd paid for this house with her own money. No one could take it away from her. Turning again, she asked her daughter, 'Can you walk Lola tomorrow?'

Lola was the family pet. When Eden was tiny, the golden Labrador used to let her ride her back like a horse and for a long time after that, Lola had remained Eden's constant companion and protector. But that was before the BlackBerry had become a portal through which the teenager had vanished. Abi raised her voice a notch. 'I said, can you walk Lola before school tomorrow?'

'Get Jack to do it,' Eden said absent-mindedly.

Abi looked at her daughter. Eden had changed physically as well. Her lissom, gangly frame had started to resolve itself into the figure of a young woman. A nasty twinge of jealousy went through Abi's body. She didn't want to be reminded of the fact of her own ageing, her own sagging, especially not after her conversation with her agent. 'Jack's busy, darling.'

With effortless sarcasm, Eden grunted. 'Yeah, right.'

Marching across the kitchen, Abi snatched the phone out of Eden's hand.

'Omigod!' Eden protested, flying straight into a rage. 'Don't you *want* me to have any friends?'

'I'd like you to listen to me when I'm talking to you, Eden. I'd like you to show a bit of respect!'

Eden tried to grab her phone back. 'Respect?' she spat out. 'Why should I respect you if you don't respect my property?'

Abi held the phone just out of Eden's reach. A text pinged in.

'Give it back, Mum!' Eden pleaded. 'Please!'

Abi calmed herself. 'Let's try again. This is the part where I, loving mother, say, "Can you walk Lola tomorrow morning?" And you reply . . .?'

Eden pouted. 'Yes, OK! I can walk your bloody dog before I go to school.'

Abi gave her daughter back the phone. 'That's better. And it's not my bloody dog. It's our bloody dog. In fact, you were the one who made me buy it.'

Eden carried the BlackBerry over to the table, where she sat down with her back turned to her mum to read Lloyd's message. It looked like he was coming after all.

Dressed in his grey sweats, Jack walked into the kitchen. 'What's all the noise?'

'Nothing,' said Abi, putting on the kettle to make them both a cup of herbal tea.

Jack came across to where Abi was standing. He put his hand around her waist and nuzzled her neck, whispering something into her ear.

Out of the corner of her eye, Eden watched what they were doing. 'Get a room.'

Giggling, Abi pushed Jack away half-heartedly.

Abi Martin had been with Jack for the last two years. The newspapers had a field day when they got together, not only because of the difference in their ages – Abi was forty-four and Jack in his late twenties – but also because of Jack's gory tabloid past. And yet Abi had come to know a side to Jack that the tabs never wrote about, a naive kind of tenderness and a care for Abi's daughter that made her take his recent proposal of marriage more seriously. They'd been skirting the subject in bed just now, trying on the 'Mr' and 'Mrs' sobriquets for size. Underneath the mockery Abi sensed a moment of reckoning approaching. The only problem would be telling Eden.

Abi took the teabags out of the cup and left them on the side for the cleaner. 'I'm going to have a shower,' she said, picking up her cup.

'Another one,' said Jack, his hand fluttering round Abi's bottom as she passed by.

Abi paused by the dining table, trying to sneak a look at the text message on Eden's screen. 'I've got a charity event at the football stadium. I thought you might like to come.'

Eden angled the screen away from her mother. 'Why on earth would I want to go there?'

'Apparently, most of the players will be attending.'

Eden's interest was piqued. Lloyd supported Brighton and Hove. The club was all he ever went on about. But the thought of being dragged around the room by her mother filled her with too much dread. No one was interested in Eden. Not any more. 'I've got homework to do.'

'Maybe that school's worth the fees, after all,' Abi said on her way out of the room.

His back to the counter, Jack sipped at his fruit tea, wishing it was a healthy brown colour instead of this alarming shade of red.

Eden's thumbs played on her BlackBerry. Jack remembered his own teenage years – his first fumble, his first heartbreak – very well indeed. He and Eden had other things in common as well. They were both subalterns in this house, satellites whose job it was to orbit round the celestial body, to do Abi's bidding and to keep her feeling good about herself. 'Any plans?' he asked Eden.

Turning round, Eden looked at Jack. He had a muscular frame, piercing blue eyes and strong cheekbones. He was around the house a lot. 'No.'

Jack could tell she was excited about something or other. 'What's up?'

Enthusiastically, Eden told him about Lloyd and Katie and their visit to the cinema.

'You like this Lloyd, do you?' Jack asked.

'No,' said Eden contemptuously. 'He's a complete dork.'

Jack smiled. 'Why are you going to the flicks with him, then?'

Eden turned away.

'This Katie,' Jack said. 'Competition, is she?'

'We're BFF.'

Jack sipped at the acid-tasting tea. 'Well,' he said. 'You go ahead and have a good time.'

Looking up, Eden watched Jack leaving the kitchen. At times, he could be all right. At least he was actually interested in what was going on in her life.

Eden knew lots of people whose parents were divorced but no one in the position she was in. Upstairs, in a box in the bottom of her walk-in wardrobe, she had a tatty piece of paper that gave some basic information about her father. His name was Matthew and, although the geography was not entirely clear to her, she knew he lived somewhere in the north of England. Matthew had been picked out by Eden's mother from a list supplied by the sperm donor clinic. He had been twenty-eight years old, with light brown hair, and he played the piano for recreation and tennis for his county team.

And that was all Eden knew.

10

• • •

'I'm here to see George,' Minter said to the girl behind the bar. She pointed behind him, to a big man sitting on his own at a table opposite. Minter walked past the low stage, where a topless girl in a pink satin thong was going through her routine, and up the three carpeted steps that led to the VIP area of the lap-dancing club. Unhooking one end of the red rope from its silver stand, Minter went up to the club's owner. 'Mr Moore?'

George Moore looked up from the account books he was trawling through. He was middle-aged, with a deeply tanned face and a mane of ginger hair he backcombed into a trademark. When he extended his hand Minter saw pudgy fingers encrusted with gold sovereign rings and, around the neck of George's black roll-neck jumper, a gleaming, chunky gold chain. Gorgeous George, as he was known in the underworld, was more flash than bling and every bit as old-school gangster as his moniker suggested. Minter shook his hand.

When George took a sip from the highball glass at his elbow, he raised his pinkie. 'Mr Minter,' he said, putting down the tumbler and indicating the brown leather tub chair next to him. 'Please.'

'Thanks,' said Minter. He cast an eye around the long narrow room. 'Regency de luxe' was the best term he could find to describe the interior – grey-painted wooden panelling, purple flock wallpaper, huge gilt mirrors. This was one of three such similar establishments Gorgeous George had opened in the city, and even on a rainy lunchtime, Minter noted, it was doing good business. He counted five tables of men watching the girl disport herself on the stage.

'What can I do for you?' George asked.

Minter took the photograph taken on the pier out of his jacket pocket and laid it on the table. 'Mercy Mvule. Do you know her?'

George studied the photograph. 'Never seen her before. Why you asking?'

For waitressing at the North African restaurant in Kemptown, Mercy Mvule was paid minimum wage plus pooled tips. But she never asked her flatmate for any rent money. Freema Agyeman had offered a few times, especially once she started working as a cleaner, but each time she did Mercy refused. Freema put it down to Mercy's customary hospitality – Freema was from Ghana not Togo, but both women belonged to the Ewe tribe – but when Minter did the maths Mercy's monthly income and expenditure didn't add up. 'She's never worked for you at any of the clubs?' he asked.

George shook his head again.

'What about on the streets?'

George adopted a hurt tone. 'Mr Minter, are you suggesting I'm living off immoral earnings?'

Minter was disappointed. He still had to find the sous-chef

at the restaurant where Mercy worked. According to Freema Agyeman, Freddy the chef had been Mercy's on-off boyfriend for the last year or so. It had been a tempestuous relationship, with lots of flying plates and tearful reunions.

A loud cheer went up. Glancing across, Minter saw that the young woman was now completely nude. Turning back to George, he said, 'Your business empire isn't the issue here.'

George looked a little harder at the photo of the black woman. He read the papers, just like everybody else. He knew who Mercy Mvule was. 'Nah,' he said, shaking his head. 'Don't know her.'

Another, more localised, cheer went up. A different girl, this one in a baby-doll nightdress, was leading one of the men away from his table of stags and towards a heavy curtain made of gold cloth. 'Private dance booths,' George explained. 'You should try one sometime. Complimentary.'

Minter took another photograph out of his pocket. 'What about this woman?'

The second victim had now been identified. Jane Metcalfe was a third-year student of Fine Art at the University of Sussex. She had been reported missing by her parents, who had come down to Brighton for a half-term visit and, when they couldn't locate their daughter, had been spooked by the reports of the murders in the city. They'd called the police and an eagle-eyed PC passed the description they had given straight to CID.

George looked down again. The photo-booth shot from Jane Metcalfe's NUS card revealed her as a slightly gawky young woman with long strawberry-blond hair and a smattering of freckles. Jane Metcalfe and Mercy Mvule were different in every way. It wasn't just body shape – Jane wiry, Mercy well built – it was their colouring, their educational background, even their ethnicity. The only thing that connected them was that they both seemed to have access to ready money.

Minter had come here from the campus, where he had interviewed a group of Jane's friends. Brighton was a student town and students went Dutch on a Coke but, said Metcalfe's friends, it was always Jane who paid for cabs at the end of a good night out. She didn't have a term-time job, she wasn't getting bungs from the bank of Mum and Dad, and her student loan account was a lot less in the red than most. But in a town like Brighton there were other ways a young woman could find to earn some cash, even if she was a student of Fine Art. Not according to Gorgeous George, though. 'I've never seen her either,' he said. 'Too scrawny, anyway. Now, if you'll excuse me, Mr Minter,' he added, 'I've got business to attend to.'

'In cases like this,' Minter went on, 'it's difficult to know what to do about showing the family the remains. I mean, the killer stabbed Jane a total of fifty-three times. Can you imagine what that does to a body, Mr Moore? It's not really in a fit state to be viewed. If you were a parent, would you want the memory of your only child despoiled like that?'

For the first time in the interview, George began to look chastened.

'On the other hand,' Minter went on, 'some experts say that viewing the remains is essential, whatever state they are in, no matter how traumatic it might be. They say it's the first stage of grieving.' His eyes trained on George, Minter paused. 'What would you have done this morning, if you were me? Would you have let Mr and Mrs Metcalfe view their daughter's body?'

'Ok,' said Gorgeous George 'I'll put the word out. I'll tell my girls to be careful.'

*

'The head of the first victim was some kind of trophy, right?' Beckett asked.

Dr McGuire nodded. 'The extremities are often taken.'

In Tom Beckett's office, the two men were sitting opposite each other at the newly delivered conference table, grisly scenes-of-crime photos strewn across the table between them. 'I don't get it,' Beckett said impatiently, 'this guy doesn't leave anything behind – no fibres, no DNA, *nothing* – but the increased frenzy of the knife attack is meant to suggest a disintegrating personality.'

Dr McGuire looked at Beckett. 'Have you located the clothes belonging to either victim?'

Beckett shook his head. 'Not yet.'

'As your pathologist points out in the PM,' said Dr McGuire, 'the wrists of both victims show clear ligature marks. The women were absolutely at his command, yet he neglected to sexually assault them.'

'You mean he has some kind of sexual dysfunction?' Beckett suggested.

'I'm not here to speculate. I've interviewed enough of these men to realise I'll never fully understand their motives. But the lack of bodily contact between this perpetrator and his victims might explain why you've failed to obtain any forensic evidence. And it is certainly anomalous.'

In the field of forensic psychiatry Dr McGuire was a rising star. Beckett had seen his name on the speakers' lists of numerous conferences and his services had been recommended to the Brighton SIO by two separate murder detectives from the Met. Not for McGuire the psychological insights offered by the profilers of yesterday – he wouldn't even call himself a profiler, his business card instead announcing him as a 'behavioural investigative adviser'. McGuire had something a lot better than moonlit flashes of inspiration. He had data.

He was somewhere in his late forties, with steel-rimmed spectacles and short, dark hair and he had driven down to Brighton this morning from somewhere on the other side of the M25, where the department he ran occupied an entire floor of a country house owned by the National Police Improvement Agency. For the agency, McGuire managed the growing national database that was said to contain the details of every serious sexual and violent assault committed in the UK.

Beckett watched as McGuire pored over the photographs on the desk, turning them this way and that in order to get a better look at the victims' wounds, sometimes putting two of them next to each other for comparison, pausing every now and then to note his observations on his pro forma. Dr McGuire's handwriting was small and neat and precise.

'Why use a blowtorch?' Beckett asked. 'If he wanted to make identification difficult, or if he wanted to take trophies, why not remove her head, like he did the first time?'

Ignoring him, McGuire opened the folder which he'd brought into the room and handed Beckett a couple of printouts. 'The database has flagged up two linked cases. Burning the face in such a ritualised fashion is extremely rare, certainly a lot rarer than taking off the hands and feet. The first case is from Birmingham, a sociopath who pulled three women off the streets. I interviewed him last year in a secure unit as part of a research project I was doing.' He let Beckett read the notes. 'As you can see, he is a very disturbed individual.'

Beckett had moved on to the second case, which remained unsolved. Two years ago, a young Glaswegian woman had been abducted, bound and hooded. Her assailant had poured lighter fluid over the material of the hood and set it alight. Luckily, the woman's screams had alerted a passer-by, but her attacker escaped.

It looked promising. The assailant had not verbally abused his victim, nor had he tried to touch her or sexually assault her. The police in Glasgow even had a suspect but there'd been insufficient evidence to charge him and Beckett didn't recognise his name or his description from the lists of suspects Brighton and Hove had drawn up for their own murders. Disappointed, he said, 'We've screened all the offenders in our area with a history of violence against unknown women.'

'It's a common misconception' said McGuire in a patronising tone of voice 'that assailants like these graduate from minor sexual offences to full-blown murder, but I'm afraid that's simply not borne out by the data. What you need to do is to look at *all* offenders within a nine-mile radius of the bodies, even those with convictions for, say, burglary.'

Beckett had taken a firm dislike to Dr McGuire. There was his manner for one thing. Then there was the expensive pen McGuire was using, the initials *LM* engraved on the silver at the side. It might have been a gift, of course, but something about McGuire told Beckett that, as well as being a little vain, the scientist lived very much on his own.

'This is a town with a quarter of a million people in it,' Beckett told McGuire. 'Screening *all* offenders will take for ever.'

'Maybe,' said McGuire flatly. 'But otherwise, I'm afraid, there's not much point.'

'What if our guy's not even from our patch?'

McGuire fixed Beckett with his stare. 'That's very unlikely. A nine-mile radius is the optimum search area.'

There was a knock at the door and Minter stuck his head round.

'Come in, Minter,' said Beckett. 'This is Dr McGuire. He's not a profiler. Apparently, they're not called that any more. Dr McGuire here is a behavioural investigative adviser.' He turned to the other man. 'This is my oppo, DI Minter.'

Minter was still getting used to being addressed by his new rank. 'Good to meet you, sir.'

McGuire nodded curtly.

'I talked to Vincent Underhill's psychiatrist this morning,' Minter said to Beckett. 'He's convinced Underhill didn't commit the murders.'

Quickly, Beckett explained who Underhill was, and his importance to the investigation. For a moment, McGuire looked puzzled. He said, 'This murder certainly doesn't fit what we know about schizophrenic killers.'

Beckett stood up, the printout from McGuire still in his hand. 'I'm going to get going on this Glasgow case. Minter, you stay here with Dr McGuire and go through the PM.'

When Beckett left the room, Minter and McGuire began to pore over the post-mortem report on Jane Metcalfe, noting down the differences and similarities to the first Brighton murder. It took more than half an hour and by the end they had concluded that it was almost certainly the same perp. Even the wound profiles were the same.

'Have you been given somewhere to work?' Minter asked, closing his notebook.

'I've got a desk in the DC's room.'

'If you need somewhere private, I can find you an office.'

'No, that's fine. I like being in the centre of the action.'

'OK,' said Minter, unsure whether that was really protocol. He got up to leave but stopped in the doorway. 'I wanted to ask something.'

'About the case?'

Minter hesitated. 'Not about this one. But it might be related. Do you know anything about manic depression?'

'Bipolar disorder isn't something I come across a lot.'

Minter nodded. Psychopaths were sociopaths now and manic depressives had become bipolar. He was catching on. 'Can you tell me what age the symptoms of bipolar disorder start to manifest themselves?'

'Onset varies enormously.'

'What age is the median?'

'Late twenties would be regarded as typical.'

Minter nodded.

'Why did you want to know?'

But Minter didn't reply.

11

In her bedroom, Eden Martin checked Facebook. Linking to her friend Katie's page she saw that it had just been updated with a photo showing Lloyd's face goofing off over his plate of food in Nando's.

Eden threw the phone onto her bed in despair. Despite what she had told Jack earlier on this evening, she liked Lloyd a lot. He might not live in a big house and his parents might have ordinary jobs but he made Eden laugh. He was fun.

She heard her mother coming up the stairs. A moment later, there was a soft rapping at her door. 'You awake, darling?' said Abi, pushing the door open and sticking her head around.

Eden had the second bedroom suite, with its own palatial en suite and two sash windows overlooking the Downs to the rear of the house. She liked to keep the room dark, illuminated only by a desk lamp and the glow of her laptop where she'd been watching catch-up TV.

'I had a great time at the football stadium,' Abi said. She was hiding something behind her back.

Eden could always tell when her mother was a little tipsy. 'What have you got?'

Abi walked into the room and held out the striped blue and white football shirt. 'Ta-da!'

'It's a Brighton shirt,' said Eden, unimpressed.

'It's not just any old Brighton shirt,' Abi said sashaying over to Eden. 'It was part of the charity auction,' she explained, holding up the shirt so that Eden could see where the first team had all signed it. 'Jack said you'd find a use for it. Can't think why. But I bid for it anyway.' Abi pointed to one of the signatures scrawled on the front of the shirt in thick black Sharpie. 'That's Ruben Thingummy's signature.' Abi smiled. 'Ruben took me into the player's bar. He's a very naughty boy.'

'Ruben Kennedy!' exclaimed Eden, jumping to her knees on the bed. 'Hold it up so I can get a picture!'

Jack was fantastic, Eden thought, snapping another photo with her camera phone. This shirt would get Lloyd's attention all right. Ruben Kennedy was his all-time hero. Lloyd would be much more interested in this than in the chicken at Nando's, or in Katie. She texted the picture straight to his phone.

Abi knew enough not to interfere with Eden's electronic biosphere, but she could see how right Jack had been about the shirt. The tabloids could say what they liked about Jack, but when it came to helping her stay in touch with Eden, Jack was as good a spy as any. And Abi was glad that she'd caught her daughter in a better mood. 'I've got something to tell you,' she said.

'What?' said Eden absent-mindedly, looking at her phone waiting for Lloyd to text back.

Abi grabbed her daughter's hand. 'Jack's asked me to marry him!'

'Really?'

'Yes, isn't it amazing?'

In Eden's eyes, Jack could do no wrong. Hadn't he got her the football shirt? 'That's great!'

Abi already had this conversation planned out. 'It'll be a long engagement.'

There was a pause 'When you do get married, will Jack become my dad?'

Abi hesitated. 'You've already got a dad.'

'That's different, though. You picked Matthew out of a brochure.'

'It wasn't quite as simple as all that,' Abi demurred.

By the time she'd hit her thirties, Abi's breathless enchantment with her own success had begun to fade. She decided she needed to feel more love. She was greedy to have it and greedy to give it, too, and once she'd admitted that to herself, every fibre in her body began to yearn for a child. She felt the press of it in her flesh. At work, a black and murderous mood would descend on Abi every time a female colleague told her they were going to have a baby, her angry despair reaching its nadir when she had a researcher sacked for daring to bemoan the behaviour of her one-year-old. Abi found some pretext about the quality of the girl's work, of course, but she couldn't hide the truth from herself. A couple of months later, when she had still not met a suitable man, she decided to go ahead and have a baby on her own.

Having Eden completed Abi. She carried the growing baby for nine months in her tummy and she swore the little girl would have all the things she hadn't. Ever since then, she'd given Eden everything – everything, that is, except a father.

'Would you like Jack to be your dad?' Abi asked Eden.

'I suppose he could adopt me.' Over the years, she'd gone over all the various ways of securing a father for herself, including once considering going up north to hunt for Matthew.

'He could.' A pang of guilt went through Abi. 'He could.' She put her hand up and stroked Eden's cheek. 'You know what I think?'

'What?'

'If it looks like a dad and sounds like a dad, then it probably is a dad.'

Eden wasn't so sure. 'Maybe.'

'Anyway,' said Abi, 'there's lots of time to find out.'

She had no idea how wrong she was.

In the deserted car park Minter got changed into his running gear. He set the GPS system on his Suunto training watch, pocketed his mobile and fitted the band of the head torch that would light his way. When he jogged up the side of the first hill the moon was hanging big and low in the sky, illuminating the Downs with its silvery light, close enough, it seemed, for Minter to reach out and touch it. He ran along the promontory for a couple of miles, disturbing from the undergrowth a family of foxes and passing an old barn where a hunting owl perched on the roof. Warily, it swivelled its head to track Minter's progress. The wind whipped into his face, bringing the blood to his ears, making him grateful for his insulated running suit. When he reached Rackham Hill Minter lengthened his stride, settling into an easy rhythm. Even under these conditions – in the dark and cold – it felt good to be out here.

He kept his gear in his car and ran at least twice a week. He raced for the challenge of beating his own best time and for the rush of the endorphins.

Ahead of him, the hills spanned the shadowy horizon from east to west. Dipping and rolling, they lined up one behind the other as far as the eye could see, like the shoulders of sleeping giants. As he ran on, the detritus of his day began to fall through Minter's mind. There was the move to Hollingbury. That would be OK. As a child he'd gone from home to home so often that after just a year or so in any one place Minter sensed the time had come to move on. Kevin Phillips, however, would be more of a problem.

There was history between the two men. The first case Minter had worked in Kemptown had been an investigation into Brighton's most violent and well-organised heroin supplier, Russell Compton. Halfway through, it became obvious to Minter that someone on the team was selling information to Compton's gang and, for a time, his suspicions fell on Phillips. In the end Kevin had been exonerated but not before he had spent an uncomfortable three hours with the officers from Professional Standards, who had arrived in Brighton to pick over the bones of the corruption allegation. The mud that stuck from that had driven Kevin out of SOCU and into CID. It was meant to be a fresh start.

Minter ran on across the side of the hill. In the distance, he could see the deep white scars of the old chalk pits shining eerily in the moonlight.

Overnight, a file of evidence concerning a recent series of unsolved murders in Leeds was on its way down to Brighton and Minter had already talked at length to the senior investigating officer. Two prostitutes had been slain in the northern city and in terms of MO there were similarities to the Brighton murder: the perp had a taste for knives and took trophies from the corpses of his victims – heads and hands – to enjoy at his leisure. The Leeds squad had lifted fingerprints and DNA samples from the crime scenes but they hadn't been able to charge anyone. The lab results had come back; the fingerprints and DNA they'd obtained from Vincent Underhill and which were all over the suitcase didn't match any of those in the Leeds case. The alternative was that the Leeds murderer had drifted down to Brighton to resume where he had left off. 'If that's right,' the Leeds SIO had warned Minter, 'that body in the suitcase won't be your last.'

But the killer in the north had been disorganised and opportunistic, picking on streetwalkers because they were easy targets, and leaving lots of forensic evidence. By contrast, the Brighton killer had been scrupulous, even methodical. That meant either he had learned from what had happened in Leeds or that the Brighton killer was someone different.

Minter accelerated across the hillside, pounding out a faster rhythm. He tried to clear his mind by focusing on the one-two slap of his running shoes against the chalk, reminding himself that the ideas that floated up from his subconscious at these times often proved to be the best ones. But the near-hypnotic state of reverie didn't come and Minter's mind continued to spin out in all directions until, finally, it fell upon the scene that had been welling up inside him ever since this morning.

Minter and his mum were on the bus out of Brighton. It was the day of his sixth birthday and she said they could go upstairs. They sat right at the front and Minter pretended to drive, jigging about on the seat as he turned the imaginary wheel and imitating the sound of the bell. But he didn't allow himself to become totally lost in the play. He couldn't afford to. Every now and then he glanced across at his mother to check on her, watchful for any sign that her mood might change. But she just sat there laughing at him, her long hair tumbling over her shoulders.

'One day sunshine, the next day rain' – that's how Lucy Minter used to explain her illness to her son. For now it was all sunshine.

They got out at the top of the hill and walked over to the famous lookout. It was a hot summer's day and there were lots of people about, walking or picnicking or flying their kites on the hillside. Minter and his mother went into the café. For once it seemed that money was no object because they had lunch together and after that she bought them both an ice cream from the van in the car park. They sat down on the bench, Minter licking greedily at the soft vanilla, wondering when his birthday present would arrive.

When he was finished, his mum took a hanky out of her pocket, wetting it first with the tip of her tongue before dabbing at the stains around his mouth. But she didn't get angry – she just tucked the hanky into the sleeve of her top and sat back on the bench. 'Lovely here, isn't it?'

Minter was impatient for his present. He stared glumly down at the Weald.

She giggled.

Minter turned towards his mum to see her outstretched hand, the palm flat and a crumpled wedge of purple tissue paper sitting proudly in the middle. 'Happy birthday, love!' she cried.

Minter grabbed the tissue paper from her and started unwrapping. Inside there was a gold chain and a medallion.

He held it up by the end so that the sunlight flashed off the bright gold. It wasn't what he wanted. He wanted a scooter.

'Here,' said his mum, taking the chain from her son and using her fingernails to pull back the clasp. She put it around his neck and did it up, patting it as it dangled there on the chest of his T-shirt. 'It's called a St Christopher,' she said. 'It's to protect you on all your travels.' She patted the medallion on his chest again.

Minter picked up the medal and turned it face up so he could see the image stamped there. In the circle of gold a man with a grizzled beard trudged waist-high through the swollen waters of a river, a boy riding safely on his shoulders. Minter glanced across at his mum. He knew she couldn't afford much. 'Thanks,' he said, a little reluctantly. He had really wanted the scooter.

'You're a special boy.'

They settled back on the bench to admire the view. For the first time, Minter looked at the hills above the city where he lived and noticed how beautiful they were. He inched across the bench, snuggling close to her, but she pushed him away, and when he looked up at her she was biting her lip. 'Mum?'

'I'm not feeling so good.'

These black moods swooped down out of nowhere. At home they made her take to her bed and close the door of her room, ignoring his clamour for company and even his pleading for food. He would sit there on the floor outside her door, listening to her wailing. 'Did we spend too much money?'

When she turned to face him tears were standing in the corners of her eyes. She ran her fingers down his cheeks. 'You're a clever boy. You'll work it all out one day.'

But he never got the chance.

That night, Minter woke up coughing. He leapt out of bed and struggled through the billowing, acrid smoke towards the door, on the other side of which the fire roared and crackled. He grasped the handle of the door but it burned his skin. He had no choice though. Gripping it tightly for the second time, he yanked it open.

The fire surged into the room, tongues of yellow flame shooting along the ceiling above him. The light fitting exploded immediately, dripping flames onto his bed and setting the blankets alight. The fire snickered along the walls as well, catching the curtains. Within moments, the whole room was ablaze.

In its eagerness to be inside, the fire had batted the door straight back into the boys face, knocking him to the floor. It saved his life. The flashover scalded his cheeks but the fire itself passed right over him. When he came to, red embers danced giddily in the air above him and he could feel coal-points of heat settling all over his face and hands. Coughing, swallowing smoke, he got to his knees. He was in a little island of safety between the inferno in the hallway and the fire raging in his bedroom.

There was the crash of exploding glass and a sudden whoosh of rushing air. In the window, he saw a figure through the flames and, behind it, a ladder. The fireman was the last thing Minter saw before he passed out.

From Rackham Hill, the course began to descend quickly, the flints on the ground twisting at Minter's ankles. He went headlong, his hands out either side of him in an effort to keep his balance, his flexed knees groaning.

At the bottom of the hill he joined a farm track. After the

ceaseless rain, tractor tyres had pressed the mud up into crests as soft as fondant. Minter's running shoes slipped straight through them into the pools of icy water below. He climbed a five-bar gate and jumped down the other side, mud spattering his trousers up to his knees as he landed. He had reached one of those rare parts of the Downs that had been ploughed instead of being left as pasture. In front of him, the track skirted a large field but the course Minter had planned ran straight through it. He paused a moment to catch his breath for what was going to be a very difficult traversing.

'One day sunshine, one day rain,' that's how she'd explained it to him then. Now Minter could give it another name, it's proper name. Bi-polar disorder.

Did he have it, too? Certainly, it would explain the way he could go with very little sleep, sometimes for a week at a time. It would explain the terrible sadness he would often feel, and the way at other times his thoughts would start to race – and the sudden bursts of energy that compelled him to run these hills for hour after hour. Would the curse of mental illness be his mother's final gift?

Minter slipped his hand inside his training jacket and touched the little gold medallion. When he was six years old the medal had rested on his chest but now that he was grown it dangled awkwardly below the tips of his collarbones. He turned it over in his fingers, feeling the thinness of the gold, the raised impression of the little scene, the warmth of the alloy where it had been so close to his moving body. All the time he'd been in care, the medallion had been a kind of magic charm, a talisman. Even in the dark days at Hillcrest, as long as he had the St Christopher Minter felt he wasn't completely on his own. His mother was watching over him. Wasn't that what she'd promised that afternoon out on the Downs? That one day he would understand it all.

Minter started running across the ploughed field. The mud sucked his feet down, clutching at his running shoes so that at every step he had to wrench them free. The muscles in his calves began to pull terribly and his breath came in ragged pieces and the beam from his head torch bounced crazily off the deep brown furrows. Every now and then he took a misstep and staggered sideways across a few of them, at one point even tumbling to his hands and knees in the mire. Minter got up again but towards the middle of the field the furrows were waterlogged and his pace slowed to a weary trudge. Then he did what he always swore he never would. He stopped running.

Minter heard the high-pitched stutter of a redwing. His breath made wreathes in the freezing air and steam rose from his head and shoulders. Panting, he put his hands behind his neck and fiddled with the clasp of the chain until at last he'd prised it open. He looked down at the medal in his hand. It didn't seem magical at all now. It seemed cheap and ordinary, the kind of trash you could pick up for a few pennies from any high street jeweller.

The chain played out until it was held just on the pad of Minter's thumb, then it was gone, landing in the soft mud at his feet without a noise, becoming a faint, yellowish gleam in the darkness.

12

• • •

'And … out!' said the voice in Abi's ear. The adverts began. They were on the home straight now – eight twenty-eight a.m. and just the final celeb interview to go. In her earpiece Abi overheard her favourite director share a joke with someone up in the gallery. Everyone sounded relaxed, pleased with their work this morning. She looked to her left, where the floor manager was leading guest Dan Hegarty out onto the set. 'Hi!' said Abi, getting up from the famous sofa and air-kissing Dan expertly on both cheeks at the same time as ensuring he didn't smudge her make-up. 'So good to see you again.'

Hegarty was the new face of TV wildlife. He had the long nose and thin lips of good breeding and the kind of ruddy tan that could only be obtained at this time of year from the world's more expensive ski resorts. Posh totty was in right now, even if it came in the dim variety, and they were lucky to get him on the week his new series went to air.

'Thanks for having me, Ms Martin,' Dan said, basking in the glow of Abi's most radiant smile. Abi's co-host Simon shook Dan's hand and they all sat down. Someone came over and with difficulty attached a radio mic to a blob on Dan's Aran jumper.

'How have you been?' Abi asked.

'Excellent. I've been excellent.'

Dan might have gone to Marlborough but he was still a bit of an action man. He'd thrown over his place at Exeter in favour of two years spent radio-tagging sea turtles off the coastline of Sri Lanka and he got his first presenting job when he was waiting tables in a London restaurant where a female producer took a shine to him. That night, the producer had Dan for dessert. His big break in TV had been a kind of tip.

'Dan,' Abi enthused, 'this new series of yours is going to be *massive.*'

'Do you think?' Dan smirked.

'Absolutely,' said Abi, her eyes twinkling. Dan Hegarty was the perfect eight thirty interviewee: one hundred per cent premium English beefcake with a side order of Planet Earth. The kids packed safely off to school, the mums at home would lap him up.

'The second series has already been commissioned,' said Dan. Leaning forward, pleased to be getting the hang of these conversations, he said, 'Why don't you come on, Abi? You'd be awesome.'

Abi had seen the preview tape and the clever segment where a celebrity came face to face with their most feared wild animal. 'That would be so exciting,' Abi said. 'The only trouble is, I'm not sure if I'm scared of anything.'

Feeling a little left out by all this excited cooing, Simon leaned across. 'Yes,' he said, 'all the animals would be terrified of *her.*'

Abi was going to put Simon down but she could hear the tension return to the voices in her ear. She winked at Dan and mouthed, 'Good luck!'

'Welcome back,' Abi said to camera two. 'And we're joined for the last half-hour by wildlife god Dan Hegarty.' The crew smattered applause. 'Dan's got a new series starting next week and I can tell you it's not to be missed. This time, instead of backpacking his way across the Andes, Dan's taking the plunge deep underneath the surface of the world's oceans, getting up close and personal with some of the planet's most amazing and endangered creatures.'

In big close-up, Dan turned on his frowning, jut-jawed, eco-warrior expression.

Abi said, 'Let's take a look at some of what he found.'

Tony Evans, the breakfast show's producer, was up in the gallery for the last half-hour, standing behind the director and watching the show on the bank of monitors. He was looking in particular at camera three – the two-shot of Abi Martin and Dan Hegarty that came up after the VT. On the screen, Abi flirted with the guest relentlessly, her hand even reaching across to touch his knee after Dan delivered the punchline to a funny story about his organic smallholding in the West Country. The difference in age between Dan and Abi made their banter look a little creepy. Even Dan seemed to sense it too. He was leaning back a little on the sofa as if he was trying to get away from her. 'That woman has no shame,' said Tony Evans.

'Back to guest,' the director instructed camera two. Without taking his eyes off the monitors he turned his head slightly in Evans's direction. 'Good show today.'

Evans didn't reply. His eyes had moved over to Simon's close-up. Excluded from the chat, the male presenter was looking bored, not even bothering to check his running order as they headed for the commercial break. Evans glanced across at the medium shot of the whole sofa, imagining how Sonia Lewis would look in between Simon and the guest. Sonia's perky glamour would soon rouse Simon out of his torpor, he thought, and if it was Sonia sticking her tits in Dan Hegarty's face then he wouldn't be mountaineering the sofa in an effort to get away from her.

The door to the gallery opened and one of the young production assistants snuck in behind them. 'Excuse me, Mr Evans, but there's a call for you.' When Evans didn't even look at her, the production assistant held out the mobile phone. 'Mr Evans?'

'Fuck off,' he muttered. In his mind Evans was calculating the exact sum of money the company would have to pay to cancel the remaining three months of Abi's contract.

The production assistant looked worried. 'I thought you'd want to take it. It sounds urgent.'

Evans ignored her.

'It's Abi's boyfriend.'

On the monitor, they went to more VT of Dan's new show. At last, Evans looked at the production assistant. 'What are you going on about?'

She was still holding out the mobile. 'I really think you should talk to him.'

Sighing, Evans snatched the phone away from her. 'Hi, Jack.'

'I want to speak to Abi!' Jack shouted. 'Just put me through to Abi!'

'She's on air, Jack,' said Evans wearily, as if he was talking to a little boy. 'She can't talk to you right now.'

There was wind playing across the microphone of Jack's phone. 'Fuck that! I don't care about that! It's Eden!'

The director and his assistants in the gallery could hear the frantic tone in Jack's voice. This time they all turned their heads to see how Evans would respond. He stepped to the back of the narrow room and said in a low voice. 'I don't know what you're talking about, Jack, but if you ring Abi's phone in an hour or so I'm sure she'll pick up.'

'She's fucking gone! Eden's disappeared! Someone's taken her!'

Evans paused, realising that Eden must be the name of Abi's brat.

'I've got to speak to Abi. *Now!*'

'She'll call you back,' said Evans, pressing the button to end the call and handing the mobile back to the production assistant.

There was an awkward silence in the room. They could hear Abi's voice on the playback from the studio, asking Dan Hegarty a question. 'We could always go to some ads,' suggested the director. 'Simon could anchor the rest of the show on his own.'

Evans was watching the monitors again, looking at the time codes. 'Abi's a pro,' he said. 'She'd want to see out the last few minutes.'

'What?' said the production assistant. 'I don't think so.'

Evans glared at her. 'Tell you what, Jessica or Jocasta, or whatever your fucking name is, why don't you make yourself useful and go and make some tea?'

*

The body was on the top floor. An amateur photographer had discovered it just an hour before. He had trespassed into the abandoned industrial building on a main road seven miles west of Brighton, hoping get some moody black and white shots of the factory's decay. He got a lot more than he bargained for.

Beckett's shoes clanged up the metal staircase, his fingers disturbing decades of fine cement dust on the handrail. The interior of the building around him – the floors, the huge mixers, the giant slurry pipes – was all covered in grey.

Brushing his hands clean, Beckett hurried up the next flight of stairs. Through one of the broken windows in the far wall he glimpsed the massive limestone quarry scooped out of the hills behind the factory. He could hear more police sirens and, from somewhere above, the echoing conversations of the Scenes of Crime officers. When his mobile rang Beckett didn't break stride as he snatched it out of his pocket. 'What?'

'Is that Detective Chief Inspector Tom Beckett?'

Beckett's feet banged against the metal walkway as he crossed from one side of the building to the other. Ahead of him, he could see the arc lights. 'Who wants to know?'

'My name's Keith Miller. I'm the chief crime reporter on the *Daily Mail.*' He waited for some kind of response – most police officers cultivated Miller with a sense of deference at least – but none was forthcoming. 'If you've got time,' he said a little more warily, 'I wanted to ask you a few questions.'

Surely, Beckett thought, this Miller hadn't been told already about the discovery of the third body? 'I don't know how you got this number,' he said, 'but I suggest you ring the Press Office.'

'We're running a story tomorrow about your lack of progress in the Brighton serial killer case. I thought you'd want the right of reply.'

Beckett stopped. 'You been speaking to Andy Griffin as well, have you?'

There was a pause on the other end of the line. 'Is it true you have no usable forensic evidence?'

The police had been very cagey about the lack of forensics – it wasn't something Griffin should know. 'I told you,' said Beckett, 'speak to the Press Office.' Turning the corner, he hung up.

The third body was illuminated by the two sets of arc lights SOCO had set up in this dingy corner of the factory. The victim had been chained by both wrists to a block and tackle in the ceiling and left suspended a couple of feet off the ground. Instead of being taut, as Beckett would have expected, there was a strange slackness about her naked body. She looked like a marionette, a puppet on a string. 'Anything?' he said, walking slowly over and addressing himself to the four paper-suited officers moving on their hands and knees beneath her.

'Not so far,' said the SOCO in charge.

The body swayed gently from side to side in the breeze. She was young, about the same age as Mercy Mvule and Jane Metcalfe. Her straight brown hair hung down round her breasts, breasts that had been slashed until all that remained were shapeless ribbons of flesh. Her head lolled down onto her chest. Beckett had to move closer to be certain of what he'd seen.

He was right. Her eyeballs had been removed, the sockets blind, clogged with dried blood and tissue. The odd slackness of her body was the result of the terrible beating she had received, one that had been delivered with the help of something metal, by the look of it. Every one of her joints was bruised, every major bone broken. It had been systematic.

'I want you to look really carefully,' Beckett told the sergeant, his voice rising. 'I want a fingertip search of the entire factory. If there's one bit of forensics, I want it bagged and up at Hollingbury by lunchtime. Understand?'

'Yes, sir,' said the sergeant.

On the other side of Brighton, the police car slowed to a halt on the Downs. 'Have you found her yet, sir?' asked the female officer as soon as she got out. The school-ma'am hat she was wearing had a band of black and white squares around its crown and was pulled down low across her brows. It made her look severe.

'No,' said Jack breathlessly. 'I've been all over.'

'How long have you been looking?'

'I don't know. Half an hour or so. I came out here when I realised Eden was late for school.'

'Is that the dog she was walking?'

Jack had Lola on a lead now. The Labrador hunkered down by his side, a worried expression on her face as if she knew something was wrong. 'This is Lola,' Jack said. 'When I found her, she was whining.'

At this stage, the officer wasn't too worried. Teenagers were prone to running away. But leaving the dog behind was a little odd. 'You told my colleague that Eden is thirteen?' she said, taking out her notebook.

'That's right.'

'And what's her date of birth?'

Jack hesitated for a moment, causing the first note of

suspicion to waft over the policewoman's face. With an effort, Jack remembered.

'And are you the father?'

'No,' Jack said. 'I guess you'd call me the stepfather.' The word sounded strange in his mouth.

'And where's Mum?'

'She's at work in London.'

'Does she know what's happened?'

'I've just tried to ring her.' The policewoman's eyes narrowed. 'She works on TV. They're in the middle of a broadcast.'

The policewoman knew she'd recognised Jack Bellamy's name. And now she knew where from. There were always photographs of him, usually standing next to Abi Martin, in the celebrity magazines she read at the hairdresser's. Suddenly, this routine call had become very interesting. 'Can you give me a description of Eden?'

'She's tall for her age,' said Jack, putting his hand up to just below the level of his chin. 'About so high. Long hair. Blonde.'

'What about her clothes?'

Jack cast his mind back to Eden in the hallway this morning as she took the lead down for Lola's walk, the dog barking excitedly at Eden's feet. 'Her school uniform.' He described the dress, the blazer. 'And a brown raincoat,' he added.

The policewoman scribbled it all down, estimating Eden's height as five foot five. 'Eye colour?'

'Blue.'

'Thank you, Mr Bellamy,' said the officer. Putting away her notebook, she cast her eyes over the open farmland. Far away to her right, the village of Falmer nestled at the bottom of a fold of land. To her left, a series of fields ran down to the white cliffs where the last of the sea mist was evaporating. She was standing in an excellent vantage point but the little girl with the eccentric name and the famous mother was nowhere to be seen. There were plenty of places where she might have conceivably fallen and twisted an ankle, or simply gone to hide – barns and farmhouses, copses, dew ponds, hillocks – but there were also lots of country lanes and roads criss-crossing this part of the Downs, raising at least the possibility that the teenager had been taken and was right now on her way out of the locality.

The officer turned to the radio clipped to her lapel and pressed a button. When the call was answered she told the dispatcher her name and police number and asked to be called back by the duty DI regarding a missing thirteen-year-old girl by the name of Eden Martin. After adding the address she signed off and turned to Jack. 'Can you show me where you found the dog?'

'Over there,' Jack said, pointing to the bottom of the little valley.

All of them – the PC, Jack, the Lab – walked down the slope towards the ditch at the bottom, which was lined on either side with by a thicket of hawthorn. 'Lola was here on the bank,' said Jack.

The police officer nodded. She pushed her way through a gap in the hawthorn and saw a stream at the bottom of the ditch. Even given all the rain that had fallen these last few days, it wasn't much of a current – nowhere near deep enough to carry a girl the size of Eden away. She looked across the stream towards the slope rising up from the other side. The bank wasn't particularly steep but the vegetation all along the banks was very thick. That was where someone could have seized her. Eden's violated body might still be lying there.

'Have you been across?' she asked Jack, who was standing right behind her.

'I told you. I've been all over. She's not there.'

He sounded very certain. The policewoman glanced down the stream, to the windmill and the roofs of the houses in Rottingdean village and out towards the sea, where the sky lowered ominously.

When the radio chirruped into life it was the duty DI from Kemptown station calling back. Eden Martin wasn't on the Child Protection registers so the DI didn't sound too concerned. But he was still sending two more units to help with the initial search of the area.

'Is that it?' said Jack when the policewoman told him. 'No helicopters?'

'The chances are very high that Eden will be found in the next hour or so, and that she'll be safe and sound.'

Inside, though, the policewoman wasn't so sure. She had a bad feeling about this one.

13

• • •

At Meadow View Psychiatric Hospital Dr Jones was in the cafeteria. He was sitting at one of the tables, on a moulded plastic chair with its legs bolted to the floor. Opposite him was a young man in his twenties with a bewildered expression on his face. He was mumbling something. After a moment, Jones caught sight of Minter and asked to be excused. The man stared after him.

If anything, the circles under Jones's eyes had got a little darker, his blond hair a little more dishevelled. 'Another new admission?' Minter asked, nodding towards the café table.

'Yes,' said Dr Jones. 'Came in last night.' He glanced back at the man. 'All of my patients tell me they're going to kill themselves. Very few of them actually manage it, of course.' For a moment it looked like, for Jones, that was the subject of some regret.

'How's Underhill?'

The only other lead they had on the victims – the unexplained money – had been busted this morning. It turned out that Mercy's boyfriend, the chef at the Kemptown restaurant, was a generous man with a sideline in selling weed; and in her last year at uni Jane Metcalfe had decided to blow a small inheritance left to her by a godmother. So the police had nothing to link the girls at all and no reason why they'd been selected by the killer. And now there was a third victim – the third in as many days.

'Sorry,' Dr Jones told Minter, 'I know I was meant to call you.'

'What happened at the tribunal?'

'It got a bit heated.'

'You told them Underhill was a person of interest in a murder investigation, didn't you?'

'Of course I did. But they were also told by Vincent's social worker that the police have formally dropped the charges against him. Is that correct?'

Minter nodded.

Dr Jones shook his head. 'She was a bit of a harridan, this lady. She wants the committee to write to your boss lodging a complaint against the police doctor who declared Vincent fit to be interviewed.'

'What was decided?' Minter asked, praying that an extension to the assessment order had been granted in the absence of a section.

'Well, in the circumstances, we had to come to a decision based on our psychiatric assessment. Vincent shows increased insight into his illness. And he has demonstrated a readiness to continue taking Risperdal.'

'Where is he now?'

'That's why I wanted to call you. He's not here.'

'What?'

'The tribunal felt that, in the circumstances, Vincent's

needs would be best addressed by a community treatment order. He'll be coming back here every Tuesday to review his medication.'

'You are kidding me, aren't you?'

'If Vincent breaks the terms of the order then he can be sectioned immediately.'

'And that was it? You just let him go?'

The doctor nodded. 'I'm afraid so.'

Minter looked at his watch. 'What time did he leave?'

'About forty-five minutes ago. We're a hospital, DI Minter. We're here to treat people, not to detain them.'

'You mean you needed his bed.'

'I don't think comments like that are particularly helpful.'

But Minter had already turned away and was heading for the door.

Splashing through the rain in the car park, he told the police dispatcher to let him know straight away if there were reports of a man answering Vincent Underhill's description behaving oddly in the city.

'Now, Victoria,' said Vicky Reynolds's mother, putting her hands together. 'Sherry. Dry or sweet?'

'Whatever,' said Vicky. Her mother was the only person in the world who still called her Victoria.

They were standing in the living room of the chocolate-box cottage in West Sussex where Mrs Reynolds lived on her own. It was at the end of a country lane and it had a thatched roof and distant views across dunes to a wide and sandy beach. The room was modestly furnished, with two small sofas and an inglenook fireplace.

Mrs Reynolds looked disappointed. Her lips pursed. She

was slender, with the kind of upright posture that made Vicky always feel that she herself was slouching.

'Well,' said her mother, 'you can have the same as me, then.' With that she left the room, returning in a few moments to hand Vicky her sherry, saying, 'Chin-chin.'

'Any nibbles?' said Vicky.

Mrs Reynolds looked Vicky up and down. 'Lunch will be fifteen minutes. And you need to watch your figure.'

Vicky had sat in court on many different occasions and seen the many ways in which the guilty could get off. There were lazy QCs with poorly prepared briefs and razor-sharp defence counsels, and juries who were swayed by cons who brushed up nicely. But while criminals walked free every day of the week, no one and nothing ever escaped her mother's censure. Her rule was far more rigid and unbending than that of any law.

'I had a lovely letter from Marjorie Clarke,' her mother added.

'Oh, really,' Vicky replied, steeling herself with a large swig of sherry. She had gone to the same private girls' school as Marjorie Clarke's daughter, whose name was Vanessa, and afterwards both of them read law at university. But while Vanessa Clarke had gone on to do her articles in a well-known London commercial firm, Vicky had gone to the police training college.

Vicky couldn't resist the bait. 'How's Vanessa?' she asked.

'She's bought a house,' Mrs Reynolds said delightedly. 'Imagine that! A whole house! In London!'

Vicky hoped that it was somewhere louche and up-and-coming, like Lewisham.

'I think Marjorie said it was Dulwich. Somewhere very chic like that.'

Vanessa Clarke had a sister. Vicky waited for the second shoe to fall.

'Heidi's pregnant with her second.'

Vicky put her sherry glass down on the side table just a little too hard.

'You know,' said Mrs Reynolds, looking at her from out of the corner of her eye. 'It's not too late for you to take up the legal cudgels again. Marjorie said that law firms are always on the lookout for bright young graduates.'

'I'm fine where I am, Mum.' Vicky looked around the room. 'I mean, you and Dad did all right.'

'He put you through that expensive school, darling. If that's what you mean.'

Vicky stood up. She'd only been in the house half an hour and she'd had enough already. 'Have I got time to go to the loo?'

Mrs Reynolds waved the word away, wishing it was still possible to call it 'lavatory'. 'Yes, of course.'

Upstairs, Vicky washed her hands and looked in the mirror, reminding herself to see the ridiculous side of her mother's genteel frustration. She left the bathroom and hesitated at the top of the stairs, listening to the familiar rattle of plates going onto the warming rack on top of the cooker. She was about to go down when she had second thoughts and crossed the landing.

In her father's bedroom, the furniture hadn't changed at all. There was the same bed, the same heavy oak wardrobe against the far wall. Vicky went over and opened the doors of the latter. Her mother had filled it with her autumn clothes, the outfits and coats hanging there in an orderly row, some of them in dry-cleaning bags. Pushing them back along the rail, Vicky found her father's old uniform right at the end. She pulled it out of the wardrobe and held it in both hands, one hand clasping the wooden hanger, the other supporting it at the small of the back. It was the blue serge dress uniform of a chief superintendent in the Metropolitan Police Force and, with its gold-braided epaulettes at the shoulder and its rows of medals across the chest, it felt weighty. When Vicky put her face closer to the material there was still a lingering scent of her father, a whisper of the aftershave she used to buy him as a birthday present every year. She brushed a piece of lint from the jacket. 'Miss you, Dad.'

She'd like to talk to him right now. He would know what to do about her faltering career and the absence of a boyfriend.

'Whatever you do,' Mr Reynolds had said to Vicky when she told him she was joining the force, 'don't you dare marry a police officer.'

'More soup, Victoria?'

'No thanks, Mum.'

With a scraping noise, Mrs Reynolds put the lid back on the tureen. They were in the fussy back parlour of the cottage. On the table there was a cruet and crystal water glasses but not a whiff of booze. Vicky laid her soup spoon down carefully in the bowl. 'Do you think Dad was happy here?'

Mrs Reynolds dabbed her mouth with a napkin. 'What a strange question.' She put the napkin back into her lap. There were so many ways she had found to stop conversations turning awkward. Napkins were one of them – kind of punctuation to the speech of others. 'He did wonders with the garden. Have you seen the roses this year?'

Vicky had read that many men suffered a major episode

of ill health soon after retiring. They couldn't adjust to the sudden change of pace, the loss of purpose, status, even identity. Neither had her father been keen on moving to the cottage on the coast as soon as he stopped working. It took him away from the few friends he had.

'Your father was very glad when he retired,' Mrs Reynolds said definitively, standing up from the table and collecting the soup bowls. 'The Met worked its officers too hard.'

Vicky sat there, stymied. She waited until her mother had returned from the kitchen with the main course. Then she said, 'I asked you a question, Mum.'

'What's that, dear?' said Mrs Reynolds.

'Do you think Dad was happy here when he retired?'

Mrs Reynolds looked down disapprovingly at the food on her plate. 'And I said it was a very strange question. Of course he was happy here. Why shouldn't he be?'

Vicky's mobile rang. Bending down to retrieve it from her bag, she had a brief and urgent conversation with Detective Chief Inspector Grant, one of the SIOs she'd met the day before at Hollingbury.

'I've got to go,' she told her mother. 'A girl's gone missing.'

The storm that had been massing out to sea finally broke over the city, the rain teeming down. On the seafront, Vincent Underhill had left the café, where he'd been shouting at the customers, and was now standing at the entrance to the derelict West Pier, staring out to sea. The rain ran down his neck from his thick, matted hair, beading on his bushy eyebrows, gathering in the corners of his eyes. It streamed down his cheeks and tasted salty on his cracked lips, turning his long black woollen overcoat into a limp and oily blanket.

But Vincent Underhill didn't seem to notice he could survive everything that the natural world could throw at him. His clothes would dry again, just as his hands, which were little more than claws in the morning, always seemed to unbend.

His eyes were fixed on the sea, watching for a sign. But none came. The wind howled instead, shoving wave after wave onto the beach, where the white horses frothed and foamed and clutched at the stones, dragging them down the shoreline. They sloshed around the rusted metal legs of the ruined West Pier, where the remains of the two pavilions – the larger dance hall further out, the concert hall closer to the shore – rose and fell with the swell, the rusted stanchions that showed above the waves groaning under the weight. As Underhill watched and waited, the wind ripped another grey metal panel from the roof of the concert hall. It twisted in the wind for a few moments then smacked down onto the surface of the water.

Underhill put his hand into one of the pockets of his coat and turned the plastic bottle the doctor had given him over and over, feeling the tumble of the little green tablets as they revolved inside the jar. The pills gave him terrible stomach cramps. He took the bottle out of his pocket and tossed it into the surf. He tried to remember the day he was supposed to go back to the hospital but all that came to mind was the overheated little room and the cigarette burn on the fabric of the chair he'd been sitting in. It was hard, brittle, waxy. He wasn't going back to the hospital again.

He began to see little flecks of light on the edge of his vision. They were gathering behind him. He turned to see the curlicues of light scamper towards him. Their hateful voices tucked themselves inside the wind like echoes. *You think that you've escaped, don't you, Vincent?* they squealed.

You think you got away. You think he's coming to save you, don't you, Vincent? But he isn't. He isn't! You're a fool, Vincent Underhill! A fool!

Underhill put his hands up to his ears so he wouldn't have to hear them. He turned around. Across the skyline of Old Brunswick thousands of the creatures were settling on the rooftops and on the chimney pots of the Regency buildings. As Underhill watched they launched themselves into the sky. The noise of their beating wings suddenly filled the air. 'Master,' Underhill said desperately. 'Don't leave me here.'

But the voices were right. Underhill had been abandoned. Laughter came instead – gleeful, high-pitched, spiteful laughter. The grey-black sky above the city was blossoming into swarms of the sharp-tongued demons. *Vincent! You belong to us!*

When he closed his eyes, Underhill saw an upturned face with white teeth. The black woman was looking at him as if only he could save her life. 'Please, master,' he prayed. 'I did what you told me to do.'

Underhill turned to the sea again and ran towards the old pier.

His way was blocked by a chain-link fence put there after the fire to stop vandals climbing onto the unsafe structure. But directly over his head, the demons were circling, forming themselves into the shape of a tornado – a hammer head at the top, a sharpened point at the bottom. Underhill waved his arms about to fend off the first of the swooping attacks. He jammed his hat further down on his head. They would use the hole in his head to get inside him. They'd swoop down through the air and tunnel inside him, invade him, cram his wretched body with their leathery wings. Possess him at last.

With a cry, Underhill jumped up on the fence panel. His fingers grabbed the metal wire, his boots kicking for a better purchase. Somehow, using the same sudden access of strength he had found at the police station, he got up one side and straddled it before throwing himself to the ground on the other side. Above his head, the demons swooped ever closer.

At one time the promenade was linked to the pier by a wide boardwalk made of wooden slats but dereliction had removed the timbers and now there were just the rusted supporting beams that led towards the hulking metal skeleton of the pier itself. Underhill inched across the foot-wide beam to the left, his feet slipping on the wet metal.

The beam met a platform on which had been erected a wire door festooned with barbed wire. Underhill tried to slide the bolt across but it banged against the thick padlock. Above him, the dark legions were thickening all the time as more and more of the infernal creatures joined the swarm from the direction of the city. With renewed vigour, Underhill put his foot around the edge of the door and tried to squeeze himself between the loops of barbed wire. His thick overcoat took the worst of it. It ripped in numerous places and one of the coils pressed through his shirt and dug into the side of his chest. Underhill yelped in pain but he pushed himself on, desperate to flee the creatures in the air. The wire stretched out and tautened as a second length of barbs burrowed deep into his cheek and the beating of wings all around him suddenly intensified in volume. Underhill put his hand up and grabbed the tearing loop where it was attached to the frame of the door. The barbs dug deep into his palm and the pain was extraordinary but he yanked it for all he was worth until one by one the rusty fastenings began to pop out of the door post. He plucked the metal thorns out of his face and chest and threw the loop down into the raging sea.

On the seafront road, Minter's car screeched to a halt. Getting out, Minter caught sight of an unmistakably massive figure on the pier. He blessed the police dispatcher for calling him so promptly.

Having freed himself from the wire, Underhill was stranded between the security gate and the wreckage of the first pavilion. Minter dashed across Brunswick Lawns towards the candy-striped ticket booth at the entrance to the pier. The hours he spent in the gym paid off as he scampered up the wire fence panel and pivoted over the top, landing catlike on his feet the other side.

Minter peered out through the foul air to where an exhausted Underhill sat perched on the side of one of the rusted beams, his hands either side of him grasping at the metal. His face was turned towards the crashing sea thirty or more feet below. Minter looked down at the chopping, frothing water. It was more than deep enough for Underhill to drown in – *if* he survived the drop, that was, because the storm had littered the sea with debris from the pier. Long iron stanchions stuck out of the waves at crazy angles, ready to impale him.

'Vincent!' Minter yelled. 'Stay where you are. I'm going to get help.' But every word was immediately torn to pieces by the wind and it didn't look like Underhill could hang on for much longer.

Minter took off his sodden suit jacket and wound it as tight as he could around his wrist. He traversed the first few feet of the right-hand beam and made the platform, gripping the upright of the security door then, using the bundled material of his suit jacket to protect his hand, started yanking at the remaining loops of barbed wire. As soon as an entire section was clear he stepped around the door.

The beam on the other side was narrower and at first Minter's foot slipped but then he found his balance and started tightrope-walking towards where Underhill was still sitting.

The wind smashed rain into Minter's face. He wobbled dangerously at times, glancing ahead every now and then at the concert hall looming over the cowed figure of the vagrant. There was a lull in the storm and he risked walking faster but then a sudden gust punched him in the back and he completely lost his footing.

His right knee smacked painfully against the metal beam and his leg bounced over the side, his face hitting the metal as he tumbled over the edge. On the way down, his chin was split open by one of the huge rivets on the beam but as he fell towards the water, Minter still had the presence of mind to reach out with his hand and grab hold of the slippery metal beam. With a wincing physical effort, he swung his other hand across and dragged himself level, bending his leg over and clambering awkwardly back to his feet.

Underhill had seen what had happened. His face was crooked with fearful incomprehension. Blood was running down from the gash in his own face and his skin peeped through the rips in his clothes. Behind Minter he watched in horror as the light converged and bent and rifled towards him. Down the tunnel came thousands of the creatures. Underhill tried to stand, his leg flailing over the side of the beam as he pushed himself upright.

He was on his feet now and running. 'Stay where you are!' Minter yelled, expecting Underhill to fall at any moment.

But as Minter watched, Underhill reached the platform on

which the concert hall swayed in the storm. Minter followed him, leaping the last few feet to land on the platform as well.

The storm had reached the very peak of its strength. It was lashing at the pier, making the girders groan beneath Minter's feet. When he looked down he could see the boiling sea through the floor and the ambitious waves reaching up to get him and the rotting stanchions wrapped in bright green seaweed. When he put his foot onto the nearest wooden floorboard that seemed to be intact it went straight through, his feet wavering over nothing. Minter looked up to see Underhill running through the maze of decorative iron posts that stood at regular intervals, heading for the far side of the pavilion. Minter had no choice. He had to follow. Leaping from one floorboard to the next, Minter raced him to the back of the concert hall.

Ahead of him, Underhill had stopped at the edge. The walkway that had once made it so easy to stroll between the two pavilions had long since fallen into the sea and between them now was just a chasm. Directly in front of him there was nothing but storm and, forty feet away, its outline blurred by the pouring rain, the dance hall looming out of the gathering darkness. Underhill glanced behind himself, to where the creatures were swooping through the posts. For a moment, his mouth moved soundlessly but then he made up his mind. He turned and jumped into the sea.

Dashing forward, Minter saw the vagrant's dark form wheel in the air once before it splashed down into the swell. Without hesitating, Minter jumped too. The cold water shocked him, clutching its cold fist around his heart. The freezing tang of the salt water erupted in his throat.

He broke the waves and gasped but it was even worse on the

surface, where the towering waves slapped him in the face and deluged his head and shoulders. He turned in the water but he couldn't see Underhill anywhere, just the peak of the next wave against the sky. He let the swell rock him back and forth then he duck-dived beneath the surface.

Minter opened his eyes on silted, green gloom. The fury of the sea had suddenly been reduced to a murmur. Swimming further down, Minter caught sight of a dim shadow in the water. Desperately, he swam towards it but by the time he was there it had gone and his hands clutched only moving water where the body had once been. The effort of swimming had robbed Minter of the last of his breath and he made quickly for the surface. He took two deep breaths, dragging as much air into his bursting lungs as he could, and dived again.

The storm tide was dredging up sand from the seabed. The further he descended the less he could see. By the time he reached the place where he thought Underhill had been the figure had vanished completely and all Minter could see were green shadows. He swam against the undertow of a huge wave as it retreated from the beach and kicked again, moving further down to where Underhill might have sunk. His hand brushed against a jagged piece of metal and the iron tore his skin. Minter ignored the pain and pushed down even further, his hands fluttering in front of him.

Nothing. He pushed for the surface again.

Minter was nearly spent now. This would be his last chance. He thrashed the waves on the surface, moving himself a little further away from the beach, knowing instinctively that the tide was on the turn. Filling his lungs with air once more, he dived down.

This time, after more than a minute underwater, he caught

sight of a dark smudge. It was suspended in the gloom, rolling over in the current. Minter kicked towards it. His outstretched fingers closed around the soft material of the collar of Underhill's coat but then the vicious undertow of another giant wave loosened his tenuous grip and shoved him away from the lifeless form. Swimming furiously back, Minter grabbed hold of a clump of Underhill's hair. The blood made it slimy but Minter pulled at it hard enough to drag Underhill towards him. He wrapped his other arm around the bulk and swam for the surface.

When Minter broke the waves he cupped Underhill's chin in his hand to keep his mouth out of the water then started making for the shore. There was a low, grinding sound above him and to his right as a run of five or six panels were uprooted from the concert hall roof, each one as long as Minter was tall. With a series of thunderous claps they landed in the water around him.

By the time he got to the beach, Minter was all in. He dragged the vagrant up the stones and staggered out of the water. Through the pelting rain he could see the lights of the ambulance and fire engine on the seafront road and the uniform of a paramedic running down the beach towards him with a tank of oxygen.

Minter laid Underhill on his back and knelt down on the pebbles beside him. He bent his ear to his mouth, listening for his breath. He felt his neck for a pulse. The paramedic arrived and put the oxygen mask over Underhill's face. A few moments later Underhill sat up, vomited seawater and spluttered back to life.

14

• • •

'Bloody hell,' muttered Vicky, turning the corner at the top of the hill. Abi Martin's house was under siege. Satellite vans blocked the progress of Vicky's car and tele-vision crews scampered to and fro across the private lane, fixing cables to generators. A legion of paparazzi had parked their scooters on the grass verge and crowded round the entrance gates. One of them noticed Vicky's arrival. Within moments she was surrounded, blinded by a hail of electronic flashes. Anxious not to be scooped, reporters hurried over to the car as well, yelling out their questions at the official-looking woman in the driver's seat. 'Was Eden taken by the serial killer?'

A uniformed sergeant fought his way through the crowd to Vicky's car and she held her open warrant card up to the windscreen. 'Right, you lot!' cried the sergeant, barging the photographer next to him so hard that he almost fell over. 'I'm going to open the gates to let this officer inside. So you better get away from her car. And if any of you so much as take a step inside the property, I promise you that you will be arrested for trespass. Is that clear?' There were some resentful mutterings about a promised press conference but eventually the journalists did as they were told. Vicky's car crawled forward through the crowd. Ahead of her the gates opened slowly.

The driveway looped up the hill, around topiary hedges and a rose garden. The enormous white house had a red-tiled roof, and the pair of bay trees guarding the huge wooden door added to the impression of a Spanish hacienda. Vicky parked her Astra beside a red Porsche and walked past a plashing fountain towards the house.

Normally, the only thing an FLO would know about the family she was going to work with was what the SIO could tell her but that certainly wasn't the case here. Vicky knew all about Abi Martin. She'd been at school when Abi first presented the national news on BBC television. In those days Abi had been blonde and that in itself got her talked about a lot, the fuss about her appearance even percolating down into Vicky's teenage world. She paid more attention a few years later when the story of Abi's IVF treatment hit the papers. That time the former news presenter, who had no partner, was branded by the tabloids as a self-obsessed celeb bent on acquiring a 'designer' baby. And more recently, Abi had hit the front pages yet again, this time regarding her relationship with Jack Bellamy. Now she was a 'cougar'.

When another uniformed officer answered the door, Vicky entered a hallway that resembled a stage set. The wide oak staircase in front of her had a landing halfway up and there was a crystal chandelier suspended from the ceiling. The flooring was chequerboard black and white tiles and the antique wooden tables were freighted with enormous vases of exotic, perfumed white lilies. 'Where's Ms Martin?' Vicky asked the officer.

'She's upstairs,' said the policewoman. The weary expression she allowed onto her face suggested that babysitting Ms Martin on her own had not been an easy task. She pointed to a door on Vicky's right. 'The lounge is through there, ma'am, I'll go and get her.'

The split-level living room stretched out endlessly in front of Vicky like a football pitch. On the higher level there was a seating area around an open fireplace and a baby grand piano with photos in silver frames displayed on its closed lid. Crossing the floor on the lower level, Vicky sat down on one of a pair of barge-like sofas. Its fabric was silky to her touch. Real silk, she thought, getting out of her satchel the things she'd need to complete the victim profile and glancing around the luxurious room. All this stuff, Vicky marvelled, just for chatting on breakfast telly. Vicky slogged her guts out for less than twenty-five grand a year, including overtime, less her tax and pension – and that was under threat – and half of what was left to her at the beginning of every month was blown just on rent. She knew that it was envy that made her think this way, she knew she had to expunge it from her mind. *Put aside your prejudices and preconceptions,* she heard the trainer say. *Deal with the family as they are, not as you think they should be.* But Vicky couldn't help it. Just this once, she was going to let herself indulge the feeling. Get it all out of her system once and for all. Maybe, just maybe, Abi Martin had this coming.

The door from the hallway opened and Abi herself appeared. Vicky got up, the paperwork she'd gathered in her lap falling to the floor.

'Is there any news?' Abi asked. 'Have you found her yet?'

'I'm afraid not.'

Abi's shoulders dropped.

'I'm Detective Constable Vicky Reynolds. I think Detective Chief Inspector Grant mentioned I would be coming over?'

Abi was distracted. She'd taken her TV make-up off but hadn't put anything on in its place. She looked older as well as smaller than she did on television. 'I don't care who you are,' she said. 'Where's Jack?'

'Mr Bellamy is still out helping with the search.'

Abi looked at Vicky as if surprised to find her there. 'And why aren't you out searching as well?'

One by one, all the positive scenarios – the friend's house Eden had gone to without telling anyone, the accident that had put her in the hospital – had disappeared. The police were hoping that Eden had run away and that, especially now the storm had started, she'd give it up and head for home. What had started out this morning with a single officer walking the Downs behind the house had already turned into a major operation. The police helicopter with all its imaging equipment had been sent over from its base at Shoreham Airport and more than fifty officers had been assigned to help in the search. They were out there now, walking at a snail's pace across the hillside, positioned a few feet apart from one another, their faces turned intently to the ground. 'The child rescue alert was issued an hour ago,' Vicky explained to Abi Martin. 'By now every police force in the country and every broadcast outlet is aware that Eden is missing. We've set up a Major Incident Room and also what we call a Red Room with two dedicated telephone lines that will come into operation should we receive a ransom demand and are forced to open negotiations.'

Abi Martin was not reassured. 'There's a murderer running

round this city. He doesn't negotiate. He's not interested in ransom.'

'I've spoken to the officer leading the investigation into the murders. He tells me that Eden is a good ten years younger than the victims. He doesn't think the cases are connected. I know you'll be imagining the worst, Ms Martin, but there's a very good chance that Eden will be home before dark.' Vicky indicated the other sofa. 'Would you like to come and sit down?'

Abi stared at the young woman in the cheap Marks and Spencer suit with the contrast stitching and the ingratiating manner. 'Remind me why I should be talking to you.'

'I'm here to support you, Ms Martin. And I'm going to keep you up to date with what we're doing. The Family Liaison Officer acts as a kind of bridge between the family and the investigation.'

'That comes straight out of a manual,' Abi snorted. In the course of her career as a journalist she had worked with the police lots of times. She knew they never lifted a finger unless there was something in it for them. 'What you mean is that you're here to eliminate Jack and me from the inquiry.'

The truth of Abi's remark threw Vicky off her stride. It took her a moment or two to find her place in the script again. 'I'll aim to share everything with you. At times there may be certain things I can't tell you but that will only be because I've been instructed to do so by the senior investigating officer.' Vicky sat down and put the victim profile onto the coffee table. She took an MP3 recorder out of her satchel and placed it next to the paperwork. 'I've got some questions to ask you about Eden. There's rather a lot, I'm afraid, but I need to build up as complete a picture of her personality and life as possible. I know you want to be doing something practical right now,

I understand that, but believe me, Ms Martin, what you tell me, no matter how insignificant it seems, might turn out to be the very thing that leads us to your daughter. So why don't you sit down?'

Reluctantly, Abi walked over to the sofa. 'How long will this take?'

'I'll be as quick as I can. Please. Sit down.'

Abi sat down opposite Vicky on the second sofa.

Vicky smiled apologetically. 'Do you mind if I record our conversation? My note-taking's not as efficient as it should be.'

Abi looked askance at the little silver recorder. 'I suppose I'm used to it.'

Vicky began to congratulate herself on how she'd recovered things. 'Now,' she said, turning over the front page of the victim profile.

Family background. Abi was an only child whose parents had both died some years before. 'Does Eden have any contact with her birth father?'

Abi bridled.

Vicky noted her tetchiness on this subject. 'I understand that Eden was born following IVF?'

Abi remained silent.

Vicky remembered the lurid headlines. 'I'm not here to judge you, Ms Martin.'

'You know I used an anonymous donor.'

'Hasn't there been a change in the law?'

Abi nodded. 'The year before Eden was conceived. But the change isn't retrospective. There was no contact with the father at the time and I don't want there to be any in the future. He doesn't know anything about Eden and I want it kept that way.'

'Even so,' Vicky demurred, 'I think we have to find him in order to eliminate him from our inquiries. I assure you, Ms Martin, we can talk to the father in such a way that he finds out nothing about the case. We won't even mention Eden's name.' She paused. 'What IVF clinic were you treated at?'

'Is this really necessary?'

'I'm afraid it is.'

'The Queen Adelaide Clinic in Harley Street.'

Vicky made a note on her form then turned to Eden herself. She had a wide circle of friends and was doing well at school. It seemed the nanny did a lot of the fetching and carrying for Eden and, if she couldn't do it, it was Jack who stepped into the breach. 'Eden has a mobile phone, doesn't she?'

'She had it with her when she left the house. I gave the number to DCI Grant.'

'What about computers?'

'She has an Apple notebook.'

'Do you monitor her use of social networking sites?'

'The computer has security installed.'

'Do you know what the settings were for the browser?'

'No.'

Vicky was always surprised how little time parents devoted to keeping tabs on their offspring's parallel existence on the internet. 'So Eden hasn't said anything recently about meeting someone new online?'

'If she had,' said Abi, 'I would have told your superior officer. I'm not stupid.'

Vicky nodded. 'Would you have any objection to us examining all the mobiles and computers in the house?'

'No,' said Abi, getting up from her chair and rubbing her palms together. 'Go ahead. Anything.'

'I know that this is difficult, Ms Martin.'

Abi turned on her. 'You keep saying that. You keep saying you know how I feel. You keep *empathising.* Do you have any children of your own?'

Vicky looked down. 'No.'

'Well, then, stop saying you understand, because you don't.' For the first time, Abi saw how young Vicky was. 'How many times have you done this before?'

Vicky looked at her. 'I was in the Serious and Organised Crime Unit for two years. Before that—'

'I mean *this.* This liaison officer job, or whatever you call it. How many times have you done *this*?'

Vicky had to be honest. 'This is my first assignment.'

'Your first assignment?' Abi said incredulously.

'I've had specialist training. I have experience of other major crime investigations.'

Abi stood over her. 'And I've been to the chief constable's residence in Lewes on numerous occasions. If I'm not convinced by your performance, DS Reynolds, I won't have any hesitation in asking him to replace you.'

Vicky swallowed her pride. 'Of course, that's your right.'

Abi looked outside. 'Where's Jack?'

'I have some more questions, Ms Martin.' There was an edge to the way Vicky spoke now. Sometimes, the trainer had said, you had to be firm early on. No matter how high and mighty Abi was, Vicky had a job to do.

Seeing the warning look Vicky was giving her, Abi sat down again.

If Eden had run away for some reason she might well have taken some extra clothes, or some money. Vicky said, 'I think DCI Grant asked you to go through Eden's belongings.'

'That's right. Nothing had been taken. Everything was there in the room. Just like she left it.'

Vicky made a note. 'I'd like to go through the family finances now.'

They weren't poor. The salary Jack drew from the production company he was a director of was five times what Vicky earned but it paled into insignificance compared to Abi's extravagant income. With all the other work, in the last tax year they pulled down well over two million pounds.

The next question wasn't on the pro forma. It was just for Abi Martin. 'Have you ever had a stalker of any description?'

'There was a weirdo a few years ago,' Abi said. 'He used to write to me every day. Sex fantasies for the most part. When he started turning up at the studio I told the police in London. They went to see him and it stopped.'

Vicky made a note to contact the Met. 'These letters, did any of them mention Eden?'

Abi shook her head. 'No. But ever since then I've used an assistant at Kitchen Sink to answer all the fan mail. I just sign the photographs.'

Vicky wrote down the name of the production company and then moved on to previous events. 'Have there been any changes at home recently? Anything that Eden might have found difficult to deal with?'

'Far from it.'

'What do you mean?'

Abi looked at Vicky cautiously. She knew how leaky the police could be.

Vicky saw her hesitation. 'Everything you say to me is confidential, Ms Martin. The only person I share it with is my SIO.' Mentally ticking herself off, Vicky corrected her lapse into police jargon. 'My senior investigating officer, that is. And anything Detective Chief Inspector Grant does with it is treated strictly on a need to know basis.'

Abi looked at the police officer. 'We've been talking, Jack and me, about getting married.'

'And did Eden know about this?'

'I had a conversation with her. I didn't say it was going to happen, but I kind of broached the subject. I wanted to sound her out before I gave Jack my decision.'

'So Jack proposed to you?'

'Not in so many words.'

'When did the conversation with Eden take place?'

'Last night.'

'How did Eden react?'

'She was happy for me. She likes Jack.'

'What did she say?'

Abi looked at her defiantly. 'Eden didn't run away, if that's what you're thinking.'

'Was Mr Bellamy aware that you had spoken to Eden about the possibility of getting married?'

'Yes,' said Abi. 'I mentioned it to him when we went to bed. Why on earth shouldn't I?'

'No reason at all.'

'I told you, Eden likes Jack. They get on really well.'

Vicky nodded. 'I'm glad.'

Abi's mobile rang and she answered. Judging by the conversation that followed, it was Jack Bellamy who had called. Abi took the phone out of the room to talk to him, closing the door behind her.

When Abi didn't return, Vicky slipped the victim profile into her satchel and walked across the floor and up the step. She went over to the piano and looked at the framed photographs on the lid. There were older shots of Eden, one or two with a pony that she evidently adored. Vicky found what looked to be the most recent, a shot of Eden in a restaurant, her face beaming at the camera. In the picture, she hovered between girlishness and womanhood in a way that made Vicky catch her breath.

Don't get overinvolved, said the voice inside Vicky's head. It was still a matter of prioritisation: some things happened quick-time, some things happened slow. It was the same job in a different guise: Vicky was an investigator, just like her father had been.

But as an investigator, Vicky had been shown the data. In the majority of child abduction cases the child was either let go immediately after being sexually assaulted, or murdered within the first twenty-four hours. How on earth was Vicky going to support Eden's family through either of these scenarios? How on earth was she going to stop herself getting involved?

PART THREE

15

• • •

Oxford, June 1996

Martin Blackthorn put his eyes to the lens of the electron microscope he had just calibrated to a magnification of five and a half million. In the lens, the edge of the human cell appeared like a halo. Stained a deep green, the speckled DNA gathered pin-sharp in the darkness of the interior. The needle end of Martin's pipette loomed large, its hollowness clearly visible.

Martin had carried out this procedure a thousand times before but in this obscure laboratory tucked away in a corner of the science block he had been working all night long and now his hand began to waver. He jerked the pipette forward a little more and its sharpened point nudged against the wall of the cell, causing the circumference to bulge a little. Another jerk and the needle penetrated the cell wall but missed the nucleus altogether, coming out the other side. 'Damn!' he cried.

He was throwing the ruined slide away when a woman came into the lab. 'Oh,' she said, surprised to find him there. 'I didn't know this was booked.' She was tall and a little plump, a couple of years or so younger than Martin was, with a round face and long, reddish-brown hair.

'That's all right,' said Martin, glancing at the clock. 'It's my fault. I should have left an hour ago.'

Smiling, the girl nodded at the barrel of the electron microscope. 'Finish up first.'

Ignoring her, Martin continued shutting down his computer.

Julie Foyle was something of a nerd herself and mistook his pique for shyness. She said, 'I've not seen you around college.'

Martin gathered up his notes. 'I keep myself to myself.'

'I'm Julie Foyle,' said the woman, stepping forward and offering him her hand in a gesture she regretted immediately because it seemed way too formal. 'First year postgrad.'

His handshake was limp. 'Martin Blackthorn.'

Julie's eyes narrowed. 'Are you one of Professor Deaver's assistants?'

Martin shook his head.

Julie tried to steal a glance at the scribbles in the last of Martin's notebooks. 'What are you working on?'

Picking up the pad, Martin stuffed it into his bag. 'Is Professor Deaver your supervisor?'

'Yes.' Julie made a face. 'If I could ever get to see him.'

Deaver was the leading geneticist in the department. 'His team are working on stem cell extraction,' Martin explained.

'I know.' Julie hadn't told anyone, but ever since she'd arrived in Oxford from her red-brick university, she'd been feeling a little lost. 'I've wasted a whole year on enzymes,' she said. 'I was thinking of changing my proposal. I've got interested in the Hox.'

Martin nodded. The Hox gene was the first to become

operative within the human embryo: it told the foetus where the arms and legs would go. 'The Hox hasn't evolved for millions of years,' he said.

'You know about it?' Julie asked.

Martin put his bag over his shoulder. 'A little.'

'Could you help me with the rewrite of my proposal?'

Martin hesitated.

'Please,' Julie begged. It seemed she really was in trouble with her thesis. 'Come round to my digs. I'm on the Cowley Road. Number one hundred and forty-five. The upstairs flat.'

Martin felt his cheeks begin to redden. 'I've got to go.'

'And does anyone know why we grow this plant?' asked the tour guide. The class had come into the Palm House, the biggest of the glasshouses at Oxford Botanic Garden.

'Which one?' asked an excited boy, wriggling his way to the front.

The tour guide pointed again at the delicate-looking, pink-white flower with a starburst of darker purple at its centre. 'There. Do you see?'

The boy nodded.

'Its scientific name is *Catharanthus roseus* but most people call it Old Maid.'

There were a few ambitious guesses as to the remarkable nature of the plant.

'Just a year ago,' the tour guide went on to explain, 'this plant was in danger of extinction. Now, thanks to cultivation, it is used as a medicine. The essence of *Catharanthus roseus* produces a chemical that can be manufactured into a drug. That drug is used to treat cancer. So, believe it or not, this little plant saves lives.'

There were gasps of appreciation from the children.

'Now, if we walk through the Palm House we'll come to some other interesting specimens.'

The teacher waited to join on the end of the line. It had been a very long term and he was glad of the chance to take a back seat. He was about to set off after the others when he caught sight of a figure standing outside the greenhouse, his hands and face pressed to the steamed-up glass. For a moment he thought it might be one of his charges but when he took a closer look he could see how big the boy was. Somebody else's responsibility, he thought gratefully, following the crocodile of children as it passed beneath a giant tree fern.

Outside, John Slade turned away and walked past the greenhouse. He sauntered along the cinder path that ran alongside the Cherwell, where some punts had been tied together in the middle of the river.

He was fourteen now and puberty had left its stamp on him, bending his form into a different shape, rewiring much of his brain. It had left John with a heavy, protuberant brow and a wispy moustache and a figure that had filled out considerably. Beneath his T-shirt, John's chest and arms were knotted with the kind of muscles an Oxfordshire agricultural labourer from the last century would have been proud of. As he walked through the Botanic Garden, his big, powerful hands hung down by his sides.

The next greenhouse was smaller but had the same hipped design, the roof pushing itself up into the vaulted blue sky.

The interior of the insectivorous house was airy and bright. Either side of a central path, the soil looked damp, almost boggy. There was no one about so John took his time examining the pods hanging from one of the bushes. Each pod was about four inches in length and tapered towards the bottom, where a green tube connected it to a single, outsize leaf. As John watched, a fly buzzed around the top of one of them. Intrigued, John leaned closer, watching the fly land and walk around the lip, coming close to the precipitous drop but never quite falling in. It took off again and John followed it to where it settled, this time on the leaf of one of the lower-lying plants a few feet away.

The outside of the leaf was bright green, shiny, hard as plastic. The other side, however, was a luscious pink, soft and dewy with nectar. The fly walked round and round, becoming drowsy as it drank. For a few tantalising moments it looked like it was going to get away again but then, as if a switch had been thrown somewhere deep inside the brain of the plant, the leaf snapped shut like a clasp and the fly was trapped. It buzzed angrily, its antenna and a single crushed wing waving between the sharp points of the hairs that had closed together to imprison it. After a few moments, the buzzing began to wane and the antenna slipped back inside.

'I've been looking for you,' said a voice. Standing up straight, John turned to find a breathless Martin Blackthorn standing behind him.

'You're an hour late,' said John Slade.

There'd been a time, not so long ago, thought Martin, when John would never have dared to speak to him like that. 'Come on,' he said. 'Let's go for a walk.'

The boy shrugged. It made no difference to him where they went.

They left the gardens and walked across Magdalen Bridge. Martin glanced across at the teenager, a little frightened by the extent of the physical changes the last few months had wrought within the boy. Unlike the smooth waters of the ageless Cherwell, John Slade's mind had recently become turbid as well as shallow – and more than a little treacherous. When he looked at the benighted boy, Martin could tell that all his plans were coming to fruition, that all his efforts to nurture the lad were about to pay off handsomely. But now, for some reason, the very thought of that filled Martin with dread and fear.

At the far end of the bridge they walked through the famous gates and went down the steps towards the river. The unexpected heat of a fine late summer day had drawn lots of people to the water meadow, including the party of local school children from the Botanic Garden who had gone there for a picnic lunch. Elsewhere, office workers sat and chatted on the grass and, along the bank, couples lazed in each other's arms.

Martin and John walked along the river path. Leaving the people behind, they slipped under the shade of some trees and headed downriver to the boathouse.

The vegetation became much thicker and in front of them a moorhen strutted in and out of the undergrowth. Martin saw how quickly its little scarlet beak attracted Slade's attention, and the way the boy's head moved with alacrity to follow the bird's progress. It was only during these moments of pursuit that John Slade really came alive, it seemed, his eyes moving quickly beneath his beetling brow. But then, all of a sudden, he seemed to lose interest. 'You're getting bored of being cruel to dumb animals, aren't you?' Martin asked.

John stared at him, still a little surprised whenever Martin knew exactly what was going through his mind. They walked on past the mill in silence.

At Magdalen College, Martin's studies were going well.

He was beginning to publish some of his findings and they'd attracted the attention of a couple of professors who were vying for him to become their assistant. But it was the notice of Professor Deaver, Julie Foyle's research supervisor, that Martin really wanted to get. So he had rebuffed the other two suitors, preferring, for the moment at least, the solitary path of his own experiments, his own discoveries. But now Martin was moving ever closer to finishing his PhD and soon he'd need an academic job – preferably one at St John's – and he wanted to impress.

After the rushing waters of the weir pool, the river broadened out again and the bank became a grassy knoll. 'Let's sit down there,' Martin said, suddenly very tired.

They scrambled up and sat in the sunshine. A punt appeared around the bend in the river. Martin watched the young man in the rugby shirt get his pole stuck in the weeds, much to the apparent amusement of the young woman lying in the prow. Imbued as he was with the self-confidence of his class, the young man wore his incompetence lightly. When the pole slipped out of his grasp he merely laughed along with her and snatched it back. Martin glimpsed the bottle of white wine chilling in a net bag off the side of the boat. It made him think about the cramped railway cottage where he had been brought up and the maddening vulgarity of his parents. Martin had got to Oxford entirely under his own steam. His parents had given him nothing.

He fixed his eyes on the young woman in the punt. She was dressed in a white blouse with a gypsy collar, the cotton ties dangling down over her bosom. Martin smiled, waving at the glamorous-looking couple. 'Nice day for it,' he called out across the slowly moving water. The man grinned and waved back and the girl was about to do the same when she caught sight of John Slade and something odd about the couple on the bank made her lower her arm and turn away. Growing thoughtful, she trailed her fingers in the water on the other side of the boat.

'Do you see her?' whispered Martin. Slade's eyes had already begun to move. They both stared brazenly at the girl, drawing a reproachful backward glance from the man standing up in the boat as it glided past.

Martin looked away, scanning the river banks, speculating on the opportunities for concealment they presented. But it was too late. The punt was already beginning to vanish round the next bend in the river and the couple's easy laughter floated tantalisingly back to him on the bank. Not for the first time, Martin cursed his own inhibited nature.

Sighing, dismissing the thought from his mind, Martin lay back on the grass. Closing his eyes, he allowed the sun to soothe his weary body and troubled mind. Thoughts of the research fellowship Professor Deaver was bound to offer Martin once he'd read his PhD thesis mingled with images of the girl he'd just met in the lab. She had a kind face and she'd obviously been impressed by Martin's knowledge of the Hox. He imagined them sitting in the kitchen of her flat on the Cowley Road, talking long into the night about their work. He even pictured himself living there with Julie, returning from college to find her waiting for him.

Martin snapped awake. He must have dozed off for a minute or two. Glancing down the slope, he saw the waters of the Cherwell sliding by in dappled sunlight. It was idyllic, almost dreamlike. Refreshed by his nap, Martin felt a lot better.

Sitting up, he realised he was alone. When he looked down, he could see that his bag – the one containing all his lab notes as well as the knives he'd brought for John – had gone. 'John?' he said, getting to his feet. 'Where are you, John?'

The young man poured wine into a mug and gave it to his girlfriend. They'd pulled in past the bend and dragged the punt up onto the bank, then scrambled up the slope towards the clearing.

'Thanks,' she said, bending her head to sip the cool wine. Her boyfriend poured another for himself, drinking it a little more greedily. Putting it down on the grass, he leaned across to kiss her. 'Not here!' she giggled.

'It's term time,' he said. 'No one's going to come this far.'

She started to enjoy the way he nuzzled her earlobe. His hand stroked the bare skin on her shoulder, moving down towards her breasts. 'What's that?' she asked suddenly, looking round.

'It's nothing,' he whispered, moving in for another kiss.

But she turned her head away from him. 'I heard something. Something over there.'

With a sigh of impatience, the man stood up and took a step over to where she had indicated. 'There's nothing here.'

Martin Blackthorn watched them from the other side of the clearing, where he was hidden by the trees. Like the woman, he had heard something moving in the thicket but he had also seen something too – a flash of the dun-coloured shirt John Slade had been wearing.

'There!' the woman cried, pointing again.

Excited by the thought of what was coming next, Martin held his breath.

The man in the rugby shirt laughed uproariously as the moorhen dashed out of the undergrowth. He shooed the bird away, clapping his hands, pursuing it down the bank. But as he came back up towards his girlfriend, he caught sight of Martin and his expression suddenly changed. 'Oi!' he said, racing after the peeping Tom.

Martin tried to run but the Oxford blue soon caught him up. Grabbing Martin, he rammed him up against one of the tree trunks. 'That's how you get your kicks, is it?' he said, punching Martin in the stomach. Winded badly, Martin crumpled to the ground. The man kicked him hard in the stomach, doubling him up again.

'Stop!' cried his girlfriend, who had followed them into the bushes and who was now looking at Martin with pity in her eyes. 'Leave him!'

For good measure, the man bent down and punched Martin one more time in the face. Turning away, he took the woman's hand and led her back to the clearing. Coughing, grovelling on the ground, Martin heard his retreating voice say, 'I taught him a lesson all right.'

Martin tried to catch his breath. His lip was swollen and his ears were ringing from the blow to the side of his face. When he rolled on to his back he saw John Slade towering above him.

'Are you OK?' asked Slade.

'Help me up!' said Martin, infuriated. It had happened again. He'd been humiliated. And, this time, even John Slade had seen it.

Reaching down, Slade helped Martin to his feet. He glanced towards the river, from where the sound of the punt plopping and splashing into the water could be heard. Lifting the flap of Martin's bag, Slade took out the wrap of knives that was lying at the bottom. 'I'll go and get them. I'll bring them back here.'

Martin was brushing himself down. Quickly reaching out an arm, he stopped John Slade. 'Let them go!'

Slade looked at him. 'I don't want to. You looked after me. You stopped Kelvin hurting me.'

The moment he stared back into John Slade's cold grey eyes, Martin knew that the servant would soon outstrip the master. Before, that very thought would have sent a shiver of anticipation down the length of Martin's spine. Wasn't this moment, after all, what Martin had been striving for, the reason he had done all of those unspeakable things? Yet now, standing in the thicket, the shiver that went through Martin's body was not of anticipation. It was one of stark terror.

Martin Blackthorn wondered what he had done.

16

Abi lay in bed, listening to the wind gust outside her window. The curtains remained open because she wanted the light from her room to be visible on the Downs behind the house. It was dark now and she had cried all the tears there were inside her and uttered every prayer she knew. Whenever she closed her eyes, all she could hear were Eden's screams.

The little world. Eden had led her there. For most of Abi's life she'd been at the centre of her own world: career, lovers, clothes, houses and holidays, everything was to her taste, all of it down to her hard work and her hard work alone.

The little world. So small and circumscribed that sometimes it had driven Abi to distraction. A world of pushchairs and playground swings, of tender, bruised feelings, of first words, first steps, first shoes; a world of afternoon naps and grumpy teatimes, of cutting the crusts off sandwiches and the clean smell of plasticine. It was the first time Abi had ever really fallen in love and she wrapped herself up so tightly inside her child that she forgot who she was. That was the trick of it, in fact. Abi had become someone else entirely, someone she actually liked. 'Come home, darling,' she whispered into her pillow. 'Please come home.'

But after just two years she'd left the little world of her own accord. The truth was, she was bored. She couldn't do it any more. She wanted her own world back.

The guilt was tearing her apart. Hadn't she been sitting in the back of the Mercedes being driven up to town this morning – it seemed like a lifetime ago – reading the notes on Dan Hegarty, planning what she'd say to the Sky executive at the Wolseley, never once wondering what Eden was doing.

If only she'd called. Just a single thought, a single telephone call. Let the nanny take the dog for a walk, or Jack could have done it for once. Then the little world would have remained intact, and it would have still been waiting for Abi when she got home.

A single thought. A single telephone call. That's all it would have taken.

Downstairs, Vicky was finishing typing up the HOLMES-compatible version of Abi's statement when, from the hallway, she heard the front door open and close.

She glanced up towards the window in time to see an officer leaving the house, a large transparent evidence sack containing the family's computers gripped in his right hand. In the security light above the door, Vicky watched him put the sack into the back of an unmarked estate car, get in the front and drive off down the hill. At Hollingbury, the various laptops and iPads would be booked and tagged by the ladies in the evidence centre before going off immediately for forensic examination.

On her own computer, Vicky saved the file and emailed an

encrypted version to the HOLMES clerk at Hollingbury. She wished that she was there instead of here for the duration. At CID headquarters, the operation would just be up to speed, officers running in with details of promising sightings. Vicky wanted to be there with them. *Doing* something.

The door to the living room opened and the police search adviser came into the room. 'Just to let you know we've finished searching the property, ma'am.'

Vicky got up and walked towards him. Reaching out a hand she pushed the door to. 'Anything?' she asked in a low voice.

'We've checked everything. There's no false walls or hidden compartments and there's nothing in the water butts but rain.' The POLSA shook his head. 'The girl's not in this house.'

'Thanks,' Vicky said.

The POLSA left and, as the sound of another car engine faded into the distance, Vicky knew that the first flurry of visits had come to an end. Around her, the house settled back into an uneasy silence, as if it was shrinking around the hard and nubby fact of Eden Martin's vanishing. It hunkered down, waiting for news.

For lack of anything else to do, Vicky went into the kitchen and made some tea. Waiting for the kettle to boil, she checked her watch. Half past eight. Officially, her shift finished in half an hour but at this early stage she knew she'd be staying at the Martin house well into the night. She poured hot water over the teabags in a couple of mugs. Being an FLO wasn't just tea and sympathy, she'd told Minter yesterday. Squeezing out the teabags, she wondered if that was true.

The tea wasn't for Abi Martin.

Outside the house, the PC on the door had donned his rain

cape and was sheltering as best he could beneath the porch roof. Even this far away from the cliffs, the rain carried with it a tang of salt. Vicky could taste it on her lips.

'Thanks, ma'am,' said the young PC as he took the cuppa out of Vicky's hands. 'That's lovely.'

Vicky pulled the collar of her coat up. 'What time you here till?'

He took his first sip. 'Right through until the morning. We're short-handed.'

Vicky looked at the rainclouds scudding quickly across the moonlit sky and the land running away to the dark sea. The silent, reproachful mansion loomed up behind them. Somehow it felt bad, talking about the weather.

The sergeant from the gates came trudging up the drive, something large gathered in both his hands. It was only when he arrived inside the circle of light from the porch that Vicky could properly make out the two massive bouquets of flowers.

The sergeant crunched towards her across the last bit of gravel. 'A delivery van's just dropped these off,' he said. 'We wondered if Ms Martin would like to see them.'

Vicky examined the bouquets. Each one was wrapped in cellophane and had a message card tucked beneath its curly ribbon. The first bouquet, the largest and most ostentatious, came from Abi's agent, Jean Dawson. The other was from Tony Evans, the producer of the breakfast show. *Take however long you need* was the typewritten message. 'Leave them in the kitchen,' Vicky told the sergeant.

The sergeant had a kind face. 'There's teddy bears and all kinds of things. People have started leaving them.'

'Thanks, skip,' Vicky said. 'I'll ask Ms Martin what she

wants doing with the flowers. The rest of the stuff can wait.'

The constable opened the door to let the sergeant into the house.

Vicky looked away again, her eyes settling on the village of Rottingdean lying in the valley at the bottom of the slope. Framed by an upstairs window, a small female figure pulled the curtains in a back bedroom of one of the houses. A moment later the big light in the room was replaced by the dim glow of a night light. Vicky imagined the woman hugging her child a little tighter as they said goodnight. Then her attention was grabbed by a slew of flashes coming from the bottom of the drive. The gates opened again and a car started speeding up towards them. Jack Bellamy was home.

In the hallway, Jack took off his waterproof jacket, his biceps straining at the material of his checked, short-sleeved shirt. His short, gelled hair was soaking wet. 'They're calling off the search for the night,' he said to Vicky, taking off his mud-caked walking boots. 'Why are they calling it off?'

'There's no point in searching any more,' said Vicky. 'Visibility is too bad. But the helicopter has thermal imaging equipment on board: it will continue sweeping the area. And at first light they'll start again.'

Jack looked up the stairs. 'Where's Abi?'

Vicky wanted to interview Jack before he and Abi talked. DCI Grant had told her to take a careful look at him. With Eden out of the way, he was the sole beneficiary of Abi Martin's considerable estate. 'Ms Martin is resting. Perhaps we could have a word?'

Jack looked at her suspiciously. 'OK.'

They went into the living room and sat on the same sofa

and Vicky started working through the pro forma, the little red light of the MP3 recorder blinking slowly on the coffee table. Jack was curt throughout and sometimes got frustrated – 'Your boss asked me that already,' he kept saying – but on the whole he was cooperative. Listening to his replies, Vicky realised she couldn't fit a cigarette paper between what he was telling her now and what Abi had told her earlier on this evening. They even agreed on Eden's favourite supper dish – the fish pie the nanny cooked.

Jack told her how he usually took Eden to school in the mornings. Vicky nodded. 'In many ways,' she commented, 'you're acting like a parent would.'

Jack nodded. 'We get on really well, Eden and me.'

'Does that include disciplining her?'

'I tell her off if she's being mouthy, but mostly I leave that kind of thing to the nanny.'

'Have you ever hit Eden?' Jack was a powerful man. Perhaps something had got out of hand.

'Of course not!'

Vicky nodded. 'Have you ever been jealous of her?'

'Why would I be jealous of a kid?'

'Well, before you came along I can imagine Abi and Eden were pretty much a tight-knit unit. I mean, they've been on their own ever since Eden was born.'

'Maybe that was part of the attraction.'

'You mean Ms Martin having a child was something that attracted you to her?'

Jack's temper flared. 'You ought to watch what you're fucking saying.'

Retreating, Vicky said, 'I'm sorry, sir. I didn't mean anything by that remark.'

'Broken pieces have a way of finding each other,' said Jack sullenly.

'Meaning what, sir?'

'My parents were divorced when I was little. My dad moved away. When I started living here it felt good. It felt right. We were like a family.'

'And how would you describe your relationship with Abi now?'

'We're getting married, aren't we?'

'You're getting on well, then?'

'Yeah, of course.'

'What do you do for a living, Mr Bellamy?'

When Jack flashed a grin, his teeth were perfect: a lot of work had been done on them. 'Kept man, aren't I?'

'Does it bother you, what the newspapers say?'

'Nah. It's complete bollocks. I do all right. I own a company called Tequila Productions. We make *Celebrity House Swap*. You seen it?'

Celebrity House Swap did just what it said on the tin. 'It's very good,' Vicky lied.

'Cheers.'

'Although I hear it's a tough time in the TV industry at the moment.'

Jack winked at her. 'Don't let them fool you. The second series of *House Swap* has just been commissioned.'

Jack's salary might have been confirmed by his tax returns but Vicky had also seen his charge sheet. 'Do you still take drugs, Mr Bellamy?'

'Everyone does a bit of coke now and then.'

'I don't.'

'Well, maybe you should try,' said Jack. 'Might chill you

out a little.' Vicky stared at him. 'I went into rehab after I met Abi. I haven't touched drink or drugs since.'

Vicky nodded. *Abi Saved Me From Drugs Hell* had been one of the tabloid headlines from the time when Jack's affair with Abi had been made public. With Abi, Jack had found redemption – that was the angle that had won the red tops round, at least.

'I'd like to talk to you about what happened this morning,' said Vicky. 'When you tried to speak to Abi at the television studio and Mr Evans wouldn't put your call through.'

'OK,' Jack said suspiciously.

'You told Mr Evans that someone had taken Eden.' Vicky looked down at the transcript. 'Those were your words. "Someone's taken her." '

Jack looked puzzled. 'Yeah? So what?'

'What made you so sure that someone had abducted Eden?'

Jack's eyes narrowed. 'What do you mean?'

'Well, teenagers often run away. But you were very definite, Mr Bellamy. You clearly said, "Someone's taken her." '

Jack shrugged. 'You think the worst, don't you? I mean when a kid goes missing.'

'Do you?'

'Yeah. It's all those horror stories about paedos and stuff.'

Vicky turned the page. 'I need a comprehensive list of your recent movements.'

Jack was getting impatient again with the questioning. 'I've had enough of this.'

'This is important, Mr Bellamy. It's possible that whoever snatched Eden might have been watching her for some time. It might help us establish a link to the abductor.'

'Abi needs me right now.'

'She can wait a little longer. We can't afford to miss anything, sir. For Eden's sake.'

Reluctantly, Jack started going through all the places he'd been in the last week. On Monday morning and Thursday afternoon he'd been in meetings at the Brighton office of Tequila Productions. He'd done the school run every morning except Tuesday, when the nanny had taken a turn. He'd spent Wednesday at a spa. Thursday night he'd been up in London at a party and Friday night he'd been to a club down in Brighton.

'Anything else?' Vicky said.

Jack shook his head. 'No.'

'The Porsche outside is yours, isn't it?'

Jack nodded. 'It's a GT3.'

'Must have cost a lot.'

'List price is one hundred and thirty thousand – and I specified lots of extras.'

Vicky tried to look impressed. 'Does anyone else ever drive it?'

Jack had been in police custody before and he knew the way interviews worked. He knew that if he said someone else had driven the Porsche, the DC would ask him straight out for a name. 'Nobody drives my car without my permission.'

Day and night, selected traffic cameras in Sussex captured images of all the registration plates of the cars that drove past them – not just the ones that were speeding. If they were lucky and it turned out that one of these had recorded Jack's Porsche to a destination not included in the list he'd just given Vicky, the police had something they might be able to trip him up with.

'Does that mean,' Vicky asked him, 'that, other than you, no one has driven the Porsche in the last week?'

'That's right. Now, if you don't mind, I'm going to see my fiancée.'

As soon as Jack had left the room, Vicky's mobile started to ring. She took it out of her bag and saw from the illuminated screen that DCI Grant was calling her. She listened to him for a minute or two, finding what Grant told her difficult to believe.

On the A23 the cars hurtled past the layby, their lights punching holes through the night. A car indicated and pulled over. When it had come to a stop, Keith Miller, the crime reporter from the *Daily Mail* who had rung Tom Beckett this afternoon, bent down to see inside.

The window wound down. 'Get in,' said Kevin Phillips.

Miller slid in beside the cop. 'Where we going?'

Phillips gunned the engine. 'Nowhere.'

They joined the traffic driving out of Brighton. Phillips turned to the journo. 'How much do you earn a year?'

Miller shrugged. 'Including bonuses, about seventy grand.'

Phillips whistled through his teeth. These days, money was on his mind all the time. It was all he and Fiona had talked about late last night after Kevin had got home – all they talked about, that was, when they weren't screaming at each other or listening to the sound of their children crying in the bedroom they had to share. Suddenly, Phillips pounded the steering wheel with his fist. 'Nine years of my fucking life I've given to this poxy job!'

Miller was worried he was going to lose control of the car. 'It's not my fault, mate.'

They left the main road and came to a roundabout. Phillips drove his car round and round, studying all the exits carefully as he went, the tyres squealing because his foot was too heavy on the accelerator.

'What the fuck are you playing at?' said Miller, bracing himself against the door.

Phillips glanced in the rear view mirror. 'Making sure no one's following us.' He took the last exit and after a few more minutes of driving, stopped in a quiet layby in the countryside. He got out of the car and walked around and yanked open Miller's door. 'Get out.'

'Listen, mate,' said Miller, doing as he was told. 'I'm on your side. You and me, we're just doing our job.'

'Lift your arms out to the side.' When Miller complied with the request, Phillips started patting him down. 'I wouldn't put it past you to record this.'

Miller took a brown envelope stuffed with cash out of the pocket of his raincoat. 'Is this what you're looking for?' Phillips took the envelope and riffled the edge of the used fifties. 'It's all there. I counted it out myself. Five thousand pounds.'

Phillips put the envelope away. It was enough to pay the bills for a couple of months. Enough to get the bank off his back.

But it seemed Miller, at least, wanted more. 'You know any of the team on the Eden Martin case?'

Phillips hesitated. 'I'm a good friend of the FLO.'

Miller's ears pricked up. 'The family liaison officer?'

'That's right.'

'She's in the house all the time, isn't she?'

'That's her job.'

It was Miller's turn to whistle. 'Just you take a look at the front pages tomorrow, Kevin. That abduction's going to blow matey away. Your new body will be lucky to make the third lead.' He nodded at the bulge in Phillips's jacket. 'I'll pay top dollar. It'll make that look like peanuts.'

'What kind of intel you looking for?'

Miller shrugged. 'How Jack and Abi are coping. Any juicy gossip on them. And, even better, something on the girl.'

Vicky would get the blame. 'The FLO's a mate. I'm not doing that to her.'

'Think about it, Kevin. I'm talking more money than you pull down in a year. More money than *I* pull down in a year.'

Phillips wasn't a bad cop. 'I'll see what I can do.'

Vicky was still wondering what to do with the information Grant had given her when she heard the sound of hurried footsteps on the stairs.

Abi Martin burst into the living room. 'I've remembered something!' she said, breathlessly. 'Something important!'

'What?' Vicky asked, standing up.

'Yesterday morning, at the studio, when Charlie was driving me home, there were some autograph hunters standing round the gates. I didn't take any notice. They're always there. And always the same group.'

'So?'

'It just came to me. There was someone I hadn't seen before.'

Vicky picked up her notebook. 'Can you give me a description?'

'He was wearing a parka and the hood was up. I didn't really get a chance to see his face. But he was a big man.'

'You mean big as in fat?'

Abi shook her head. 'Not so much fat as broad. And tall.'

'Taller than Jack?'

'About the same height.'

'Would there have been someone on the gate we could talk to? A security guard?'

'Yes!' Abi exclaimed. 'He'll be able to give you a clearer description.'

Vicky had been warned it would be like this. During sleepless, tormented nights, the parents would revisit every single moment leading up to their child's disappearance. The smallest detail became overloaded with sinister intent. Most often, what stuck out in their minds turned out to be entirely innocent: the man waiting at the school gates was somebody's uncle; the unfamiliar car belonged to a neighbour. Vicky hesitated, wondering if Abi's rudimentary description of the man really merited a quick-time response. She looked more closely at the older woman – at Abi's crumpled designer dress, at her make-up streaked with tears, at the way anxiety had ravaged Abi's face, lending her eyes that terrible, haunted quality – then she picked up her mobile and speed-dialled the number for the HOLMES clerk.

'That's done,' said Vicky, putting down her phone. 'They're going to call the emergency contact at the studio to see if they can get the details of the security guard.'

'Will they get back to you?' asked Abi frantically, convinced that the man in the parka had something to do with Eden's disappearance.

'As soon as they hear anything.' A little relieved, Abi sat down on the sofa.

Vicky said, 'Officers from Greater Manchester police visited Matthew this evening.'

'And?'

Vicky sat down next to her. 'There's nothing to put him under any suspicion.'

'Did they tell him who Eden is?'

Vicky shook her head. 'The officers said they wanted to interview him regarding a spate of burglaries that had occurred in his neighbourhood.'

Abi looked down at her hands in her lap. 'Thank you.'

'We can be subtle when we need to be.'

Abi looked across at Vicky. 'How old are you?'

'Twenty-five.'

'I know you don't have any kids. What about a boyfriend?'

Vicky felt embarrassed. Then she realised that asking questions was what Abi Martin did for a living. It was normal – therefore good for her. 'No boyfriend,' Vicky said. 'The job makes it difficult. A lot of the male officers I work with . . . well, let's just say they're not my type.'

'A woman in a man's world, eh?'

'You know that feeling, do you?'

Abi's eyes went upwards. 'There you go again with the empathy.' This time, though, she didn't seem angry. 'In my world, there are no glass ceilings.'

Vicky took advantage of the new intimacy that had been established. 'Tell me about the clinic where you had your treatment.'

Abi cast her mind back to the worst year of her life. The hormone injections she administered herself turned her stomach into a pin cushion. They ruined her skin and gave her terrible crying jags but the worst of it was the fortnightly journey to the clinic. Each time Abi would set off filled with hope and every time she left she was shattered with disappointment. Hiding her tears behind a pair of dark glasses, she put her head down and ran the gauntlet of reporters, feeling her dreams dying with every step she took. She started to believe that the pavement was littered with them. 'The clinic assured me it wasn't any of their employees that leaked the story,' she told Vicky bitterly.

At the time, Vicky had been going through her feminist stage. She distinctly remembered the howls of disapproval when it emerged that Abi Martin, newsreader and presenter, was trying to get pregnant using anonymously donated sperm. For a time, she turned into public enemy number one. How *dare* she try for a baby without a man in tow?

'The IVF didn't work at first. They advised me to give up after the third cycle. But I refused. I wanted to keep going.' Abi looked at Vicky. 'I told you. I'm used to getting what I want. I fell pregnant the fifth time round.'

It was no good. Abi couldn't be strong any more. She started to cry.

Vicky went to sit down next to her. 'Now I know why you called her Eden.'

Abi nodded. She turned to look at Vicky. 'Don't put off having your children. Our bodies aren't made that way.'

Vicky said, 'Were the clinic pleased with the way things went?'

Abi wiped her eyes with a tissue. 'The pregnancy was textbook.' She noticed the anxious look on Vicky's face. 'Why are you asking me all this? What's this all about?'

'I took a DNA sample from a lock of Eden's hair this afternoon.'

'Yes. And a swab from me and Jack. What about it?'

'We created a profile for all three of you. It's just procedure. But I'm afraid there's a problem.'

'Of course there is. Jack isn't Eden's father.'

'This isn't about Jack. It's about you. There's no easy way of saying this, Abi. I'm afraid you're not Eden's mother.'

Abi snorted. 'Run the tests again.'

'The polymers have been rerun three times. There is no mistake. Half of Eden's DNA comes from Matthew and the other half comes from a woman we don't know about.'

Abi held her hand in front of her mouth.

'The most likely explanation,' Vicky went on, 'is that the laboratory made a mistake. It happens around once in every three thousand cases, when the wrong egg is taken out of storage and used for implantation.' She paused. 'I'm sorry.'

Abi's mind turned somersaults. This morning she'd been told that her daughter had gone missing and now this woman was insisting that Eden wasn't hers. 'I don't believe it!' she cried.

'Ms Martin, I know this is really difficult.'

'Shut up! I've had enough of your evil insinuations! Get out of my house!'

'Ms Martin—'

'Get out!'

'I'll go,' Vicky said, standing. 'But here's my card. If you need to get in touch there's a pager number on the back. You can call me any time. Day or night.' FLOs rated their relationship with the target family on a scale of one to three and in the Martin household they'd just reached level three – crisis, breakdown.

Getting to her feet as well, Abi took Vicky's card and tore it into shreds. Letting the pieces fall to the floor, she pointed to the front door.

Brighton had another pier. The council, ever aware of the need for self-promotion, had rebranded it Brighton Pier, but the locals kept on using its more seaside-sounding name. In the middle of the night the Palace Pier stood deserted, the lights all off along its considerable length, the funfair rides at the end stilled and shadowy against the dark, cloudy sky. Nearby, two figures ran down onto the shingle from the promenade.

'It's freezing!' shivered Lorna, a woman in her late twenties with a slightly mannish haircut.

'I'm not cold!' cried the other.

Michelle was in her first term at Brighton University and tonight, at the first ever lesbian club night she'd gone to, she'd met the woman called Lorna. At half past three in the morning, the chemicals Michelle had ingested before she'd gone out were still coursing through her veins, filling her with excitement and anticipation. Every fibre in Michelle's body told her the wild kiss she'd just shared with Lorna heralded the true beginning of her life.

'Come on!' she yelled out triumphantly, grabbing Lorna by the hand and making her run across the stones.

'We shouldn't be out here,' Lorna said breathlessly as she ran. She glanced back along the beach, to where someone might be hiding behind the shingle dune. 'It isn't safe.' But she still let herself be led by the younger woman closer to the waves, further away from the road and streetlights.

Michelle threw her head back, delighting in the cold. She wasn't yet nineteen, with mousy hair and a sexy button nose. 'No one can tell me what to do! Not any more! I'm free!'

They had arrived at the water's edge. It was black and silky. Michelle kissed Lorna on the lips again.

Lorna could feel the thrill of danger now as well – it overtoppled her nerves. She shoved her fingers into the waistband of Michelle's jeans and tugged at the hem of the cotton shirt.

Michelle giggled and pulled away. 'Come swimming with me!'

'No!' Lorna insisted. She had lived in Brighton for years and she'd heard all the stories about clubbers diving into the sea. 'It's too cold.'

Michelle looked her in the eyes. 'Are you scared?'

Lorna kissed her. 'Darling, I just want to stay alive.'

Michelle glanced at the crashing, whispering surf. 'But it looks so inviting.'

'Stay here with me,' said Lorna.

Michelle nuzzled Lorna's neck. It was a marvellous feeling to be embraced like this, to be caught by Lorna, to be held.

'What's that?' said Lorna.

Her voice had changed, becoming tense, and when Michelle looked up at her she could see that Lorna was peering over towards the side of the pier. 'What?' she asked, looking across as well.

'There,' Lorna instructed her, pointing. 'That thing bobbing up and down.'

Sure enough, when the moon slipped out of the cloud cover it reflected on something rising and falling with the swell. 'It's tied to the pier,' said Michelle.

Lorna saw that she was right: a rope suspended the object from one of the iron struts underneath the boardwalk. Letting go of Michelle, Lorna turned and walked closer, the shingle stirring restlessly at her feet. The sea shifted, revealing more. 'Oh, God.'

The sea tilted, revealing the naked body of a woman. Her hands and feet had been removed and she dangled there, strangely incomplete.

17

• • •

'She'd been suffocated,' Beckett told Dr McGuire the next morning. 'A plastic bag over her head. A clear plastic bag, so he could watch her die.'

'You don't know that,' McGuire corrected him.

In his office, Beckett stopped pacing. 'I don't know what?'

'You don't know that he wanted to watch her die. You're making assumptions again.'

The train station, the mews in Brunswick, the cement factory: each time, the concealments had become more elaborate. But the fourth victim was different. Her body had been hung out for all to see on the city's most famous landmark. Serial killers had rituals – things they did all the time – and Beckett knew that in the end it was this that got them caught. But, no matter how twisted, the Brighton killings seemed to show no rhyme or reason. That left Beckett with the uncomfortable feeling that the killer, whoever it was, wanted to toy with the police. 'So what does the computer say this time?' he asked McGuire.

There doesn't seem to be much of a pattern at all. I can find lots of matches for the individual murders but this amount of variety is unique. It's fascinating.'

'I'm glad you find it interesting,' said Beckett, sitting down opposite McGuire at the conference table. 'Listen, I know how you hate speculation and psychologising and all that, but you must have formed an opinion about this guy.'

McGuire made a pious face. 'I don't rely on opinion. Nor do I rely on assumptions. I rely on facts. I shouldn't have to remind you that the opinion of so-called profilers has sent innocent men to prison.'

'It's not an innocent man that's giving me nightmares, sir. Right now, I could use some insight into the killer's state of mind. So, go on, Dr McGuire, take a leap in the dark. Let's take the third victim as an example. What might be significant about the fact he spent so much time and effort breaking every bone in her body?'

'Using a claw hammer hardly constitutes a thorough knowledge of anatomy, if that's what you mean.'

'What about the eyes, then? Why would he do that?'

McGuire leaned forward. 'Do you think removing her eyes might be symbolic in some way?'

Beckett shrugged. 'Maybe.'

McGuire nodded. 'You mean our man couldn't bear for her to look at him? Maybe he wants to be caught. Maybe he wants all this to stop.'

'Isn't that their unconscious wish?'

McGuire laughed out loud. 'Do you want to know what I think, DCI Beckett?'

'Enlighten me, sir.'

'I think you're beginning to panic. Now, let's talk about

something useful. What about the Glasgow case I gave you the details of yesterday?'

'The suspect is in prison,' Beckett said. 'He was convicted of another aggravated rape last year.'

'Pity. That looked promising.' He stood up. 'I've set up a remote link to the database. I'll go and upload the details of the latest murder and see what it comes up with.' He was talking as if the murdered woman was an item of missing stock.

At the door, McGuire turned around. 'By the way, can I have hard copies of all the PM photographs? We like to keep our archives as comprehensive as possible.'

'Ask Minter.'

Beckett had already dismissed McGuire from his mind.

'Another milestone in my brilliant career,' Vicky said. She'd come to Sussex House for an early meeting with her SIO, a meeting that had just finished.

'Don't be too hard on yourself,' Minter replied. 'It must happen to all FLOs.'

'Yeah,' said Vicky disconsolately, 'but not their first assignment. And not their very first day.'

'From what I've heard, it was never going to be an easy one.'

Vicky felt a little buoyed. 'That's what Grant said.'

'So what's going to happen now?'

'He thinks I'll get back in there once Abi Martin has calmed down. In the meantime, he wants me out of harm's way.' She looked at her watch. 'He's asked me to go to London.'

'Why London?'

'That's where the IVF clinic is where Eden Martin was conceived.'

Minter looked puzzled.

'It looks like the clinic made a mistake,' Vicky explained. 'Apparently it happens about once in every three thousand cases.'

'And this time it was Abi?'

'That's right. Eden Martin isn't Abi Martin's biological child. She belongs to someone else.'

'Bloody hell.'

Vicky nodded. 'That's right. Grant's sending me to London to tie up any loose ends.' She smiled ruefully. 'If that's the right expression.' She sipped at her coffee. 'I heard about your promotion.'

'It's only acting up.'

Vicky hid the jealousy she felt. 'You'll sail through the exams. You've got it made, mate.'

Kevin Phillips came into the room. 'I didn't think you'd want to hang out with the likes of us, Vick,' he said. 'I thought you were hanging out with celebrities these days.'

'Very funny, Kevin,' said Vicky.

Screwing up his fists, Phillips pantomimed wiping away some tears. 'Or did the waterworks get too much?'

Her voice a little barbed, Vicky said, 'Good news about Minter making DI, isn't it, Kev?'

'Yeah,' Phillips agreed. 'Brilliant.'

'I've got to go,' said Vicky, getting up from the chair. 'I'll see you later.'

Minter and Phillips both said their goodbyes, then Phillips turned to Minter and said, 'Tom's called a briefing for this evening. He wants you to give an update on Underhill.'

Dr Jones had called from Meadow View Hospital, where Vincent Underhill's short-term memory had started to come back. 'OK,' said Minter. 'As a matter of fact, I was just on my way to the hospital.'

When he was alone, Phillips took his mobile out of his pocket. Looking at the screen he could see he had three missed calls from Fiona and a couple of texts. Ignoring them, he rang another number.

It was answered on the fourth ring. 'Keith Miller,' said the world-weary voice.

'It's DS Phillips.'

'It didn't take you long to call.'

'You're not going to believe what I just heard.'

18

• • •

The Queen Adelaide Clinic was at the top end of Harley Street in London. In the waiting room, Vicky sat opposite a glamorous-looking woman dressed in brown leather trousers, her wrists adorned with gold, her make-up perfect in every detail, her age indeterminate. She was flicking through the pages of a glossy magazine and when the receptionist brought her in a cup of tea – Earl Grey, lemon – she thanked her in a husky voice with an Eastern European accent.

Vicky looked around the rest of the room. Everything in it bore the authentic, understated stamp of affluence. It was in the hipped legs of the antique furniture and the plush of the carpet and the brass lights over the original oil paintings. Amid all this refinement, Vicky felt a little vulgar. She glanced surreptitiously back at the Russian woman, noticing how, beneath the sheen of lipstick, the woman's bee-stung lips had been treated with a little too much Botox.

Outside, another limousine hushed along the London street, which had been treating the maladies of the great and the good for over two hundred years. Now the women getting in and out of the Mercedes were all foreign and the nameplates on the buildings suggested there'd been another change. As well as private hospitals, this end of Harley Street was made up of cosmetic surgeons and assisted conception clinics. It wasn't illnesses as such that the doctors here were treating, it was the symptoms of ageing. If you were a woman with enough money, it seemed, you didn't have to suffer that affliction.

Getting up from her chair, Vicky picked up a copy of the clinic's brochure from the coffee table. On the inside front cover there was a large photograph of a woman in her forties holding up her newborn baby, who was swaddled in a fluffy white towel. The photo could only have been taken a couple of hours post-partum. The mother hugged the chubby infant tightly, one hand reaching forward to touch the baby's perfect flecks of fingernail. She looked blissfully happy and just a little awed, as if she still couldn't believe her baby had arrived.

Vicky could only imagine the magnetic pull that pictures such as this one must have exerted on Abi Martin. For her, the idea of having children never loomed particularly large. Vicky was young, she told herself. She still had lots of time. But deep down, if she was honest, Vicky harboured a nagging worry that she lacked the vital warmth, that quickening pulse, which would make her ready for motherhood. It was her own mother's fault, she suspected. From Mrs Reynolds, Vicky had somehow imbibed the idea that children were an encumbrance – a messy, tiresome chore and something to be endured. It wasn't a surprise, then, that at home Vicky was fascinated less by the domestic realm and more by the world her father inhabited.

She remembered very well the day she found out what an important job her father did. She was standing at the window of her bedroom in the rambling old rectory in Hurstpierpoint. Outside, her father was striding down the garden path in his uniform. To Vicky's juvenile eye, he looked so smart and purposeful. There was an official car waiting for him in the road, with a driver in the front dressed in another uniform, the engine of the car still running. Vicky watched in breathless admiration as her father tucked his shiny-peaked cap under his arm and opened the garden gate. He paused on the other side of the flint wall and looked back up at the house, spying her at the window and waving happily. Then he got into the official car and was gone, off to protect other boys and girls from the bad men. The car that took her father off to London confirmed the importance Vicky's father had to the wider world but it held something else for Vicky as well, which was why she lingered at the window after her father had gone. To Vicky, the car held out the possibility of adventure.

It wasn't just IVF that the Queen Adelaide offered, Vicky read. They had pioneered techniques for the screening of embryos for genetic traits and along with this service they now offered third-party egg donation, egg sharing and the services of gestational carriers. These last, Vicky learned from the brochure, were women who volunteered to have the fertilised egg of another woman implanted into their wombs and carry their baby to term, at which point the Queen Adelaide's client would reclaim possession. Vicky was a little shocked by the idea. It seemed there was no end to the lengths a clinic like this one would go to in order to procure a baby. There were no boundaries the scientists wouldn't cross to transcend the limits imposed by nature.

'Ms Reynolds?' said a voice.

Vicky looked up to see an overweight, middle-aged man in

a grey suit. 'I'm Mr Chalmers,' he said, advancing. His handshake was limp and his nerves manifested themselves in a kind of obsequiousness. 'I'm the business manager here,' he said. 'We spoke on the telephone this morning.'

Vicky said, 'Thanks for seeing me at such short notice.'

'Not at all,' said Chalmers, the light flashing on one of the lenses of his glasses. 'It's very good timing, in fact. Mr Kent has a window now. If we're quick, we'll just catch him.'

Vicky followed Chalmers up the stairs and across a narrow landing where a stained-glass window overlooked the street outside. Mr Chalmers knocked at one of the heavy doors and waited. Glancing down, Vicky noticed how shiny Mr Chalmers's shoes were. From inside the room, a voice called out, 'Come!'

The consulting room was a blur of dark wood and Mr Kent's rich cologne. The doctor himself was sitting behind a desk decorated with an old-fashioned blotter and a pair of silver ink pots on a stand. The walls of the room had been painted rose-pink and Vicky glimpsed a studded Chesterfield examination couch peeping out from behind a lacquered Chinese screen. Smiling, Mr Kent stood up to greet her. He was tailored immaculately in a pinstriped suit with purple lining in the jacket. He had silvery-white hair and when he shook Vicky's hand his skin was soft and dry.

Vicky and Chalmers occupied the two chairs in front of the desk and Kent sat back down in his wing chair. 'I believe,' he said, 'you wanted to talk about Mrs Abigail Martin?'

Vicky nodded. 'She was a patient of yours.'

'That's right. I remember her well. A very forceful woman.'

Mr Chalmers tempered Kent's statement. 'Ms Martin was concerned about the issue of confidentiality.'

'She was right to be,' said Vicky.

The business manager shook his head sadly. 'Most regrettable. We launched an investigation as soon as we found out the press had the story. I'm glad to see all our employees were exonerated.'

'As if the poor woman didn't have enough to deal with,' Mr Kent put in.

Vicky turned to him. 'Tell me about Abi Martin's treatment.'

Kent had obviously reacquainted himself with the details of the case. 'Ms Martin was thirty-four years old when I first saw her.'

'Is that old for IVF?'

'Nowadays we treat women up to forty-six. Forty-seven next year, if we get the approval. But at the time, I suppose thirty-four was considered to be the median. No one was particularly surprised that it took some time for Ms Martin to conceive. We tried enhanced IUI first.'

'We take the basal temperature of the patient,' Mr Chalmers explained, 'to establish the optimum time for insemination.'

'But that didn't work,' Mr Kent went on. 'It took four more cycles of IVF before she finally conceived successfully. A little girl, I think. I delivered her myself. A private room at the Queen Charlotte's and Chelsea. The very room, I believe, where certain younger members of the royal family came into the world.' He smiled urbanely. 'We were all so pleased.'

Mr Chalmers wrung his hands. 'Perhaps you can tell us why you've come here this morning, DC Reynolds.'

When Vicky explained, the ingratiating smile fell from his face. He was frowning darkly now, already anticipating another, more ominous letter plopping onto his desk from

Abi Martin's tenacious solicitor. The Queen Adelaide carried hefty public liability insurance for just this eventuality but the harm a court case would do to the clinic's reputation was incalculable and Mr Chalmers was already thinking of his damage limitation strategy.

'The Queen Adelaide has been licensed to carry out IVF since the earliest days of assisted conception. Nothing like this has ever happened before. You've read our latest HFEA inspection report, I take it?'

Vicky nodded. She had been on the regulator's website. The Human Fertilisation and Embryology Authority had given the Queen Adelaide a clean bill of health. 'But mistakes happen,' said Vicky. 'I've informed the HFEA and they will be sending in a team of inspectors to look into the matter. That's not really my concern, Mr Chalmers. My concern is with the criminal investigation into Eden's disappearance. An investigation, by the way, that takes precedence over the HFEA's.'

Mr Kent shot out a cuff and glanced at a watch that gave off an impression of bejewelled weightiness. 'I have a patient in a couple of minutes,' he said, looking directly at his colleague.

Mr Chalmers got up from his chair. 'Thank you for sparing the time,' he said, almost bowing and scraping in his readiness to be gone.

Outside the room, Mr Chalmers closed the door.

'If it's on the premises,' Vicky said, 'I'd like to take a look at the laboratory.'

Mr Chalmers's manner changed completely, from the unctuous to the brusque. 'Very well.'

Back on the ground floor, Vicky followed the business manager through reception. They stopped at a door marked *Private* at the end of the hallway. Mr Chalmers's index finger jabbed at the alphanumeric keypad and the lock was thrown. 'The security codes are changed every week,' he said gruffly.

In going from the public areas of the clinic to the laboratory, they travelled from the antique to the modern. On the other side of the door the deep carpet ended, replaced by sterile white floor tiles and fierce ceiling lights. There were white-painted bars at the windows and cameras on the walls. They entered a white room with a sink and a bank of grey lockers. Chalmers squeezed alcohol rub out of a dispenser on the wall and washed his hands thoroughly. Vicky did the same. From a hamper in the corner he handed her a little bundle of freshly laundered and neatly folded surgical scrubs. Protective gear donned, they went through another door into the inner sanctum of the lab itself.

The long, windowless room ran the width of the rear of the building and had been partitioned into three separate areas. 'This is where the IVF is carried out,' Mr Chalmers said, indicating the area to their left.

It seemed to be the largest, with three workstations arranged along a lab bench. At each workstation there was a microscope with a revolving set of lenses, a centrifuge, some Petri dishes, a miniature fridge and a tray full of long needles, each in its own sterile wrapping. It was nearly lunchtime and there was no one working.

'IVF is our bread and butter,' Chalmers went on. 'We do upward of three hundred cases every year. It's a simple procedure.' He pointed at the centrifuge. 'This is what we use to select the best sperm from the donor semen. We call it "washing and spinning". The fertilisation itself takes place outside the womb, in one of those glass jars. IVF: *in vitro* fertilisation. Fertilisation in glass.'

Vicky nodded. 'What could go wrong?'

Chalmers ignored her sarcasm.

Vicky wondered if he realised what a contribution he was making to the ever-increasing redundancy of the male of the species. 'Where are the eggs kept prior to fertilisation?' she asked.

'I'll show you.'

They went into a chilly side room where a dozen aluminium canisters were lined up against the wall. Each one was waist-high and shaped like a torpedo and sat in its own trolley. Chalmers went across and wheeled one of the canisters out of the line. When he unscrewed the top there was a hiss of escaping gas and a cloud of liquid nitrogen tumbled down the side. 'Don't worry,' he said, seeing Vicky take a step back. 'It's an inert gas. It can't harm you.'

Vicky approached. She peered down through the clearing fog as Chalmers lifted the top of the metal rack clear of the sides of the canister. There were six compartments running round a central rod, each compartment containing about a dozen glass straws. 'Every one of those contains an egg,' said Chalmers. He pointed with his finger to the numbers printed on a label stuck to the side of one of the straws. 'That's the unique serial number given to each egg. Whenever they take an egg out of storage the technician has to sign for it.'

'Have you still got the records for Abi Martin?'

'Of course.'

Vicky nodded. That was what she had come for: the name of the technician who had made the mistake. 'I'll need copies to take with me.'

Chalmers nodded.

'Do the technicians stay here long?'

'They come and go.'

'What kind of people are they?'

'They usually have some kind of scientific background. But they don't need to be very highly qualified.'

Vicky looked down at the canister. There was room inside for about five more rings of egg. She did the maths. Around three hundred eggs in a canister and twelve canisters in all. That was three thousand six hundred eggs.

Chalmers seemed to reading her mind. 'During a typical IVF cycle, a healthy young woman can produce up to twenty eggs. At one time we would implant two or even three fertilised eggs in order to enhance the chances of success, although now that is officially discouraged.'

'To reduce the incidence of twins and triplets?'

'That's right.'

'How many were implanted in Abi Martin?'

'Her successful cycle involved three eggs. We talked to Ms Martin about the dangers but she was adamant. If necessary, she said she preferred to have a twin reduction.'

'Terminate one of the foetuses, you mean?'

'We wouldn't use that word.'

Vicky looked at the canister brimful of women's eggs. 'How long do you keep the eggs for?'

'Initially for a period of ten years. After the end of the treatment, we move them to a larger storage facility. If the client wishes to store them any longer than ten years, there is a small annual charge.' A thought seemed to strike him. 'Bearing in mind what has happened to her daughter, Ms Martin might be interested to know that we still have her eggs. She might want to try again.'

*

On her way out of the clinic, Vicky stopped by Chalmers's office to pick up the paperwork on Abi Martin's treatment. The business manager escorted her off the premises and, with evident relief, closed the heavy black door behind her.

On the street, Vicky took her mobile out of her bag and rang the HOLMES clerk in the MIR at Hollingbury. She read out the name of the lab technician and asked for a check to be run, a current address to be found. With any luck, she could get this done by the end of the day. She had one more appointment. She was meeting Abi Martin's agent in the West End. On the telephone this morning, Jean Dawson had sounded very grand and not a little insincere. Putting her mobile away, Vicky hurried towards the nearest tube station.

She didn't take any notice of the sleazy-looking man who passed her on the other side of the street, clutching in his hand a reporter's notebook. Keith Miller stopped and looked across the road, spotting the brass nameplate of the Queen Adelaide Clinic.

Mr Chalmers's day was about to take another turn for the worse.

19

• • •

It was only just after lunchtime but the railway station concourse was busy. People were still leaving Brighton for business meetings up in London or arriving in the city for early Christmas shopping. Standing in the middle of the concourse, Minter looked up at the electronic announcement board, scanning for the Littlehampton train, the crowds bifurcating round him, heading for the platforms or for the exit.

He slipped his finger between the two top buttons of his white work shirt and touched the small gold disc hanging there by its chain. The night of the run, when he'd faced up to the truth about his mother, something had made him go back to rescue the medallion. He'd retraced his steps through the quagmire of the ploughed field and found the St Christopher on top of one of the soft furrows. He'd picked it up, rubbed away the dirt and slipped it into the pocket of his running trousers. It seemed Minter's journey was far from over.

The Littlehampton train appeared at the far end of the platform, where, under the edge of the glass canopy, an unwarranted piece of dazzling blue sky was peeping in for the first time in days. Its brakes grinding, the engine slowed to a halt in front of the buffers. As the doors slid open, a smattering of passengers got down and made their way over to the turnstiles. The driver got out of the front and walked towards the station office, pausing to share a few words with his replacement. It was only then that a big man got down slowly from the last carriage.

It took Minter a couple of seconds to recognise Vincent Underhill. Since the last time they'd met his beard had been shaved off and his hair had been cut and the change had taken at least a decade off his age. He started walking towards the turnstiles and Minter saw that Underhill's shambling gait had changed as well, his stride a great deal less constricted. His heavy black greatcoat had been replaced by a blouson jacket and a pair of brown casual trousers that were second-hand but nonetheless clean and freshly pressed. Behind him was the male nurse Dr Jones had sent along as a minder. Minter walked over to the ticket barriers to meet them.

Underhill hesitated in front of the turnstile, staring down at the plastic jaws, a woman waiting impatiently behind him. 'You need your ticket, Vincent,' Minter said from the other side. Underhill looked up at Minter, frowning a little in recognition before fumbling in the pockets of his jacket for the little piece of card. The woman behind him tutted and hurried on to another turnstile. At last Underhill located his ticket. 'Put it in the slot there,' Minter told him. Underhill glanced nervously to his left and right then followed the example of the other passengers by holding the edge of the train ticket up to the front of the turnstile. The machine grabbed it out of his fingers and he recoiled. The gates opened and he was through. 'Your ticket,' Minter said, pointing at the card sticking out of the return slot. Underhill looked at Minter and then back at the turnstile. He took the ticket from the slot and examined it suspiciously, as if unable to account for its sudden reappearance, then he put it back in his pocket.

As if seeing it all for the first time, Underhill looked around the vast interior of the echoing station. His eyes flickered from a student with an enormous backpack standing at the nearby ticket machine to a young woman queuing at the coffee stand. Blinking, he looked up into the high glass roof, where a pigeon was trying to settle on one of the blue-painted cross beams. It was just like Dr Jones had said, Minter thought as he watched the vagrant. Vincent Underhill was Rip Van Winkle, emerging groggily from his long, benighted dream.

'Vincent,' said Minter, succeeding in getting his attention this time. 'I'm a police officer. I spoke to you yesterday. Do you remember?'

Underhill stared at Minter. He recalled tottering on the side of the pier in the storm. He remembered being under the waves and someone pulling him out and dragging him onto the beach. Slowly, he nodded. 'You helped me.'

Minter smiled. 'We went for a little swim.'

Underhill's eyes narrowed. 'Yes.'

'Good. Now let's see what else you can remember.'

Underhill looked uncertainly at the nurse.

'It's OK, Vincent,' he said. 'This won't take long. Just answer Mr Minter's questions as well as you can.'

Minter led them behind the WH Smith's concession. The CCTV camera that had filmed Underhill dropping the suitcase and walking away was still there, screwed halfway up the wall, but the bloodstain on the floor had been scrubbed away.

Underhill looked around. 'Why are we here?'

'You were here a few days ago. You had a suitcase with you. Do you remember?'

Underhill shook his head.

'You don't remember carrying a suitcase, Vincent?'

'No.'

Minter indicated the spot. 'You left it here. You put it on the ground.'

Underhill grunted. He looked at the nurse. 'Can we go back now?'

'Please, Vincent,' Minter said. 'It's me that needs *your* help now.'

Underhill looked at him. His voice croaky, he said, 'I'm sorry. I don't remember.'

Minter pointed to the entrance. 'You came in from over there with the suitcase in your hand. Then you walked over here and put it down on the ground.'

Underhill started to look worried. 'I told you! I don't remember!'

Minter sighed. 'Perhaps we should go outside.'

They walked beneath the arch and came out by the taxi rank. To Minter's left, Trafalgar Street led down the hill into Brighton's bustling North Laine. It was a well-known tourist district and, as such, well covered by cameras. To his right was an all-night café and the little line of shops. If Underhill's story was true at all, Minter thought, he had probably stumbled across the suitcase somewhere between the station and Seven Dials, in one of the quiet, tree-lined residential streets just beyond the all-night café. Uniformed officers had already conducted inquiries in the area. Apparently no one had seen or heard a thing.

Minter showed Underhill a picture from the camera above the entrance to the station. 'That's you, isn't it?'

Underhill looked at the dark figure in the photograph. Saying nothing, he gave it back.

Minter felt his frustration begin to grow.

Five minutes later, back inside the station, a train was waiting to take Underhill back to the hospital. Having checked the time of departure, the nurse settled Underhill into a seat and stepped down onto the platform.

'Sorry about that,' he told Minter.

Minter glanced at Underhill through the window of the carriage. The schizophrenic was sitting bolt upright and staring out. Minter would have given anything to know, to really know, what was going through his mind. 'How is he doing?'

'Dr Jones says he is showing insight into his condition.'

'What does that mean?'

'He's beginning to know the difference between what is real and what is happening only in his mind.'

'How long until he makes a full recovery?'

'Even with the new pills, that could take months.'

Minter didn't have months. He didn't even have hours. Getting on the train, he went to sit opposite Underhill.

He was still staring out the window but now the direction of his gaze had changed. He was looking into the far corner of the station, at the frontage of WH Smith's.

'What is it, Vincent?' Minter asked. 'What can you see?'

Underhill swallowed hard. His hand was shaking. From outside, an announcement was made about the train's imminent departure.

'Vincent,' Minter said, leaning forward. 'This is important. A woman's been killed.'

Underhill didn't take his eyes off the people milling around the branch of WH Smith's.

'Vincent,' Minter urged him. 'If you don't help us, more women are going to die.'

Underhill turned his head. 'She died?'

'Yes,' said Minter, leaning in even closer. 'She was killed. Her name was Mercy Mvule.'

'The brown woman.'

'Yes. You talked to her on North Street, by the bus stops. What did you say to her?'

Tears welled up in Underhill's eyes.

'Who told you to pick up the suitcase?'

Underhill muttered, 'The voices aren't real.'

'Listen to me, Vincent. This one is real. It's the voice of the man who killed Mercy Mvule. That person is real.'

Underhill covered his face with his hands. 'The doctor told me the voices weren't real. None of this happened.'

'No!' Minter said, reaching over and prising Underhill's hands from his face, forcing the schizophrenic to look at him. 'Mercy is dead, Vincent. We know it wasn't you who killed her. But the man who did used you to get rid of the body. He set you up, Vincent. He wanted you to take the blame. Who was it, Vincent? Who told you what to do?'

But Underhill wasn't listening any more. His eyes were blank and the expression on his face was catatonic.

They should have got a bigger room, thought Detective Chief Inspector Grant. He was sitting at a table at the very front of the press briefing room. Behind him was a blue banner bearing the Sussex Police logo and in front of him was a jostling, bad-tempered herd of journalists. He was distracted from the lights of the TV cameras by the sight of a photographer dashing to the front and kneeling down before the table to grab a low-angle shot of Abi Martin, who was sitting next to Grant. On her other side was Jack Bellamy.

'Right, ladies and gentlemen,' said Grant. 'Shall we get started?' Slowly the din in the room subsided. 'I'm going to read a short statement then Ms Martin will also read a statement.' He cast his eyes around the room. 'There will *not* be an opportunity for questions.' Ignoring the murmurs of protest, Grant went on, 'The search for Eden Martin now involves more than 350 officers drawn from Sussex Police and two other constabularies, Kent and Hampshire. As of two p.m. today, the team has carried out more than 400 house-to-house inquiries, dealt with more than 2,000 phone calls from members of the public and stopped over 500 cars. It is the biggest operation of its kind that this force has ever known.' What he didn't say was that, so far, every lead had come to nothing and that they'd quickly been reduced to clutching at straws. Grant looked up, locating the television camera from the BBC and looking down its lens. 'Let me make this direct appeal to the person, or persons, holding Eden Martin prisoner. It is not too late to return Eden safe and sound. We have left special instructions on how to get in touch with us in the form of messages on Eden's mobile telephone. Please use these instructions.'

Grant surveyed the room, watching all the pens hurrying across shorthand pads. For all that he reserved contempt for the press, this was one occasion when he needed them to get a message out. Grant was certain that Eden's kidnapper would be watching the press conference and the messages he had just spoken about were bait. As soon as Eden's abductor switched on the phone, his location would light up on one of the telephone company's computer screens and the police would be on their way.

But Grant wasn't holding his breath. This morning he had chaired a meeting with the three senior officers drafted in from other forces because of their experience in searching for abducted children. It was the opinion of all three officers that Eden was already dead. Most likely, one of them said, it was a grooming incident that had gone terribly wrong. Eden might have screamed too loudly during the sexual assault, or even tried to escape. To get what he wanted, her assailant would need to shut her up, make her lie still. He would have hit her, or put his hands around her throat. Right now, the officer informed the meeting grimly, Eden's violated body was most likely stuffed into a storm drain somewhere or buried in a shallow grave. If that's how it had happened, said another, if he hadn't set out to kill her from the first, there was a chance that the murderer was feeling a trace of remorse. He might even be moved by the mother's wretched pleas for her daughter to come home – moved enough, at least, to let the police know where Eden's body was hidden. Then they could get Forensics going on the remains, and Abi Martin could get on with her grieving.

DCI Grant put down his statement. 'Ms Martin.'

At first, Abi didn't move. Her balled fists were beneath the table, clutching a paper tissue someone had given her. She had faced countless press packs before but this was different. She wasn't used to the sombre expressions on the faces of the journalists. She wasn't used to the awful silence. When she looked at the statement on the table the words began to blur on the page. She felt naked, raw. For a few moments, she said nothing then she picked up the piece of paper. 'My daughter,' she read, her voice trembling, 'is a healthy, wonderful thirteen-year-old girl. She likes going out with her friends and she enjoys playing piano. She is doing really well in school.' Pausing, Abi used the crumpled tissue to wipe away the tears. 'When she grows up, she is going to be a singer.' A hundred electronic camera shutters went off, sucking in the distress on Abi's face, digitising her trauma.

Vicky Reynolds slipped in the back of the room and perched herself on the edge of a seat. During the rest of Abi Martin's brief statement she had her eyes clamped firmly on Jack Bellamy, waiting for him to put his arm around Abi's shoulder or, for his hand to cover one of Abi's, to offer her some comfort.

The more people attempted to cover up their true feelings the more they tended to give themselves away. Jack didn't want to be here this afternoon, that much was obvious. He kept looking to his left, folding and unfolding his arms.

'If you're listening, Eden,' Abi struggled on. 'Please come home. You're not in trouble. I promise. Please come home.'

Her voice trailed off then Abi broke down, her shoulders heaving. For a brief moment, even the journalists were stilled by the sound of her terrible sobs. Then the shutters started again.

Abi's ordeal was over. Standing up, Vicky went out the door at the back and hurried along to the room at the end of the corridor where she knew they would take Abi Martin after the press conference. She was hoping there was a chance for reconciliation, or at least the opportunity of lending her the support Jack Bellamy had signally failed to give.

Standing up, DCI Grant moved the microphone away from

Abi and stood up himself. 'Ms Martin,' he said, indicating the other door to the side of the platform. 'This way, please.'

Inside the briefing room, one journalist's voice sailed above all the others. 'Ms Martin,' said Keith Miller. 'Is it true that Eden isn't your daughter?'

At the door, Abi froze. Grant grasped her elbow with his hand. He didn't want this descending into chaos. 'Let's go,' he said urgently.

Throwing his hand off, Abi spun round. 'What did you say?'

All eyes in the room were turned towards Miller. 'There are rumours going round that Eden isn't your biological child. Do you have any comment?'

The room exploded into action. Knocking chairs over, reporters rushed to the front of the room, where they yelled questions and thrust cameras into Abi's face. Jack lashed out at a photographer who came too close. Grant squeezed the door open and pushed Abi Martin out into the corridor, where a couple of uniformed officers held the journalists back.

Abi was ushered into the side room only to find Vicky Reynolds standing there.

'What's going on?' Vicky asked Grant, amazed at the commotion outside.

Reaching her, Abi slapped Vicky hard in the face. 'You bitch!' she screamed.

Bellamy slammed the door shut behind him. 'What the fuck was that all about?' he said to Grant.

'Ask her!' Abi shouted, pointing at Vicky. 'She told them! She told them about Eden!'

Grant turned to Vicky. 'Is that true, DC Reynolds?'

The side of Vicky's face still smarted from the slap. She

had told someone. She'd told Minter. But he wouldn't have blabbed to the press. He would have known how much trouble that would have landed Vicky in.

'Go and wait in my office,' Grant said from between gritted teeth.

'Yes, sir,' said Vicky. She turned and went towards the door. For a moment, the frenzy in the hall burst into the room, then the door was closed again and everything went quiet.

'You know we're going to sue you,' Jack said.

'You're not suing anyone,' said Grant calmly.

'Oh, yeah? Why not?'

'Because, Jack Bellamy, I am arresting you on suspicion of the abduction of Eden Martin.'

20

'What the fuck am I doing here?' Jack Bellamy demanded.

DCI Grant had taken him to the custody centre next to Sussex House. Outside the interview room, cell doors clanged and boots stamped along the corridor. Grant wanted Bellamy riled. On the edge. 'You're here to answer my questions, Mr Bellamy.'

'Couldn't we do this at the house? You've got half the world's press camped outside.'

'I thought you were used to the attentions of the press, sir.'

'Yeah, but not like this. They're baying for my fucking blood.'

The door opened and Vicky Reynolds came inside.

'What's she doing here?' Jack asked.

'DS Reynolds is a police officer,' Grant told him. 'She works here.'

Jack crossed his arms.

Grant watched him stew, wondering if Bellamy really was capable of killing Eden Martin to get closer to Abi's money.

Vicky put a printed copy of the statement Jack had given

her yesterday on the desk, turning it round so Jack could read it. 'I'd like you to go through your statement regarding your movements in the last week, and tell me if there's anything that, on reflection, you now wish to add.'

Jack stared at her. 'Why?'

'Yesterday was a stressful day,' Vicky said. 'It wouldn't be surprising if something slipped your mind.'

Grant added, 'We're giving you a chance to change your mind.'

Jack snatched up the stapled statement. His finger ran down the side of the first page, his lips forming one or two of the words, his eyes glancing up at Grant every now and then. 'No,' he said eventually. 'There's nowhere else.'

Now Vicky took a traffic camera photograph of the rear of a Porsche GT3 and placed it on the table next to Jack's statement. 'Is that your car, Mr Bellamy?'

'Is that what this is about?' Jack asked Grant. 'A fucking speeding ticket?' He looked across at Vicky. 'I told you, darling, that's a hundred and fifty grand's worth of car. I get a lot of tickets.'

Grant leaned forward. 'Just answer DC Reynolds's question, Mr Bellamy. Is that your car?'

Jack glanced at the number plates. 'You know it is.'

Vicky asked, 'And is it you driving?'

Jack made a face. 'Dunno. Could be.'

Vicky turned the first page of Jack's statement over and found the relevant sentence. 'You told me yesterday that no one borrows your car.'

Jack was beginning to realise he had been set up. 'I don't believe you people,' he said angrily. 'It's all the perverts in this city you should be talking to. Not me.'

'We're pursuing many lines of inquiry, Mr Bellamy,' said Grant. 'Of which this is only one.'

Vicky repeated the question. 'Can you confirm that you were driving the car or not?'

Jack knew the golden rule was not to lie to the cops where you could avoid it. Nodding grimly, he admitted, 'It's me driving.'

'But in your earlier statement,' Vicky went on, 'you made no reference to going to Poynings. Why was that, sir?'

Jack said nothing.

'Can you explain the discrepancy in your two statements, sir?'

'Maybe you were right,' said Jack. 'Maybe it slipped my mind.'

'You made that trip two days ago,' said Grant. 'Is your memory usually that unreliable?'

The silence in the room lengthened.

'This isn't about a speeding ticket, sir,' said Vicky. She was convinced that Jack was about to break, to tell them where he'd stashed Eden. Convinced, too, that Eden was still alive.

Jack said, 'I want a solicitor.'

'That's your right,' said Grant. 'But the solicitor will tell you that this is a reasonable question for you to answer, especially given the fact that we're up against time here. As I told you when I arrested you a few minutes ago, if you refuse to say anything under caution then that may count against you at a later date. In court.'

'Court? What you talking about court for?'

'This is a serious offence, sir,' said Grant, his temper fraying. 'We're talking about a young girl's life.'

Jack bit his lip. He seemed to be considering something. Weighing it up. 'You won't tell Abi, will you?'

'Tell Abi what?' Grant asked.

Jack hesitated.

'Tell Abi what?'

'I go to Poynings quite a bit.'

'Why?'

'I know someone who lives there.'

'Who?'

'A friend?'

Vicky said, 'Why didn't you want to tell us about this friend?'

Jack slammed his fist down on the table. 'I'm fucking her, all right! I'm fucking her and I don't want Abi finding out.'

'Are you saying,' said Grant, 'that the reason you concealed your movements from us is because you are having an affair with another woman?'

'That's exactly what I'm telling you. She lives in Poynings. She's got a flat there.'

Vicky asked, 'What's her name?'

'Debs Coglan. She works for Tequila.'

Vicky recognised the name immediately. She'd even seen a photo of Coglan on the Tequila website. Debs was one of Jack's PAs. She was young – she had at least twenty years on Abi – and she was very good-looking.

Grant gave Jack a pen and paper. 'Write down her address and phone numbers.' Jack did as he was told. Grant snatched the piece of paper out of his hand. 'Wait here.'

After a minute or so, Jack looked at Vicky. 'This is a private conversation, isn't it? Something just between you and me. Confidential, like you promised.'

Vicky shook her head. 'You know, Jack, you really are a prick.'

The door opened and Grant came back in. 'You're free to go,' he told Jack.

'Cheers,' said Jack, getting up from his chair and hurrying out.

'It checks out,' Grant told Vicky. 'Bellamy visits Coglan once or twice a week when Abi is up in London. He was there on the Tuesday.'

'I really thought we had him.'

'So did I.'

21

• • •

On the open road, Jack hammered down the accelerator of his Porsche. Air rushed through the turbo and his all-time favourite rap song started punching out of the Bose. As he sped away from Brighton, Jack was delighted that his plan was back on track. Particularly gratifying was the way that when Abi Martin's lawyer was finished with that bitch Reynolds the former cop would be lucky to get a job doling out parking tickets. On the graphite steering wheel of his Porsche, Jack drummed out the rhythm of the chorus.

Turning off the motorway, Jack pointed the Porsche into the depths of the Sussex countryside. It was getting dark now but he gunned the engine. If the cops picked him up, he'd just tell them he was going to see Debs. A spur of the moment thing.

What was the word? Yeah, 'impulsive'.

Impulsive was Jack Bellamy all over.

Ever since his first audition for reality TV, Jack had been bigging himself up like this. He'd embroidered his curriculum vitae with so many colourful threads that sometimes even he forgot what was true and what wasn't. But that didn't matter. What mattered was what people wanted to believe, he'd learned that early on. What mattered was the narrative. So when he was doing his audition tapes for his first reality show he hadn't said he was an unemployed painter and decorator. Instead, Jack had told the camera that he'd travelled extensively in India and the Far East. When he passed the live audition and got on the show, Jack had daubed a red bindi on his forehead and in episode three, after doing a session of hot yoga in the sauna, Jack had gone down on an infamous divorcee.

'Fuck, eat, pray' – that became Jack's catchphrase on the show. It had a certain ring to it. You had to give him that. Jack Bellamy was nobody's fool. He understood women and he understood TV. He'd cracked it.

But nothing could top the sensational story of Eden's disappearance. The exclusive interview on Sky, the drama-doc, the film rights – all of them would be channelled through Tequila. For the first time in his life, Jack was going to be calling the shots. He wouldn't be just set-dressing any longer. He wasn't going to have to dance to Abi's tune. Jack was going to be The Man.

He turned right, heading for a gap in the Downs, away from Poynings. After a few minutes he parked outside an old-fashioned phone box. Getting out, he walked back to the telephone and fed coins into the machine.

There was no reply. It rang and rang. 'Come on,' said Jack, worried now. He looked at his watch. It should have already been on the news. Maybe something had gone wrong. 'Come on.' All the guy had to do was drive her out onto the hills and let her go somewhere near a road. How difficult was that?

*

The rutted farm track ran for a couple of miles before petering out. Half a mile further on, the lonely caravan was hidden by some trees. Ovoid, battered-looking, its white sides had been stained by years of bad weather. Both wheels were missing and the broken axle rusted in a puddle of muddy water underneath.

When he'd snatched her from the hills behind her home, her abductor had hit Eden across the head hard enough to knock her out. Now the concussion had worn off completely but the gnawing hunger had kicked in.

Eden was starving. She hadn't had anything to eat in two days. In the kitchenette of the caravan she had been handcuffed to the metal leg of the round Formica table. Her legs had been tied together with a length of electrical flex, a gag placed over her mouth to stop her crying out and a blindfold tied around her head to prevent her seeing him. And that was how she stayed, trussed up in this cramped space beneath the table where she couldn't even sit up straight. Every now and then she stretched out her legs but after all this time every limb in Eden's body ached.

At first, things had settled into a kind of rhythm. Her captor said nothing but he turned on the tinny transistor radio every hour, on the hour, to listen to the news. He took the radio into the living area of the caravan but she overheard the news, first local radio then – as the story began to grow and grow – a national channel. Adult and in control, Eden found the newsreaders' voices comforting: they kept her connected to the outside world, told her she was not forgotten. When she heard her mother's voice this afternoon, she stifled her sobs because she didn't want to stop him listening.

Afterwards, he left. Eden could feel the vibration in the

floor of the caravan as he paced about. Maybe, she thought, his conscience had been pricked by what he'd heard. Then she heard the door bang against the side of the caravan, making the whole thing shudder a little, and fresh air rushed into the stale interior. Eden heard his feet splashing through the muddy puddles outside, heading away from the caravan.

So far, he hadn't come back.

After half an hour or so, Eden worked up the courage to try and set herself free. The gag had been done up too tightly for her fingers to shift, but after half an hour or so of trying she succeeded in loosening the blindfold enough for her to see out of one eye. Without the radio, Eden found it impossible to say what time it was but night had fallen since he'd been gone. Underneath Eden, a foraging animal was rooting in the grass. She could hear it snuffling.

The door was still open and it was freezing cold inside the caravan. There was no water or electricity so it was only when a shaft of moonlight penetrated the grubby window somewhere above Eden's head that the key was suddenly illuminated. Eden sat up as best she could. It was a small key on a simple metal ring, right on the edge of the work unit next to the old sink. The key to Eden's handcuffs.

Eden inched forward on her bottom, getting as near to the other side of the kitchenette as possible. Her arms twisted behind her. The handcuffs dug even deeper into her wrists. When she was as close as she could go, she kicked out with her foot, her heel connecting with the door of the cupboard beneath the sink. On the counter above, the keys jumped a little but, if anything, they seemed to move in the wrong direction, away from the edge. Groaning with the pain from her wrists, Eden moved herself into position for another go. This time, when she kicked her right leg against the flimsy cupboard door, it broke on its hinge and fell onto the floor, its edge digging into Eden's shin, making her shriek with the pain.

Eden heard footsteps outside. He was coming back. He'd be angry with her for trying to escape. Sitting up, Eden's fingers scrabbled to put the blindfold back in place. She lay down on the floor, pretending to be asleep, hoping he wouldn't notice the damage to the kitchen.

Heavy footsteps shook the floor. They paused a few feet away from Eden then came into the kitchenette. 'Matt?' said a voice. It was Jack.

For some reason, he sounded angry.

Eden sat up once more and made as much noise as her gag would allow her. Jack came and crouched down on the floor beneath the table. Removing her blindfold, he loosened her gag as well.

As soon as it was off, Eden yelled, 'The key! It's over there!'

Jack stood up. His back turned to Eden, he hesitated to pick up the key from the counter. Outside, the wind rustled in the trees. Jack wondered how on earth he was going to explain to the police how he had known where it was Eden was being held. Impulsive. That was Jack all over. He'd come here to find out what had happened to that idiot of an accomplice but now he'd only made things ten times worse.

'Quick, Jack!' said Eden desperately. 'Before he comes back!'

Jack made up his mind about what he was going to do. Picking up the key he unlocked Eden's handcuffs. He lifted her bodily off the floor and put her on the banquette that went round one side of the little table. Maybe it was the sudden weight loss, but at that moment Eden seemed impossibly light. Like he could have snapped her in two if he wanted to.

Bending down, Eden tried to untie the electrical flex around her ankles but she was too weak. 'I can't do it,' she said. 'Help me, Jack.'

Jack sat down beside her on the vinyl banquette. In the moonlight, he examined the drawn features of Eden's face. Her cheeks were filthy from where she'd been lying on the floor and her hair was bedraggled. He felt almost tender towards her. But he didn't want to lose it all. Jack Bellamy wanted to be The Man. 'I'm sorry, Eden,' he said. 'You should have been at home with your mum by now. That's how I planned it.'

Something in Jack's voice alarmed Eden. 'What do you mean?'

'It's not my fault. He hasn't left me any choice.'

Suddenly, Eden remembered the name Jack had called out when he came into the caravan. It hadn't been her own name. *Matt*. 'You're scaring me, Jack.'

Jack put his hands around Eden's throat and squeezed.

'Jack, don't.'

He squeezed harder, his thumbs closing round her windpipe. 'Please,' Eden whispered, her eyes widening. Jack pressed harder with his thumbs, choking her. Eden's eyelids began to flutter. 'Don't.'

Suddenly, Jack heard his name being bellowed. 'Jack Bellamy!' it cried again. 'Armed police!'

Jack yanked Eden to her feet. Reaching into the pocket of his jeans he took out the flick knife and released its blade, dragging the half-conscious Eden out of the kitchenette and towards the door of the caravan, where he shoved the girl in front of him and brandished the blade, pressing it against the skin of her throat.

In answer, the dogs started barking and there was a shouted command to stand down.

The police helicopter had been diverted here from its search of the Downs. Its powerful beam of light blazed the sides of the caravan, turning everything around it white, blinding Jack Bellamy. The downdraught rippled the puddles at his feet as, squinting, Jack scanned the uniformed police surrounding the caravan, the dogs straining at their leashes, the guns pointing at his head. 'Back off or I'll kill her!' he shouted, holding Eden as a shield and taking a step forward.

A marksman's shot zipped through the air and thudded into Jack's neck.

Eden felt the first loop of his hot blood splash against her cheek. She screamed. A moment later, she felt Jack's arm releasing her neck and heard the knife clatter against the side of the caravan. Then she saw him falling face down in the mud.

Rushing forward from the semicircle of police officers, Vicky caught Eden in her arms.

PART FOUR

22

• • •

Oxford, September 1998

'It's Martin, isn't it?'

Martin Blackthorn looked up from the textbook he was reading.

'Professor John Deaver,' said the older man. 'Pleased to meet you at last.'

Martin sprang to his feet 'Sorry, Professor Deaver. I didn't recognise you.'

'I've been out of college for a while.' With his mop of frizzy hair and his grape-coloured corduroy trousers, he was every inch the dapper don. Deaver was in his early thirties but he had the super-confident air about him of someone who knows his time is now.

'I know,' said Martin, standing up. 'I read all the transcripts from your lectures at MIT.'

Deaver preened himself. 'I trust you enjoyed them. And what did *you* get up to in the summer?'

'I stayed in halls. I was working.'

The unhealthy pallor was an occupational hazard for a scientific researcher but there was something else about Blackthorn that made Deaver feel uncomfortable. 'All work and no play makes Jack a dull boy,' he joked. 'Although I hear you're running a little late in handing in your thesis.'

'I'm afraid so, sir.'

Deaver had returned from the States as head of department. 'I want to get as much work published this year as possible. I have a few contacts at *Nature* that I would like to share your work with.'

'I'm not sure it's ready for publication.'

Deaver dismissed his hesitation. 'No one ever thinks their work is ready. How about I come round to have a chat with you during reading week? We can talk about a proposal for the article.'

'I'd be honoured, sir.'

Deaver chuckled. 'You don't have to call me "sir". We're on the same big adventure, you and I.'

There had turned out to be only twenty-eight thousand genes in the human genome – a lot more than there were in a banana but a lot fewer than in a fruit fly. But if the building blocks of human life had turned out to be fewer in number than anyone had expected, their design was infinitely complex, infinitely arresting.

Shyly, Martin muttered his thanks to the professor.

'Reading week, then,' Deaver confirmed, turning away. 'I'll look forward to it.'

When Martin sat down again on the bench his heart was fluttering inside his chest. Deaver was his academic hero and *Nature* was the most prestigious of all the scientific magazines. He watched the professor walk towards the back of the college.

Above the honey-coloured stone of St John's, the dreaming spires of Oxford decorated the skyline, as they had for generations of ambitious young men. He could almost feel his years of dullness and obscurity begin to melt away. Doors would soon be opening for Martin Blackthorn.

Putting his book under his arm, Martin followed the professor jauntily into college, walking along the colonnade of the quad until he found the staircase in the north-west corner which led up to his study bedroom. Whistling, he bounded up the stairs two at a time. On the landing, he almost crashed in to a young woman.

'I'm sorry,' he said, moving to one side.

'Martin!' said Julie Foyle.

Martin Blackthorn had never worked up the courage to visit Julie as requested in her flat on the Cowley Road to talk about the Hox gene.

'I haven't seen you for ages,' Julie said, a little reproachfully. 'How was your holiday?'

'Good,' Martin mumbled. He saw how the strapless sundress Julie was wearing showed off a deep tan. 'Yours?'

Julie glanced along the hallway to where a study bedroom door opened and closed. 'We were in Majorca,' she said. 'Malcolm's family have a place there.'

A moment later, Malcolm himself appeared behind Julie. 'Just a little place in the north,' he explained to Martin, his hand coming to rest on Julie's suntanned shoulder. 'Nothing grand.'

'It didn't even have electricity,' Julie confirmed. 'And there was a well in the garden for water.'

With his straggly beard, Julie's boyfriend certainly looked the rugged type.

'We should go,' Malcolm said to Julie. 'Or there'll be a crush at the bar.'

She seemed to squirm beneath his touch, Martin noticed. Was it because of her sunburn?

Julie turned to Martin. 'What are you doing for lunch?'

'I've got work to do,' Martin said.

'But term's only just begun.'

'I've got an article to prepare,' he told her proudly.

'An article?' Recently, Julie had been neglecting her studies. 'Is it going to be published?'

'In *Nature*.'

'Wow!'

Martin nodded proudly. 'I've just been talking about it to Professor Deaver.'

'That's great!' Along with a little pang of envy, an idea struck Julie. 'We're going to the Randolph. Why don't you come with us? Then you can tell me about the article.'

Martin thought about what Professor Deaver had said about all work and no play. In all his time at St John's, he'd never once set foot inside the famous hotel just a few hundred yards along St Giles. 'I'll just get rid of this book,' he said, 'then I'll see you there.'

'Excellent,' Julie laughed, before following her grumpy boyfriend down the stairs.

Martin climbed another flight and reached his study bedroom on the top floor, fumbling with his key in the excitement. Inside, he put his textbook on an already overcrowded desk. Through the open window the cheerful sound of conversations drifted up towards him from the quad and, looking out, he saw Julie walking out of college, her glossy hair turned a couple of shades lighter by the Mediterranean sun. Leaving the room, Martin dashed along the corridor and hurried downstairs, stepping out of the low door and onto St Giles.

He stopped. There, standing outside college by a line of chained-up bicycles, was John Slade.

Martin hadn't seen him since that day on the Cherwell. The boy was older. His bony brow was now a promontory, a bluff from under which he stared out at the world around him with a deliberate, malevolent gaze.

'Hello, Martin,' said John.

Martin said, 'It's been a long time.'

'Two years,' said Slade, a note of accusation in his voice. 'Is this the university?'

'It's my college, yes.'

Slade peered up at the mullioned windows. 'Where you go to school.'

Over John's shoulder the elegant edifice of the Randolph Hotel beckoned Martin. 'Look, I'm late for a lunch. It's been really good to see you again.'

Martin turned to go but Slade waylaid him, grabbing him by the arm. His grip was steely. 'That hurts, John.'

'Two years,' said Slade, pulling him closer. From the look of him, life had not been kind to John Slade in the intervening period. If the stare he was giving Martin was anything to go by, he was holding Martin responsible.

Mortified by the thought that Professor Deaver, or worse, Julie Foyle, might see them together, Martin said, 'Please let go of me, John.'

But John was already steering Martin into the steady flow of students and tourists. 'Let's walk.'

They passed along the thoroughfare of St Giles and turned right into Beaumont Street, neither of them saying a word. It was hot and tiny beads of sweat prickled at Martin's scalp, making his hair stand on end a little.

They entered an Oxford Martin knew very little about. He'd never been to the multiplex cinema or visited the new shopping arcades, he'd never been among the crowds.

John hadn't forgotten the knack of finding wild places. He'd learned it from Martin. They crossed a railway bridge and turned down by some allotments between two small housing estates where the path skirted potting sheds and neat rows of cultivated vegetables.

'Where are we going?' Martin asked.

'You'll see.'

They emerged onto a scrubby piece of land, the straggly path vanishing behind some houses. Soon they'd arrived at a stream with a five-foot, brick-built bank on either side. John jumped down immediately, landing nimbly on the caked mud next to the thin current of water. He turned and looked up at Martin.

'What are you going to do?' Martin asked.

John didn't reply. He just kept staring at him.

Sitting down, Martin edged himself slowly off the bank, landing at Slade's feet.

'Come on,' said John.

The stream had been diverted through a concrete storm drain. It was cool out of the sun and as they walked along the tunnel their feet splashed in the water and they had to bend over to stop themselves banging their heads against the brick-work at the top. Martin heard the birdsong recede into the distance. Glancing back, he could see the bright circle of light shrinking at the end.

Suddenly, John stopped. He sat down, resting his back

against the concrete. For a moment, the only sound was the trickling of the water. 'I come here to think,' he said, his voice echoing in the tunnel.

Martin peered at Slade through the shadows, trying to gauge his mood.

'I think about you', said Slade. 'And I think about what we did together.'

Martin said, 'No one got hurt.'

John kicked some of the tiny pebbles lying in the water. 'I got hurt.'

Martin could see his old protégé wanted an explanation as to why, all those years ago, he had been chosen. 'You . . . interested me, John.'

Even then, in the final year of his undergraduate degree, Martin had known the name of the gene he wanted to devote his life to studying. In monkeys, the MAO was called the warrior gene. In some humans, a genetic variant negated the inhibitors – principally, dopamine and serotonin – that reined in people's natural tendency towards violence, resulting in a lack of inhibition. Given the right circumstances, it meant that the person became capable of doing anything.

But how could Martin explain the science to John, whose intellectual capacity was that of a pygmy? How could he account for the way he had created *the right circumstances.*

'What we did together was intended as a complement to what I was doing in the laboratory. You were a kind of experiment.'

In the darkness, Slade's eyes flashed.

'I was seeing how far you could go.'

Slade moved fast, picking up the biggest stone from the water at his feet. There was no way Martin could defend himself from the blow.

*

The distant sound of a jet engine.

Martin came round. He was still in the tunnel. Sitting up gingerly, he put his hand to the top of his head, exploring his crown until his fingers touched the open wound. His own flesh felt wet and soft and his fingertips disappeared a little into the contusion.

When he reached the entrance to the drain, he saw John sitting on the bank twenty feet away. His back was turned to Martin and he was holding something in his hands.

'You gave me quite a fright,' said Martin when he reached where John was sitting. It was a little injured bird that Slade was holding. It was a swallow, Martin saw, its face a shiny blue. Every now and then, its head swivelled but mostly it stayed still, trapped inside Slade's fist. The creature's odd passivity reminded Martin of the mouse in the basement room in Oxford Science Park, just as the expression on John Slade's face recalled the way he had looked that day when they first met. There'd been a kind of gentleness, almost innocence, about the boy.

Now, as then, John said, 'What do you want me to do?'

Martin smiled. 'You should do whatever you want to do.'

With an almost casual twist, John snapped the bird's neck. He opened his hand, letting the tiny body fall at Martin's feet.

23

• • •

Eden was home at last.

Abi raced downstairs to meet her in the hall. 'My baby!' she cried, hugging Eden tightly.

As soon as she saw her mother, Eden dissolved into tears. Resting her head against Abi's chest, she whispered, 'It was horrible!'

Abi had said so many prayers. In the course of these last two terrible days and nights, she had cursed herself so many times for leaving the little world behind, but now she had a second chance. Miraculously, it was here again, in her arms, safe. And it would never go away. She wouldn't let it.

'Let me look at you,' she said, standing back and reaching out her hands to hold Eden's gorgeous face. She moved her fingers down to touch the bandage on her daughter's neck. One by one, she lifted the girl's red-raw wrists and bent her head to kiss them.

'I'm OK, Mum,' said Eden who was still crying. 'I'm OK.'

Abi noticed Vicky Reynolds standing in the doorway behind her. It was an unwelcome reminder that this wasn't quite over.

Abi had already been warned that a court battle over custody of Eden was likely, especially if her biological mother had not been successful in her own IVF. But Abi wasn't scared. All the judges and the juries in the world couldn't take Eden away from her. Eden was her baby. And hers alone. She stroked her daughter's cheek. 'Let's run you a hot bath. That will make you feel better.'

'Jack's dead, isn't he?' Abi asked.

'I'm afraid so,' said Vicky.

They were downstairs, in the living room, waiting for Eden to finish in the bathroom.

Abi looked away. She had no tears to cry for Jack Bellamy. 'I wish I'd been there. I would have pulled the trigger myself.'

'We think Jack was working with an accomplice. A full search of the caravan and the surrounding area will commence at first light. Then we'll know more.'

But the technical details of the investigation had long ceased to interest Abi. Her daughter was home. That was all that mattered.

For a minute, the two women sat in uncomfortable silence. Abi glanced across at Vicky and said, 'Are you judging me now?'

'I don't know what you mean.'

'When I first met you, you said it wasn't your job to judge me. What about now?'

There was another silence. Vicky said, 'You're not the first woman to fall for a younger man.' Right now, however, she was more interested in Bellamy's motive. 'Tell me about Jack's company.'

'Tequila Productions?'

Vicky nodded. 'I've seen the books. It's highly profitable.'

'When Kitchen Sink first wanted to sign me up for the breakfast show, they sweetened the deal by offering to give me an exec producer credit on a new series they had in development.'

'So how did Jack get involved?'

'When he found out, he went on and on at me to give him the producer credit. In the end, I gave in. I thought it would be good for him to have something to do. That's when he set up Tequila. I didn't expect *House Swap* to become a hit. It's a piece of crap.'

'What exactly did Jack do at Tequila?'

'I'm not sure if anyone at Tequila did any actual work.'

Vicky decided that now was not the time to tell Abi about Debs Coglan. That could wait for another day. 'I spoke to your agent in London this afternoon,' she said instead. 'And I rang Tony Evans. Why didn't you tell me about the contract negotiations for the breakfast show?'

'Because it was none of your business.'

Vicky leaned forward. 'You should have been honest with me.'

'I couldn't afford for it to get out. OK? It would have been fatal.'

Vicky struggled hard to understand Abi's priorities. 'Fatal to what?'

'Look,' said Abi, 'in TV, most women are sacked long before they hit forty. That creep Evans was gunning for me and he'd use any trick in the book to get what he wanted. The morning Eden disappeared, I had three messages on my phone. Do you know who they were from?'

Vicky shook her head.

'One was the phone call from Jack, one was from your boss,

DCI Grant, and the last one was from a journalist from the *Sun*. The press had the story within an hour.'

Vicky persisted with her line of questioning. 'I still don't understand. Even if you lost your job on the breakfast show, Jack would have continued drawing a salary from Tequila. I've seen your joint bank statements. You were never going to go short.'

'It wasn't money Jack was interested in.'

'What was it, then?'

'Without the breakfast show my star would have faded fast. That was what Jack couldn't bear the thought of. He'd miss the premieres and the parties. He'd miss the VIP lounges in the night clubs. He'd even miss the paps. Jack couldn't go back to being a nobody. A no one. A loser.' Abi stood up. 'I'm going to check on Eden.'

As soon as Abi went upstairs, the doorbell rang. It was the sergeant from the gates. Eden was back safe and sound and the operation was winding down. 'I've told the lads they can go,' the sergeant said to Vicky on the doorstep.

Down the hillside, the lights in the houses of Rottingdean were going off one by one. Having watched the news about Eden's happy return, people were going to bed. Vicky shivered in the cold.

The sergeant took a pack of cigarettes out of his pocket and offered it to Vicky. When she declined, he took one out and lit it. 'I took a turn answering the phones up at Hollingbury,' he said, blowing smoke into the air. 'Bloody things never stopped.'

Vicky nodded. The total of calls from members of the public now exceeded four thousand.

'Some of the calls I took were abusive. About Ms Martin,

I mean. It was shocking the things they said.' He nodded at the mansion. 'She had it all, didn't she. I suppose they were just envious. Funny thing was, though, it was always women slagging her off.' He shook his head. 'Strange that. You staying long, ma'am?'

'I'll just check everything's all right in the house.'

'Okey-dokey. You look after yourself, ma'am.'

Smiling, Vicky watched the sergeant with the philosophical bent walk down the drive towards the gates, then she turned and went inside.

Upstairs, she knocked softly at the door to Abi's bedroom. When there wasn't a reply she stuck her head round.

The decor of the room gave Vicky the impression of snowy whiteness. In the middle of it all, lying fast asleep in the middle of the enormous bed, were Abi and Eden Martin.

In her fluffy dressing gown, Eden was curled up in her mother's arms, her hair still wet from the bath, her cheeks pink and healthy-looking. Exhausted, leaving the light blazing, Abi had fallen asleep next to her daughter wearing just her underwear. When Vicky walked into the room she was amazed by the narrowness of Abi's hips. She must have worked so hard to keep a figure like that at her age, Vicky thought. There were stretch marks on her tummy from where she'd been pregnant with her daughter – little silver fishes that disappeared beneath her knickers. There was no way Abi could hide those.

Gently Vicky covered Abi and Eden with the soft duvet. 'You can sleep now,' she whispered to both of them before turning away again. She switched off the light and closed the door behind herself.

Outside the gates nearly all of the paparazzi had gone and the handful that remained didn't even bother snapping Vicky's car as it drove out of the gates and set off down the hill. Only later, when Vicky thought about it carefully, did she recall the man in the parka loitering on the other side of the lane. It was only then that she could make the connection between this figure and the unfamiliar man in a parka that Abi had described lurking outside the TV studio in London

24

• • •

Micklefield, Yorkshire, November 2012

An hour earlier, and more than two hundred miles away, Minter was paying off his cab.

Feeling the bite of the northern wind, he hurried across the road and rang the doorbell of the darkened two-up two-down. He glanced at the terrace of identical miners' cottages, each one built of the same grey stone, their rooflines ascending the steep street to where the glowering profile of the hilltop had blocked out the sky at the top. Minter was about to try next door when a light went on in the room upstairs. A moment later he heard feet clattering down the uncarpeted stairs. The front door opened a crack and a woman's face – young, pale, slightly befuddled – appeared in the hands-width gap.

'Annie Russell?' Minter said.

Annie might look diminutive but she certainly had a tongue in her head. 'You fookin' woke me up.'

'I'm sorry,' Minter replied, showing her his warrant card.

'There's been some more murders, Annie. This time down in Brighton.'

Annie peered at the angry-looking stitches in Minter's chin – his souvenir from his earlier visit to the pier. 'I know,' she said. 'I read about it in the papers.'

It took a lot to frighten Annie Russell. At school she'd been a wild child. She never wore any make-up and she didn't care what the boys said about her. Even the teachers with the booming voices never intimidated her. Right now, it looked like Annie was about to slam the door in Minter's face.

'Please?' he asked. 'I've come a long way, Annie. And it's freezing out here.'

After a moment's consideration, Annie relented. 'You best come in.'

The door opened straight into the front room, where an open fire was trying to compensate for the lack of central heating. Annie sat in one of the two thrift shop chairs and indicated the other. 'Thanks,' said Minter, sitting down. Apart from the chairs, there wasn't a stick of furniture in the room.

'It took me a while to track you down,' Minter began.

'I wanted to move away from Leeds.'

'Have you got family here in Micklefield?'

'God, no. Mum and Dad washed their hands of me years ago.'

There was a feistiness about Annie that Minter liked. 'Good luck with the new start.'

For a moment all of Annie's watchfulness disappeared and a smile lit up her face. 'Ta very much.' She stood up quickly. 'Where's my manners? I'll get a brew on.'

When she went through to the back room, Minter noticed how awkwardly Annie walked. He assumed it was an injury left by one of the deep stab wounds inflicted on her by the Leeds killer. He also noticed the half-bottle of supermarket vodka by the side of Annie's chair. It was three-quarters empty, which explained why she had taken to her bed so early this evening. It seemed Annie had a lot that she wanted to forget.

Once they were sitting with their tea, Minter started on his questions.

The night it happened, Annie had scurried down an alleyway. She was wearing make-up then, lots of it, and her strappy high heels clopped loudly on the path. 'They'd already found the body of the first working girl,' she told Minter. 'I was frightened. I'm not bloody stupid. But I had to go out. I needed the money.'

Annie had taken up her usual pitch. After a few moments standing in the freezing cold, she sensed she wasn't alone. A sudden flare of panic lit up the butterflies in her tummy as she peered through the thick night to where someone was lurking in the shadows.

She breathed a sigh of relief. Her rival was a big, meaty girl with the kind of stance that indicated she wouldn't budge an inch. Sure enough, when a car came around the corner, the other girl didn't hesitate to troll to the edge of the pavement first, beating Annie to it. *'Bloody cheek!'* Annie muttered, watching her with beady, vengeful eyes. The woman was mutton dressed as lamb – way into her thirties, in spike-heeled, knee-length boots, her blonde hair piled high on top of her head. As the hatchback approached, Annie walked forward out of the shadows and both girls dangled themselves off the edge of the kerb. The driver prowled past Annie's scrawny, birdlike figure and came to a halt by the other girl. He wound his window down, taking a good look at the merchandise.

Annie watched her rival lean in through the open window, her fat arse stuck up in the air. There was a swift negotiation then the girl walked round to the other side of the car and climbed into the passenger seat. The car drew away from the pavement and was gone, its exhaust leaving a little vapour trail in the cold air. *'I hope he fookin' kills you,'* Annie said under her breath.

'Then another car came round the corner,' she told Minter.

'Do you remember anything about it? Make or model?'

Annie shook her head. She'd never been any good at cars. 'I remember the window had a winder, though, and it weren't electric. And when I got inside the air freshener smelt of marzipan.'

Minter waited for her to go on.

'He said he wanted full sex. I told him it was thirty. He said that was all right, so I got in.'

'Did he say anything else?'

'Not at first. He was excited, though. I could tell he was turned on.' Annie shuddered.

'Go on,' Minter encouraged her.

'He said he wanted to be inside. That set the alarm bells going. I told him I was feeling sick, that I didn't think I could go through with it, that I was sorry, he could keep the money and everything. That's when he got angry.'

'What did he do?'

'He stopped the car and smashed me in the face. Then he covered my mouth with a handkerchief. It made me retch.'

Minter had read the medical reports. Chloroform was what had made the car smell of marzipan.

'I kept falling asleep,' Annie went on. 'I knew I wasn't in the car any more. We were in some kind of building. I could hear a dripping pipe. He was taking off my bra and knickers. I could hear him laughing. Whooping. I tried to open my eyes but I couldn't. He had to slap me awake to get any kind of a response.' She started to cry. 'I tried to fight back.'

Annie Russell had been lucky. The Leeds police had swamped the red light district that night with undercover officers and one of them had spotted the vehicle's suspect registration plate. By the time the patrol car got to the derelict warehouse, the perp had gone but Annie was still alive. Just.

'I know that this is difficult,' said Minter. 'But can you remember anything else?'

Annie sniffed. She liked the sympathetic young police officer from Brighton. The seaside town far away on the south coast was somewhere she wanted to visit one day. 'It's a long time ago,' she said.

'I know. But please try, Annie.'

Annie didn't want another girl to die. Ever since she'd seen the story in the paper, she'd been racking her brains, trying to remember something she hadn't already told the police in Leeds. 'There is something.'

'What?'

'I kept hearing his voice. I mean, the gobshite, he kept talking to me all the time, telling me the things he was going to do, enjoying it, like. But sometimes there was another voice.' As if she was back at the terrible scene, Annie waved her hand at a space behind her head. 'He was somewhere behind me. I couldn't see him.' She shook her head. 'Mebbe I was just dreaming. Mebbe it were the drug. But they were different. The gobshite, he had a deep, growly voice. This one didn't.'

'What did he say?'

Annie shook her head. 'It were like he was telling the other one what to do.'

Within half an hour of leaving Annie's house, Minter was back at the station. On the train, sitting in the empty carriage, he made a start on the three overstuffed folders of archived case papers the Leeds SIO had given him.

Minter had started in plain clothes as an intelligence analyst. He was used to filleting paperwork – identifying inconsistencies, looking for connections, finding patterns. He had a curious mind and went about every task in the same methodical fashion. It was what made him good at his job. As the train rattled through the cloudy, starless night, he sank his mind into the case file, certain that the identity of both men was hidden there somewhere.

As the train passed through the Midlands, Minter thought again about what Annie Russell had told him. It made sense. The second man would know a lot about forensics and he would use his knowledge to ensure that no clues were left behind. He'd be extremely organised and intelligent and scientific in his manner. Nothing at all, Minter thought, glancing down at the open file on the table in front of him, like the man in the custody photograph who happened to be staring back at him. John Slade was his name. His oafish, blunted features gave Slade the appearance of an ape, not a scientist.

Minter looked up again. The train hurtled through a station too quickly for him to read the blurred name of the town on the sign. When he glanced at his own reflection in the dark rain-streaked glass, he saw how his face was crumpled and exhausted. Another hour or so, he estimated, before he reached London.

For the first time in days, Minter thought he might be able to sleep. Sleep was something he needed urgently to find, like an object he'd mislaid somewhere in his room and was now groping for in the dark. It wasn't just physical refreshment Minter craved. The knack of falling asleep would demonstrate something even more vital than that. It would mean he wasn't getting ill. Like his mother had been ill. So he rested his head against the pane and closed his eyes, listening to the rushing clickety-clack of the train upon the rails.

Then it happened. Minter slept. In the first dream, he was locked in the abandoned warehouse with Annie Russell and the two killers. He heard the animal-like whoops of delight then the other voice, calm and in control. Then the horrid sounds faded and Minter found himself running on the Downs.

Looking down, he noticed that the trail he was running on wasn't made of chalk but of broken shells. There were thousands of them. They crunched underfoot. He stopped running and bent down to take a closer look. The shells were the ones he had found in the pockets of Vincent Underhill's great-coat. Vincent was guiding his way.

With the odd, substitutive logic of a dream, the scene changed once more. Now Minter was a boy walking along a corridor in some kind of institution. A chill went through him. He didn't want to be here. He was filled with a presentiment that someone close to him was in mortal danger. Minter slowed as the corridor became dark and claustrophobic. Somewhere up ahead a fragile singing voice echoed along the tiled walls. A light appeared and he walked towards it.

It was an old-fashioned wooden telephone booth. Its louvre door was open and the courtesy light was on. The receiver dangled from its frayed wire and from it came the strains of an old dance tune. The singing lady entered the little pool of light. Her hair was white and wispy and she had two bright red spots of rouge on her cheeks. She raised her thin and bony arms to the shoulders of an imaginary partner and danced in slow-motion circles. 'Excuse me,' Minter asked her, feeling foolish. 'Can you help me? I'm lost.'

On the train, Minter woke up with a jolt. Straight away he knew it wasn't Vicky who was in danger. It was his mother.

It was Lucy. She needed him to rescue her.

Sitting up, Minter drained the last mouthful of cold coffee from the cup he'd bought at Leeds station. He looked out of the window at the endless lines of semi-detached houses and knew they had reached north London. It was gone midnight.

He turned his attention back to the batch of statements in front of him. John Slade had been one of seventy-nine regular visitors to the Leeds red light district who'd been interviewed and ruled out by the police in the early part of the investigation. The interviewing officer had appended a note saying that Slade had decent alibis and that his biog didn't match the profile given by the behavioural investigative adviser.

Minter shuffled through the contents of the last folder until he found the suspect profile. On the bottom was a scribbled signature that was difficult to read but the printed version underneath was unmistakable. It was Dr Lee McGuire.

The second man would have to know a lot about forensics. Minter remembered the two cases McGuire had pulled from his database – one from Glasgow and the other from Birmingham – neither of which had yielded anything of use. So why hadn't McGuire said anything about the Leeds case?

*

In his office, Beckett listened to Minter's suspicions on the telephone. This afternoon, he'd seen McGuire's solid silver pen lying on a desk in the MIR. When he found out that McGuire had taken to working in the room where all the confidential intel about the case was processed and discussed, Beckett had thrown a bit of a wobbly. But now was not the time to admonish his inexperienced DI on making such a simple error of judgement. 'I'll send a car to blue-light you from King's Cross,' he told Minter instead. 'McGuire's staying at the Thistle on the seafront. I'll meet you in the foyer in an hour.'

As Beckett hung up the phone he saw Kevin Phillips hovering at his door. 'You wanted to see me, boss?' he said.

'Yes, Kev. Come in.'

Phillips sighed 'Another late one.'

'What?' The whited-out windows made Beckett forget the time of day. 'Yeah, right. I've just been speaking to a mate of yours, Kevin.'

'Who's that, then?'

'A journalist.'

Phillips didn't say anything.

'Name of Keith Miller.' Getting up, Beckett walked over to where Phillips was standing in the middle of the room. 'Do you mind if I have a look at your phone?'

'I lost it a couple of days ago.'

'That's convenient. But it doesn't matter. Keith Miller told me who his informant was.'

So much for journalists protecting their sources, Phillips thought grimly.

'Why, Kevin?' Beckett asked.

'Why do you think?' Phillips said bitterly. 'I needed the money. We were going to lose the house.'

Beckett nodded. 'You're suspended on leave pending further investigations.' He held his hand out.

Phillips dug the wallet out of his jacket pocket, hesitating for a moment before slapping his warrant card down into Beckett's palm.

'I'm sorry, Kev.'

'Nah, you're welcome to it. I don't want to be doing this job until I'm sixty. I don't want to end up like you.'

Beckett shot him a warning look. 'I'm trying to do this the nice way. I could have had you arrested.'

Phillips could see exactly how this was going to play out. The fact that his career was over was just the start of it. He'd face a trial and be found guilty and the judge, wanting to make an example of him, would send him to prison. He'd wind up in Lewes jail along with all the other crims. Suddenly, Kevin Phillips felt like crying. 'What am I going to tell Fiona?'

'Tell her the truth.' No one had made Phillips take the money. But all the same, Beckett felt sorry for him. 'Go home to your wife, Kev. Tell her what's happened and ask her to stand by you. Go and see your kids.'

'Going somewhere, Dr McGuire?'

McGuire sat down on the end of the bed. He was still a little groggy from being woken by the police officers banging on his hotel door in the middle of the night. He ran his hand through his hair. 'What?'

Beckett indicated the open suitcase on the floor. 'You've been packing.'

'No,' said McGuire, bad-temperedly. 'I didn't bother to *un*pack. I travel a lot for work. Now, do you mind telling me what the hell this is about?'

Beckett nodded. 'You get around a lot.'

'Leeds, for example,' said Minter, handing McGuire the offender profile.

McGuire glanced at the report, seeing his name on the bottom. Puzzled, he looked up at Beckett. 'Am I missing something here?'

'The MO on that Leeds case is very similar to the Brighton murders, Dr McGuire. But for some reason it didn't come up on your database. Why not?'

McGuire read the text. 'Well,' he said, 'for a start, the perp didn't move the bodies after death.'

'He was very nearly apprehended in Leeds,' said Beckett. 'Maybe he's learned.'

'Or maybe there are two perps,' Minter said.

Looking from Minter to Beckett, McGuire shrugged. 'I don't know why this didn't come up on the database, to tell you the truth. Very occasionally, we get the data inputting wrong. The wrong thing gets flagged. There's rather a lot of cases.'

'That report has got your name on it,' Beckett said. 'Leeds was *your* case.'

'I told you, I'm a very busy man,' McGuire said, standing up and handing the profile back to Minter. 'My services are always in demand. Last year, for example, I was consulted on over thirty separate cases in eight different countries. I can't be expected to remember every one.' McGuire gestured dismissively to the piece of paper in Minter's hands. 'That Leeds case is very run-of-the-mill. Not like the case here in Brighton.

You know, I've already started writing up your victims for a paper I'm delivering next month in Arizona.'

'Run-of-the-mill?' Beckett said. He had heard enough. 'Where were you last Tuesday evening?'

'Did I hear you right, DCI Beckett? Are you asking me for an alibi?'

'Please answer the question, sir.'

Sighing, McGuire went over to the desk and picked up his smartphone and turned it on. 'You know,' he muttered darkly as he waited for the entry screen to appear, 'I've never been treated like this by any other force. I won't be in a hurry to come back to Sussex, I can promise you that.' A few prods of the keypad later, he said, 'I thought so. I was having dinner with a colleague.'

'Can you give me the number?' Minter asked.

'With pleasure.'

McGuire stroked a few more keys and offered the phone to Minter, who used it straight away.

'And what about Thursday?' Beckett asked. 'You left our meeting early. Where did you go?'

'As a matter of fact, I came back here to start the paper for Arizona.'

'Did anyone see you?'

'I had room service. Oh, and I couldn't sleep, so I watched a movie.'

Minter ended the call to McGuire's work colleague. He nodded at Beckett. The story checked out.

McGuire smiled at Beckett triumphantly. 'You know, the food in this hotel is really very good. If my memory serves me right, I think I had the steak.' He smiled. 'I'll put it on expenses.'

On their way out of the hotel, Minter checked the room service order and the pay-per-view account on McGuire's room and even chatted to the member of staff who'd taken up the steak Diane. There was no doubt about it. McGuire was in the clear.

'Sorry, sir,' said Minter as they walked back along the seafront to Beckett's car.

'Forget about it,' Beckett said, pulling up his collar to protect himself from the wind. 'It's not McGuire that worries me.'

Minter knew what Beckett meant. So far there'd been four bodies in four days. They were overdue for number five.

25

• • •

Oxford, October 1998

They'd had another row. Julie Foyle had stormed out of Malcolm's house. Now, ten minutes later, she was stomping along the quiet country lane a few miles outside Oxford. It was gone ten o'clock at night and when Julie reached the bus shelter she saw that there was no printed timetable. It was late October now and there was a chill in the air. Julie wrapped her coat around her and settled down to wait. A couple of minutes later she heard the sound of a car engine coming round the bend towards her. She was relieved that Malcolm had come looking for her. She hoped he was suitably abashed by the things he'd said to her earlier in the evening.

But it wasn't Malcolm's car. This one was old and it rattled – the kind of jalopy Oxford students used to get about. Going slowly now, the car passed Julie by then stopped, its engine idling.

Julie looked the other way, hoping to see the bus or Malcolm's car appear.

The car reversed until it was level with Julie and the man inside leaned across to wind down the window on the passenger's side. 'Julie?'

She bent towards the car. 'Is that you, Martin?'

'Do you need a lift?'

'Yes, I do, actually,' Julie said gratefully. 'Are you heading into Oxford?'

'Yes. You still on the Cowley Road?'

Julie opened the door. 'That's right.' She got inside the warm car. 'I haven't seen you around this term.'

The meeting between Martin Blackthorn and Professor Deaver hadn't gone well. Instead of setting up the PhD student with his contacts at *Nature* magazine, Deaver had banned Martin from even using the college labs.

'I've been busy,' Martin told Julie. 'How about you? How's it going with the Hox gene?'

Looking back, Julie realised how much of the term she'd wasted on her affair with Malcolm. 'It's not.'

'That's a shame. It's a fruitful area for research.' He glanced at her. 'Have you spoken to Professor Deaver?'

'I saw him once at the beginning of term. I had another appointment with him last month but he cancelled.'

Martin nodded.

There were steep hedgerows on both sides of the lane. 'Is this the way back to Oxford?'

'It's a short cut. How's Malcolm?'

'He passed his viva. He's working at a computer company now. They're very pleased with him.'

It didn't sound like Julie was. They drove in silence for a minute or more. Turning to Martin, she said, 'So where have you been tonight?'

'Just driving around. I was looking for someone.'

Julie laughed. 'Hope you found her.'

'I did.' He turned to her. 'You know, you should draw the curtains when you fuck at Malcolm's house.'

'Excuse me?'

'I was in the back garden.'

'Have you been spying on me Martin?' Julie asked, incredulously.

'I told you I was looking for someone. It was you, Julie. I watched you undress him.'

'You're frightening me now, Martin. I want you to stop the car. I can walk the rest of the way.'

'I saw the things you did together.'

'Stop the car!'

Martin almost stood on the brakes. He took the keys out of the ignition. 'We could have got on so well together, you and I. You would have been so good for me. It was in your power all along, Julie. You could have stopped this happening.'

The muscles of his face rippled as he struggled to control the beast within. His better nature – the affection he still felt for Julie, the dream he had of coming home to her at night – vied with his impulse to kill. 'Run,' he whispered. 'Run! Before I change my mind!'

Turning, Julie slipped her seat belt off and shoved the door open. Sprinting away, she glanced back once to make sure that Martin wasn't coming after her.

A figure loomed out at her from the hedgerow and a blade flashed in the moonlight. It nearly sliced her head off.

Martin watched it happen in his rear-view mirror as his pulse began to quicken. Getting out of the car, he walked over to where John Slade was kneeling over Julie's body, the knife rising and falling all the time.

Enthralled by the sound of Julie's death rattle, Martin looked down. All of his other dreams were coming true at once. John was the knife he couldn't wield himself, the weapon he could use to take vengeance on a world that, time and time again, insisted on humiliating him.

John Slade was Martin's better nature.

26

• • •

In normal circumstances, Vicky was proud of her flat. She'd used the small inheritance from her father to put down the deposit and so she was able to afford a respectable street in a good part of Hove. But when she got home from Abi Martin's house just after eleven it seemed ridiculously small. The flat regarded her with equal scorn. It was feeling neglected. There was a whiff of drains in the tiny passage, washing up in the kitchen and an overflowing clothes basket in the bedroom. Vicky sloughed off her creased jacket and unzipped her skirt – so much for the feminine mystique of the modern-day FLO – and left them in a pile on the floor.

She went through into the bathroom and turned the shower on. Vicky was looking forward to her day off. After that, it would be back to Kemptown and what she now thought of as her day job. She wondered if Minter would be coming back to the Serious and Organised Crime Unit, or if his secondment to CID was going to be made permanent.

Standing under the water, Vicky washed her hair and put conditioner on. At Kemptown, Minter and Vicky had been circling each other for over a year. Whenever Vicky came close to him, Minter would quickly back off. That was what he'd done the other morning when they had a coffee together. She'd come too close; he'd backed off. It was a dance they were performing. Well, she thought, stepping out of the shower, she wasn't going to chase him any more. Not if he didn't want her to.

She dried herself on a big towel. She knew that Minter liked her. She could tell by the way he sometimes grew a little tongue-tied in her presence and she could tell by the way he'd looked at her when they'd bumped into each other outside Sussex House. Vicky admired Minter for the way he did his job. There was no denying the little thrill she got when she had been told how Minter had jumped into the sea from the West Pier to save the life of some poor schizophrenic. Vicky had resisted the temptation to call Minter and congratulate him on his heroic deed.

Her house phone rang. Picking up her dressing gown from the back of the bathroom door and shrugging it on, Vicky hurried into the bedroom.

'Victoria,' said her mother. 'How are you?'

If she was honest, Vicky would have to say she was a little disappointed it wasn't Minter. 'I'm fine,' she said. Her mother never usually called this late. 'Are you all right?'

'I just saw on the news that Eden Martin is back at home.' Mrs Reynolds's voice sounded strained, like she'd been worrying about something. 'Your first job in Family Liaison worked out well. I'm pleased for you.'

Vicky's mum was the last person she would have expected to hear a compliment from. 'I took her back myself.'

'I don't suppose you can tell me who abducted her?'

Vicky had heard about Kevin Phillips, she'd learned her lesson about confidentiality. 'I'm afraid you're going to have to wait until the official statement.'

Mrs Reynolds's laugh sounded a little nervous. 'That's what your father always used to say.'

'It's really nice of you to ring, Mum.'

'You must be tired.'

'I am a bit.'

Her mother seemed to hesitate. 'I wanted to talk to you.'

'Really? About what?'

'About the thing you said the other day, when you came over. The question you asked.'

'You don't have to tell me, Mum. Not if you don't want to. It's none of my business.'

'There's no reason why you shouldn't know.' There was a pause. 'Your father could be a difficult man. It was his job, I suppose. It changed him.'

'Dad was a social drinker.'

'That's what he liked to tell people.'

Vicky remembered the study where her father used to spend so much time at the rectory. He said that he was working but he always emerged a little unsteady on his feet. She recalled, too, how her father had warned her not to marry a police officer. Now Vicky thought she knew why.

'He was never very communicative, even at the best of times,' said Mrs Reynolds. 'I suppose that's where I get it from.' She sighed deeply. 'Anyway, I should go. You must be exhausted after what went on tonight.'

Suddenly, Vicky didn't want her mother off the phone. 'I've got a day off tomorrow,' she told her mother. 'I can come and see you if you like.'

'I'm going out in the morning.'

'Where?'

'Just into Chichester.'

Vicky was intrigued by the air of mystery. 'Where in Chichester?'

'St Richard's.'

'St Richard's?' It was the local hospital. Suddenly, Vicky felt panicked. 'What for?'

'There's nothing to worry about. I've been getting dizzy spells, that's all. The doctor said my blood pressure is slightly raised so he's sent me to St Richard's to see the heart specialist. I told you, it's nothing to worry about.'

'I'll take you, Mum.'

'You don't need to bother.'

'No, I want to. What time's the appointment?'

'It's early.'

'Mum, I told you. I want to do this.'

'Well, it would be lovely. It's nine forty-five.'

Vicky committed the time to memory. 'I'll be there at quarter past.'

The doorbell rang.

'There's someone at the door.'

'At this time of night?' Mrs Reynolds said.

'I best answer,' said Vicky. 'It might be about work.'

There was another pause on the end of line. Her mother was very eloquent with her silences but for once Vicky didn't interpret it as a sign of her disapproval. Mrs Reynolds asked, 'Are you sure you'll be all right to give me a lift to the hospital tomorrow?'

'I'll be there, Mum. I'll see you at quarter past nine. And, Mum?'

'Yes?'

'Thanks for telling me about Dad.'

'That's all right, darling.'

Feeling buoyed by her breakthrough with her mum, Vicky put the phone down and did the belt up on her dressing gown and went through the lounge into the little hallway, leaving the door open behind her. 'Who is it?' she called out.

'It's Keith Miller,' said a voice. 'I'm a journalist.'

Vicky was going to enjoy giving Miller of the *Mail* a piece of her mind. His tittle-tattle had earned Vicky a slap from Abi Martin and his bribery had lost Kevin Phillips his job. 'You've got a nerve turning up here,' she said, yanking open the front door.

But it wasn't a journalist on the doorstep.

Martin Blackthorn shoved the sopping handkerchief over Vicky's mouth. Vicky smelt the reek of almonds and felt the stinging on her lips and the clutch of chloroform down her throat. Stepping inside, Blackthorn pushed her back against the side wall.

Vicky went to knee him in the groin but he was alive to that and bent his body out of the way. Putting the other hand behind her head, Blackthorn held her still. He was wiry but surprisingly strong and Vicky could feel the bonds of consciousness that tied her body to her brain begin to loosen. Terrified, she recalled what Minter had told her a couple of days ago when she'd asked him about the dismembered corpse in the suitcase. *Worse,* she heard him saying.

With whatever strength she had left, Vicky slammed her body into Blackthorn, pushing him away from her. Winded, he fell back against the other wall. Vicky tried to run out of the front door but he reached across and slammed it shut, the wooden edge cracking into Vicky's cheek and bouncing back. She cried out and Blackthorn grabbed her by her long hair. Vicky crashed to the floor. Leaning across her, Blackthorn slammed the door shut so he wouldn't be interrupted.

Vicky's heart was yammering now. Trying to get away from him, she skittered on her bottom back into the galley kitchen. Using the units, she dragged herself to her feet, her hand scrabbling behind her on the counter for a weapon of some kind, her gaze transfixed on Blackthorn as he lurched towards her.

Blackthorn grabbed the chromium toaster and smashed it against the side of Vicky's face. Looking up, the last thing she saw before she passed out were the dark pools of Martin Blackthorn's eyes staring back at her.

As soon as Abi woke up she knew that someone was in the house. Her first thought was that it was Jack, come back to get her. But the police had shot Jack in the neck. He wasn't coming back. Not in this life.

In the darkness of the bedroom, she could hear Eden's steady, rhythmic breathing. She seemed untroubled by bad dreams and Abi hoped it was so. In the bed, Abi shifted her body until it enfolded Eden. She wanted just to stay here. She closed her eyes.

There it was again. The noise. A padding. Downstairs.

Careful not to wake Eden, Abi got out of bed. She went into the hallway, which was lit by just the Tracey Emin neon piece, the words *Those Who Suffer Love* burning on the wall in glowing orange neon. Standing there, Abi had a dim memory of Vicky Reynolds wishing her goodnight.

All the police officers had gone. The house was deserted. The noise came once more, and louder this time.

Abi hurried back into the bedroom and shook Eden awake.

Groaning, Eden blinked her eyes open.

'I want you to go into the bathroom,' Abi whispered urgently.

'What?' said Eden groggily.

Abi tried to keep her voice calm. 'There's a burglar in the house.'

Eden sat up.

The sudden fear streaming off her daughter's body made Abi feel braver. Making light of the intruder, she smiled. 'Don't worry. I'll see him off the premises.'

Eden nodded. 'OK.'

Abi helped her out of bed and ushered her into the bathroom. Turning on the light, she said, 'I want you to hide. No matter what happens, stay here. Don't come out until I say it's safe. Do you understand? And lock the door behind me.'

Eden put her hand out to stop the door from closing. 'Be careful, Mum.'

'I will. I promise.' Standing outside the door, Abi listened for the sound of the bolt being drawn across.

On the upstairs landing, Abi turned on all the lights and stood still. There was no sound at all now. On her tiptoes she hurried into the home gym at the far end of the hall. Abi found Jack's nunchaku on the floor. She felt the weight of the wooden martial art flails. They were both a foot long and joined at the top by a short metal chain. Her heart started to race as she went back into the hallway and crept down the stairs.

Behind the door of the living room, John Slade listened to her approaching footsteps.

Abi pushed open the door and reached along the wall with her hand to turn on the light. When the room was illuminated, she stepped inside. She turned around just in time to see the blade coming towards her. Instinctively, she raised a hand, deflecting the knife thrust at the last possible moment. She screamed in pain as the blade went straight through her palm, twisting and severing the tendons.

Abi staggered backwards into the coffee table. As she fell onto the floor, Slade came towards her, his knife raised once again. Scrabbling to her feet, she left a bloody handprint on the sofa. The blade missed her face by inches as she ran towards the conservatory door.

Tripping up the steps, Abi sprawled across the marble. Slade was upon her in an instant, flipping her over with his giant hands like some kind of toy. He straddled her, pinning both arms down by her side with his knees. 'Where is she?' he growled. 'Where's the girl?'

Abi stared up into Slade's maniacal face. He wasn't here to rob the house. He was here because he wanted to kill Eden. He'd come for her. Frantic, Abi opened her mouth and screamed for help.

Upstairs, her ear pressed tightly against the bathroom door, Eden heard her mother scream. Trembling, her fingers closed around the barrel of the lock on the bathroom door. But her mother had told her to stay here, no matter what.

Slade smashed his fist into Abi's face. Covering her mouth with one hand, he used the other to slash at her chest with the knife. 'Where is she?'

Moving her head, Abi sank her teeth deep into the side of Slade's hand. But the pain only gave more of an adrenaline edge to the excitement he was feeling, to the anticipation of the kill. 'One more chance.'

Her eyes wide with terror, Abi shook her head. The whole house went quiet.

Eden flung the bathroom door open. 'Mum!' she shouted, running through the bedroom and out into the hallway.

Brandishing the bloody knife, Slade was already bounding up the stairs to meet her.

Screaming, Eden ran back into her mother's room and plunged into the bathroom. Her fingers fumbled with the lock but the door slammed back against its hinges – Slade was inside. Retreating, Eden put her hand out behind her until her fingers brushed against the rough-hewn concrete of the far wall. Slowly, the knife dripping blood onto the blocks of marble, Slade paced towards her.

Shaking all over, Eden got down on the floor.

Standing over her, Slade leaned in close and stared intently at the features of Eden's face. 'Yes,' he said in a low voice, a smile playing on his lips, 'I can see why he picked you out.'

Eden closed her eyes. Whatever was going to happen, she thought, please let it happen fast.

There was a crunching sound.

The giant figure of Slade tottered then crashed onto the bathroom floor. Now it was Abi standing there in front of Eden. She was covered in blood – a gaping wound in her hand, another in her shoulder – but she was alive.

Eden jumped to her feet.

Letting the nunchaku fall clattering to the floor, Abi put her good arm round her daughter and pulled her close, kissing the top of Eden's head.

'Is it over now?' Eden said. 'Really over?'

27

• • •

Vicky's mind surfaced temporarily from the depths of strange hallucinations. She thought she was in a hospital. It was the smell. Chemicals, medicines, and something else. Something sweeter – the smell of illness and physical decay. From very far away, she heard someone whistle and the clink of glass.

The next time Vicky woke she found that she could open her eyes, although at first the images were fuzzy. She felt a little nauseous in her stomach.

On the other side of the room the man who had snatched her from her flat had his back turned to her. To his side were the glass specimen jars she had heard him moving about earlier on. They were lined up neatly on the bench in ascending order of size. Vicky tried to speak but she couldn't.

Photographs had been montaged on the wall behind the bench. There were hundreds of them. Vicky looked more closely and saw that the biggest ones, the ones around which all the others had been clustered, were a series of images, each one a different teenage girl in school uniform.

They were pictured singly as they got on or off a bus, and sometimes walking down the street in pairs or threes. There was a close-up of two of the girls laughing, sharing a joke as they walked home. Someone had been following them and, from the hemlines and the haircuts, Vicky gathered that the pictures had been taken some years ago. She recognised the fashions immediately because the same styles had been around when she was growing up. Her mother would have called them tarty.

Suddenly, she drew in her breath. Around one of the old photos of the uniformed schoolgirls there were photographs of Eden Martin. Vicky looked from one to the other. The two girls looked identical. They had the same long, blond hair, the same oval face, the same widely spaced eyes. They could have been sisters.

Vicky's head was throbbing. When she rested it she realised that she wasn't lying on a hospital bed. She saw the guttering on the edges of the metal table that led towards a hole where her blood was meant to drain away. She was lying on an autopsy table. When Vicky tried to get off it, she found she couldn't move a muscle. She saw the drip stand by the zinc table and the line that led down into a cannula taped to the back of her hand. The line had been attached inexpertly: the skin around the tape had been irritated by what she now understood to be some kind of anaesthetic.

The man moved along the bench to get something and she saw the colour photographs of the last schoolgirl. There was an arrogance about the way she carried herself that told Vicky this was the leader of the little group. With her long, dark hair and voluptuous figure, she looked a lot older than her school uniform implied. She was the kind of girl who could turn a boy's head and, physically at least, she looked exactly like Vicky Reynolds.

The man turned round. Vicky recognised the dark, short hair, the intense, myopic stare. 'You're awake,' he said, approaching the table where she was paralysed. He pulled the IV line out of the cannula so that he could get at her. Leaning over, he started undoing the buttons on her blouse He had dressed her before taking her from the flat. She opened her mouth but no words came out, just a moan of protest. 'You've changed a lot since those photographs were taken,' he said. 'Your body is not so youthful.' He pulled the deadweight of her body towards him and slid the blouse out from underneath her. Breathing heavily, he bent over her again to unclasp her bra. Noticing the panic in her eyes, he said, 'Try not to be afraid. You can trust me.' He smiled. 'I'm a doctor.'

Vicky felt his clammy hands on her body. She looked away, towards the other pictures on the wall. One of the schoolgirls was black, like the first Brighton murder victim had been. Another had ginger hair and freckles. Vicky wanted to tell him that she wasn't the girl in the last photograph. That, whatever the girl had done to him, it had nothing to do with her. But another, more intuitive part of her knew that it was pointless.

His fingers trembling a little, Blackthorn unzipped Vicky's skirt and pulled it down, slipping it off with a flourish. 'But you are still very beautiful,' he said softly, taking her knickers off. 'You're blushing,' he added, apparently delighted. As soon as he said it, Vicky became aware of how her face was reddening and the blush creeping down her throat.

'Look at you now,' he said. 'You know you're about to die. You even have some idea of the pain you are going to suffer. But right now it's not the signs of fear you are exhibiting. It's shame.' He ran his hands over Vicky's body, moving from her breasts to her thighs. 'Shame is such a strong emotion. I was so ashamed of my background at Oxford. I've always been ashamed of my desires.'

Going back to the bench, Blackthorn started preparing things, taking metal instruments one by one out of a drawer and arranging them on a trolley, which he wheeled back over to the table so Vicky could see the instruments of her torture – the gleaming knives, the saws, the cleavers, even the drill with its bright circular cutting tool. He went round to the other side of the bed and attached the line to Vicky's cannula again, adjusting a dial on the drip as he did so.

Blackthorn rested his hands on the side of the table. 'Darwin described the symptoms of shame many years ago,' he mused, stroking Vicky's cheek with the backs of his fingers. 'The warmth stems from the dilation of blood vessels here. There are a lot of capillaries, you see, just beneath your facial skin.' He looked puzzled. 'The psycho-biological reasons for blushing are not so well understood. Most people believe it originates in the "fight or flight" mechanism.' He thought of Julie Foyle for a moment and her interest in the atavism of the Hox gene. 'It's a kind of throwback. Part of our more primitive nature.'

Blackthorn went back over to the bench, where photographs of the victims' bodies had been insinuated into the collage. It had taken him a little while to find his stride, to claim the women's bodies as rightfully his instead of letting John Slade take all the spoils, the way he'd done in Leeds. Now he studied the close-up of the face of the third victim, which he'd held to the flame of the blowtorch. The flesh was red and blistered and blackened in places. John Slade lacked Blackthorn's sense of artistry. He lacked subtlety. 'As a young man,' Blackthorn said aloud, 'I used to blush a lot.' He tapped the photograph of the body they'd left hanging in the abandoned cement works, the one he was especially proud of. 'Slackness of posture,' he said. 'That was another symptom Darwin described. I suppose we have the same idea when we use the aphorism "hang your head in shame".' He shrugged. 'But then, who am I to argue with such a famous man of science.'

He came over to the bed. Vicky was going to be his finest hour. Vicky would surpass all the others. 'There's an important difference between shame and guilt,' he said, picking up a scalpel from the trolley. 'I've never felt any sense of guilt. But my life has always been hampered by a debilitating sense of shame. It's taken me so long to get rid of it.'

'Which way?' Minter asked.

In the passenger seat, Vincent Underhill's bulk made the car seem small. His face was still clean-shaven. To look at him, there was nothing about the vagrant that would have alarmed anybody. 'That way,' he said, pointing with a wavering index finger.

In the maze of obscure lanes that spiderwebbed this isolated part of the Downs, they had come to a T-junction. Minter tapped the steering wheel. They'd been down this lane before. 'Are you sure?'

'No,' said Underhill, changing his mind and pointing with his finger to the left. 'There.'

Minter turned the wheel and the car climbed higher on the Downs.

Like the morning sun spreading over the hills, the gradual return of Vincent Underhill's sanity was beginning to reveal hitherto unseen objects. His description of John Slade had been correct in every detail. On the Downs, the lane came to another fork. 'Which way?' Minter asked, trying to keep his voice calm.

Slade had not been working alone, Minter was sure of that. There'd been two men involved in the Brighton murders – one to commit the acts themselves, one to direct and to clean up afterwards. It was this second perp, the more clinical one, the sinister, controlling voice Annie Russell had remembered, who was holding Vicky captive.

'That way,' said Underhill. This time, he seemed more definite.

At the top of the rise, the tarmac gave out and the lane became a farm track. They bumped along for a few minutes or so then, just as Minter was about to give up, Vincent cried, 'Stop!'

Before the car was even stationary the vagrant had opened the door. Minter took the keys out of the ignition and got out too. He glanced around. He thought he had run every inch of the hills behind his adopted city but even he had never been to this exposed and lonely spot before.

This high up, the blustery wind never stopped. It had bent the handful of stunted trees into odd shapes. Apart from these, the only vegetation was the tufts of sturdy grasses. Crossing the open ground Vincent started to look sure-footed, even nimble. Having spent so many years traversing this country, Highdown had become Vincent's natural habitat. Minter set off after him.

It wasn't long before Vincent had found a farm track leading to the summit of another hill. Minter ran up the path, his feet crunching on the chalk. Standing side by side at the top, the two men stared down into a little valley where, hidden in a corner where the landscape dipped and folded to the bottom, miles away from any road, there was a house.

'Is that it?' Minter asked. 'Is that the place Slade showed you?'

Vincent's expression was full of dread. He hesitated, suddenly unsure whether what had been lodged in one of the deeper recesses of his tainted mind was real or the product of his own weird invention. 'Yes,' he said. 'That's where He lives.'

28

• • •

Vicky woke up.

The anaesthetic was wearing off and the searing pain had started. Looking down, she whimpered.

Below the knees, the skin on both of her legs had been delicately peeled away and rolled down towards her feet. It was gathered there like stockings, its transparency rendered solid in the places where tiny gobbets of her body fat had come away with it. In the fierce glare of the overhead light he had worked by, Vicky saw the glistening red flesh of her legs.

Trembling all over, she tried to swallow her terror. *Stay alive,* she told herself. Her pulse banged in her brain and her nose sucked up little pieces of air. He would keep her alive. He would extend this period of cosseting, of play, for as long as he was able, inflicting ever more grosser pain as he took his fill of twisted pleasure until either he was satiated or Vicky was dead.

Think, Vicky told herself, trying to assemble her wits. From the information her senses could gather she forged an impression of her environment. Beneath all the chemical smells, a natural scent penetrated the bare brickwork of the room where she was being held. The loamy smell told her she was underground, in a large cellar of some kind. She tried to move her flayed legs but whatever he had mixed in the anaesthetic was still rendering her entire body immobile. She couldn't even clench her fists and when she opened her mouth to cry for help her swollen tongue didn't move. She listened. There was no sound at all. No swish of a car on a distant road, no muffled conversation – nothing that might signify life going on somewhere nearby, something that might offer her the promise of rescue. Helpless, paralysed, she was alone and at his mercy.

Footsteps moved across the ceiling and down the wooden stairs and a moment later he appeared in the corner of Vicky's vision. When he leaned over her she could see that a film of perspiration had appeared above his thin lips. 'We have to hurry things along,' he said, looking longingly at Vicky's naked body. 'I had wanted to do this properly but it seems our time together is going to be limited.' He stood up and walked over to the bench, where his implements were waiting. 'Still,' he said, picking up the scalpel. 'It's the face I'm most interested in.' Coming back to the autopsy table, he reached across to adjust the dial on the dripfeed. A moment later, Vicky felt the wooziness spread throughout her body. She saw the scalpel coming towards her. 'When I'm finished,' Blackthorn said, 'you'll be blushing all the time.'

It took Minter and Vincent Underhill a good ten minutes to scramble down the steep hillside. The house in front of them was a small Sussex barn conversion, brick-built near the ground with tarred timber sides. Walking up to the front door, he peered through the glass panels that ran from ground level right up to the roofline. A spiral staircase led up through the centre to the first floor but the house itself looked abandoned, the interior utterly devoid of furniture or decor. When Minter tried the front door he found that it was open. Turning away, he walked back towards where Vincent was standing, staring at the house as if he was expecting something terrible to burst out of it any moment. Minter took out his mobile and gave the police dispatcher his location, asking for a couple of cars to be sent straight away. Ending the call he looked at Vincent. 'Did you ever go inside?'

Underhill shook his head.

Minter could see that he was terrified. 'Stay here,' he said, turning back to the house.

Just inside the entrance, there was a door to the right. Minter opened it to find a windowless room dimly illuminated by a couple of low-wattage, red safety bulbs. The first thing he noticed were the plastic vials held in a metal clamp on the workbench that ran down the middle of the room. The liquid inside the vials glowed phosphorescent orange. Minter walked over. In the eerie light, he stared down into the shallow tank on the workbench next to the vials. It had been filled with a sticky-looking gel. As his eyes grew accustomed to the dark, Minter spied the pink strands set into the gel, like tiny shreds of fruit peel in marmalade. Some of the filaments were closer to the bottom of the tank. He had visited enough police labs to know that this was where strands of DNA were chopped and sorted for analysis.

Minter looked around. Along the wall was a tall rack of metal shelving on which had been placed various pieces of scientific equipment, including some gas canisters.

Squatting, he opened one of the cupboards under the workbench. It contained more items of equipment and, at the very back, some specimen jars. He reached inside and took one of them out. It was cylindrical, about six inches tall, the base fitting easily into the palm of his hand. Minter took a mag torch out of the breast pocket of his jacket and turned its beam against the side of the jar. Gleaming in the white light, something floated in the ethanol. It was no bigger than half of Minter's smallest fingernail and shaped like a comma with a bulbous end and four budding limbs.

Hearing a noise, Minter turned off his flashlight. It was a woman's voice, low and moaning, as if she'd only just woken up. Then suddenly it rose to an ear-splitting scream. He ran over to the door at the far side of the lab. Pushing it open, he tensed, readying himself for whatever he would find.

This room was smaller than the first but windowless again, with a strange smell about it and a sofa facing a screen on the wall. The only light source in the room was the data projector streaming images from a plinth behind the sofa.

On the screen, Minter saw an enormous close-up of Mercy Mvule's face. She had a short Afro and a large, flat nose and her wide, terrified eyes were fixed on something just outside the shot. Another scream broke from her lips then the camera started pulling out. Mercy was lying on a stained and rotten mattress, her hands cuffed to the metal frame of the bed, her mouth crammed with a rag. John Slade knelt beside her, a huge hunting knife held in his fist. As Minter watched, appalled, the camera panned down Mercy's body, coming to rest on her naked groin. Her thighs were covered with cuts and scratches and there were two deep wounds, one on each leg, that were pouring blood. Slade raised the knife into the air. A moment later, he was making excited little yelps and Minter had to look away.

His eyes fell on something on the floor at the end of the sofa. He moved forward and bent down, pushing aside the edges of a plastic bag with his hands and shining his torch inside. It was a severed head. Mercy's face was just as it had appeared on the screen – the Afro, the regally wide cheekbones – but her features had been twisted and stilled into a wordless scream of horror.

'Do you like it?' said a voice.

Minter stood up quickly, putting his hand up to shield his eyes from the fierce torchlight the other man was shining in his face.

He was a good few inches shorter than Minter but he exuded the kind of charisma that only a man carrying a gun could do. He stepped a little closer. 'Who are you?'

'Detective Inspector Minter.'

Martin Blackthorn nodded. 'You got here very quickly.'

The horrid imagery of Mercy Mvule's dismemberment flowed over the side of Blackthorn's face. On the soundtrack, Minter heard another voice, one that originated from behind the camera. Excited, it directed Slade what to do next. *'Hack her head off with the knife,'* it said. *'I want to see you remove her head.'*

Minter recognised the voice of the man standing right in front of him. 'Turn that thing off,' he said.

Blackthorn glanced admiringly at what was happening on the screen. 'We are all creatures of impulse,' he said, looking back at Minter, amused at the expression of disgust on the police officer's face. Nonetheless, he picked up a remote control from the plinth and used it to turn on the overhead light before switching off the projector. After a couple of seconds the whirring noise of the fan ceased.

'What about you?' Minter asked, seeing from the way Blackthorn was holding the gun that he wasn't used to firearms. 'Are you a creature of impulse?'

'I'm a scientist, not a murderer.'

'As a scientist,' Minter asked, 'what was your interest in John Slade?'

'Most people have a so-called good side to their personalities – some light to balance the darkness. I know that's true of me and I'm sure it's true of you, Detective Inspector Minter. But John was different. Even as a child, he was entirely made up of baser nature. In him, it was unalloyed. He had a purity that was remarkable.'

'And you nurtured his talent,' Minter said. He had seen the school reports about John Slade. Something had happened to him between the ages of ten and thirteen that had changed John Slade for ever.

'Yes,' said Blackthorn. 'I taught him everything he needed to know.'

'Which of you killed the women in Leeds?'

'The whores were all John's work.'

'How many?'

'More than you know about.'

'And what about in Brighton?'

'We took turns.'

'Who chose them?'

'I did,' said Blackthorn proudly.

'And how does Vincent Underhill fit into all this?'

Blackthorn sighed. 'When I found John again in Leeds, I convinced him he was on the verge of being caught. I told him that if he wanted to carry on taking his pleasure from the dregs of society he needed to be a lot more careful. He needed to follow my instructions, do what I told him. At first he was delighted, but eventually he became disgruntled with his lot. He hated being told what to do. When we got down here he met that fool Underhill. John thought he'd found an acolyte of his own, someone who believed he was superhuman. John wanted to dominate Underhill just as I had come to dominate him. John had become my creature.' Blackthorn smiled. 'I suppose you could say that Underhill was the creature's creature.'

'Where's Vicky Reynolds?'

'She's dead,' said Blackthorn, aiming the gun at Minter's head. 'Like you.'

When Minter came round he got up too quickly. He staggered, almost falling over the leather sofa. Regaining his balance he put his hand up to his head where he felt the sticky blood leaking from the flesh wound. He'd been right about Blackthorn's lack of experience with a firearm. Even from close range he hadn't managed anything more than a graze.

Finding the trapdoor in the floor where Blackthorn had got into the room, Minter clattered down the stairs and ran over to the metal table where Vicky was still lying. He winced.

Minter had interrupted Blackthorn before he could get further than a single strip of skin peeled back from below Vicky's right eye to the corner of her cheekbone. But that was bad enough. He tried to shake her awake. 'Vicky! It's me! Minter!' He pulled her eyelids open and saw that she was unconscious. But she was still breathing. She was still alive.

Minter yanked the cannula out of Vicky's hand and lifted her off the table. With her held tightly in his arms, he climbed the stairs and went through the room with the projector. It was as he reached out a hand to open the door to the lab that the explosion happened.

The force knocked Minter off his feet, spilling Vicky from his arms. Minter looked through the half-open door into the laboratory, where, fed by the canisters of gas, the fire had already caught. A series of smaller explosions tore through the cupboards and the shelving where chemicals had been stored, cracking the glass jars and setting new fires that soon leapt high into the air. Minter could feel the heat on his face. There'd be no fireman to rescue him now, he thought, looking across the room at the walls of flames that barred his way. And for Minter and for Vicky, there was no other way out.

He took off his jacket and draped it over Vicky to protect her. Then, picking her up again and hunching his shoulders, he ran into the burning room.

Minter leapt through the first sheet of flame, almost stumbling into a puddle of fizzing chemicals on the other side. Straightening, he could feel the sudden heat on his back and he knew he was on fire. In his mind's eye he saw himself stumbling to the floor, the funnelling fire dragging him down, his body folding over Vicky's as he succumbed.

The pain was unbearable now but Minter wouldn't give up like that. He kept going, pushing himself through the second sheet of flame and making the door that led out of the lab. His hair ablaze, Minter rushed through the living room and pushed open the front door. He fell to his knees, relinquishing Vicky before rolling over and over in the puddles outside.

At last, the fire was out. Minter came to rest on his back. He was in agony. Smoke rose from his clothes, and a hissing noise came from his blistered skin. Helpless, he saw Martin

Blackthorn walking towards him, the gun still held in his hand. Minter reached a hand out but the nerve endings in his arm were burned down to the bone. Bending down, Blackthorn pressed the muzzle against Minter's temple. This time, there was no way he could miss. The only thing Minter could do was to close his eyes.

29

When Minter dared to open his eyes again, Blackthorn was riding the sky and the gun was lying next to him in the mud. Underhill was carrying Blackthorn into the burning house.

It was all ablaze now, the fire poking through the roof. The glass at the front cracked and exploded, showering the huge figure with shards. A big piece lodged in Martin Blackthorn's chest. He screamed. Vincent's enormous figure was framed by the burning timbers of the entrance. Half-turning, he glanced back at Minter.

'Vincent!' Minter cried, forcing himself to his feet. 'Don't!'

But Vincent turned and walked forward again, taking both of them into the depths of the inferno.

PART FIVE

30

Four weeks later

Like the shoulders of giants, Minter thought, glancing up at the Downs from the road that ran parallel to the foot of the hills. It was nearly Christmas now, a cold morning but a clear one, the December sky above the hills a luminous pale blue.

It was the first time Minter had been out of the city since Blackthorn and Vincent Underhill had been killed in the fire. He was driving rather than running because his injuries had not yet healed sufficiently for him to resume training. Looking up at the hill of the North Downs, he glimpsed the white sail of a windmill that had been the residence of a composer before the Second World War. There was something of the autodidact about Minter. Largely self-educated, he had read widely so he knew the stories of all the musicians, writers and painters who shared his enduring love for Downland.

After a few more minutes' driving, Minter parked in a layby and carried on by foot. He found the bridle path that led up the side of the steep incline, where a Victorian water tower peeped dimly through the tree tops. He climbed some more, passing through the woods and the sign that someone had left behind directing him to *The Hospital*. Within a couple of minutes he came to the end of the overgrown path and stood before the main entrance.

Sticking up from the middle of the red-brick main building of Broke Hall Asylum was a clock tower and a cupola with a circular balcony running around it from which the entire hospital and grounds might be observed by the superintendent. Below this, the numerals *1882*, the date of the hospital's foundation, had been traced out in white tiles. A large portion had been gutted by fire and vandalism, and all that remained of the west wing was its brick façade, in which pieces of empty sky were framed by windows.

Walking along, Minter found a door that led directly into a six-bedded ward. Inside, the net curtains hanging from the sash windows billowed in the breeze that played through the smashed panes of glass. Years of rainwater had done a lot of damage to the interior of the room. The plaster was flaked and rotted, in many places it had fallen from the walls in chunks and, looking up, Minter saw a man-sized hole in the ceiling where the edges of the broken floorboards of the room upstairs showed through. Scattered around the ward at odd angles, the wire bed frames looked equally forlorn although one of them still bore a rotting mattress, as well as the incongruous details of a pillow at its head and even a neatly folded grey blanket at its foot. It was if this bed alone was waiting for the patient to be admitted.

As Minter looked around the ward, he wondered whether this was where his mother used to sleep after they sent her to Broke Hall after the trial. He imagined the long and fretful nights she might have passed here listening to the banshee cries of the other inmates – or even making them herself.

Outside in the corridor, he let his eyes adjust to the gloom. A couple of large ferns had rooted in the crumbling concrete in the corners, where pools of rainwater lingered and his feet crunched over debris from the collapsed skylight. He passed a series of solid metal doors, each with elaborate locks and worn-smooth brass handles and spyholes halfway up. When he pulled one of the doors open it protested with a creak. The room itself was small and cell-like. Closing the door again, Minter quickened his pace.

It wasn't long before he came to the old-fashioned telephone box.

Inside, the heavy Bakelite receiver with its dish-shaped ends dangled down from its frayed, fabric-covered cable. Minter stepped inside the booth and picked up the receiver and rested it back on its cradle. The mechanism made a brief noise like the sound of a bell. Turning, Minter half expected to be confronted by the mad old woman with the rouged cheeks.

When he was six, she had pointed the way. 'There,' she said to the little boy who had told her he was lost, pointing to the end of the corridor. 'Your mother will be in the chapel. That's where the visitors go.'

Minter carried on down the interminable corridor, pausing only once to glance into a large room where an upright piano was lying on its back, its frontage ripped off and all the delicate strings and hammers clearly visible. At last, he came to the door that was hanging off its hinges and he stepped outside into a gust of fresh morning air.

Minter entered the chapel under a porch. Inside, the sun pierced the high windows, lacing the floor of the nave with butter-yellow light. He walked between the pointed Gothic arches of the colonnade and on towards the sanctuary, where three tables had been left in front of the altar. He went round the first table and sat down in one of the chairs.

It was where his mother had sat that day, the last time he had ever seen her. Looking across the table, Minter saw himself as he had been – a frightened six-year-old boy who didn't understand why his mother had been detained here. He remembered wanting her to come home. Only he didn't have a home. Not any more.

Anxiously, the boy glanced up to his left, where the social worker was sitting on the chair beside him. From now on, it was the social worker who told him where to go and what to do.

In the silence of the chapel, Minter sat for a few minutes. Then he went to sit in the other chair, the one where, all those years ago, he had sat and waited for his mother to be brought to him.

She snivelled. Bewildered, her restless, dark-rimmed eyes searched the distant ceiling for the source of the voices she kept hearing. Just as a social worker was chaperoning Minter, a burly nurse sat beside his mother. It was this nurse who broke the silence, saying in an Irish accent, 'Lucy, your son has come to see you.'

Minter's mother didn't hear her. Neither, it seemed, did she even notice the little boy sitting just across the table from her. Her eyes darted round the church instead. 'Lucy?' said the nurse again. 'Have you got nothing to say to your son?'

Lucy's eyes settled on the nurse, then, in a hopeless gesture, she raised her shoulders and let them fall again.

The social worker and the nurse made eye contact. A nod passed between them. It was the cue for them both to get up from the chairs. The visit was at an end. Obediently, Lucy got up and followed the nurse down the stairs.

The boy watched her walking back down the nave, her cardigan wrapped around her back against the chill. 'Mum!' he called out. 'Mum!' The social worker reached down and put his hand on the boy's shoulder, although whether in a gesture of comfort or restraint it was difficult to say.

Lucy Minter was nearly at the exit when she turned.

'Mum!'

Lucy ran towards him, her slippers padding down the aisle, the nurse bustling after her, crying, 'Lucy Minter! Come back here!'

Lucy made it to the steps and knelt down in front of the boy. She patted his chest with her other hand.

He knew what she was looking for. He put his own hand between the buttons of his shirt and pulled out the St Christopher. 'I've got it,' he said, showing it her. 'I kept it, Mum.' Somewhere above their heads, the nurse and the social worker muttered to each other.

Lucy kissed him on his cheek. 'Good boy!' she whispered in his ear. 'You're such a clever boy! You'll bring it back to me one day. You'll come and get me.'

Still sitting in the chair where his mother had once sat, Minter's cheeks now streamed with the tears. He looked down at the ghost of his mother kneeling in front of him. At that moment, her expression didn't look like it belonged to a madwoman. Her eyes didn't leap from one thing to another. They were clear-sighted and looked straight back at him, as if not only did she know exactly who the little boy was but had given the boy the medal knowing that it would bring him back to her.

'That's what will happen,' she said, stroking the boy's face. 'You'll come back and set me free.'

31

• • •

Later that day, Minter visited a different kind of hospital, one that treated diseases of the body instead of the mind.

At the Royal Sussex in Brighton he was standing in the shop run by the League of Friends. From the fan of newspapers on the bottom shelf, he picked up a copy of the *Daily Mail*.

World Exclusive had been flashed across the masthead in red. In the large colour photograph that dominated the front page, Abi Martin sat on a sofa in her luxuriously appointed home in Rottingdean. Next to her, huddled girlishly close, Eden Martin stared nervously back at the camera. Abi had thrown a protective arm around her daughter's shoulder and her regretful smile hinted at hard-won lessons having been learned. The editor had headlined the story *Together Again!*

Minter read the story, picking up on Abi's quotes about Jack and how she still believed that one day she would find the right man for her – and, perhaps, if she was lucky, a proper father for Eden. A sidebar story revealed that Abi had just been offered a new, two-year contract to present the breakfast show. The producer, a man named Tony Evans, said how relieved and delighted the whole production team would be when Abi was back on the famous sofa again. Abi's fee remained undisclosed.

Minter folded the newspaper and went to join the queue at the till. After a moment's hesitation he picked the biggest, most expensive-looking bouquet of flowers out of the bucket.

Upstairs, in a side room, Vicky Reynolds was lying in bed, waiting for someone to come to take her to the operating theatre for the last of her skin grafts. 'Minter!' she said, surprised to see him.

'I didn't know if you'd be spending the night,' Minter said, holding out the flowers.

'Thank you,' Vicky said, admiring the blush-pink roses and purple hyacinths. 'They're lovely.' Remembering the scar lurking beneath her eye, she turned her face away from Minter.

He handed her the copy of the *Mail*. 'I thought you might want to see this.'

Despite herself, Vicky had been following the story every day in the tabloids. She knew that Eden's biological mother had given up any parental rights. 'Leopards don't change their spots,' Vicky said, smiling at the carefully posed photograph on the front page. Abi Martin had just paid a shocking price for all her offences against the natural order of things. Abi was a survivor. Vicky didn't doubt that a new edition of Abi's best-selling autobiography was already being ghost-written. She looked up from the newspaper. 'It's good to see you, Minter. I never got the chance to thank you properly.'

Minter shrugged. 'I was doing my job.'

It was happening again, Vicky thought. She was coming close to him and he was veering away.

But then Minter added with a smile, 'Although it did mean I got the chance of seeing you without any clothes on.'

Normally, Vicky would have come up with some kind of witty riposte or even flirted right back at him – but now she reddened. After what had happened, male attention was the last thing she wanted. 'What did you find out about Blackthorn?'

'I talked to a Professor Deaver at Oxford University. He was pretty cagey at first. I think he was worried about the negative publicity.'

Vicky rested her hands on the bedclothes. 'Did he teach Blackthorn at Oxford?'

'Not exactly. Although he did kick him out when he found out what he'd been doing. He told me that Blackthorn started his postgraduate research in the early 1990s. Back then, there was no established code of practice for geneticists and PhD students were encouraged to take risks. Blackthorn was doing some wild stuff, apparently, including stealing human foetuses donated to the college.'

'Were they the ones that you found in his laboratory?' Vicky asked.

Minter nodded. 'The last of them. Blackthorn's research at Oxford wasn't going anywhere. All his results were falsified. He was a scientist, all right, but only of the mad variety.'

A nurse came in and told Vicky they'd be ready for her in five minutes. Leaving a tray with a syringe in it on top of the cabinet by Vicky's bed, she went off to find a vase to put the flowers in.

'And one other thing,' said Minter. 'Grant tracked down the technician at the Queen Adelaide Clinic – the one who made the mistake with Abi Martin's implant.'

'And?' said Vicky.

'It looks like it was an honest mistake,' said Minter. 'The technician has worked in several clinics since then. Apparently, they're all happy with his work.'

'That's a relief.' Having spent so much time in bed these last few weeks, Vicky had had a lot of time for case theory. At one point she even suspected that Blackthorn had obtained the foetuses from the Queen Adelaide Clinic.

Minter said, 'I went to Broke Hall today.'

Vicky turned to face him properly. 'Is that where they took your mother?'

He nodded. 'There's no paper trail, Vicky.'

'The hospital was closed down, wasn't it?'

'That's right.'

Minter knew that the lack of medical records was not unusual. Back then, builders tossed entire files into skips, along with all the other rubbish.

'What are you going to do?' Vicky asked.

'Like you said, she might still be alive. I've got to find out.' He placed his hand on hers. 'Will you help me?'

'I told you Minter,' Vicky replied. 'I'm an expert on missing persons.'

'Right, Ms Reynolds,' said the nurse breezily, walking back into the room. Vicky watched fearfully as she picked up the syringe of pre-med. 'Let's get you down to theatre.'

This time when Vicky gave Minter's hand a reassuring squeeze, he squeezed back saying, 'I'll be there when you wake up.'